EARLY MORNING MURDER

"Mallory, wake up." Rachel was shaking my shoulders.

I must have been having a nightmare. I struggled to sit up, but the mattress had sunk in overnight.

I rolled back into the deep divot in the bed, pulling the sheet over my head to staunch the weak light coming through the window. I checked my watch with one open eye. "It's only six a.m. I can sleep a whole extra hour and still make it to work on time. Leave me alone."

"There's something you need to see. Right now."

I detected a slight edge of panic in Rachel's voice and flung off the sheet covering my head.

"What is it? What's so important this early?" I was groggy and grumpy. I'm not a morning person, and today would be my first day back at work since my life blew up. I wanted to hide under the covers as long as possible. I wasn't eager to test drive Thistle Park's plumbing this morning either, as there was no way to shower, only a claw-footed tub encrusted in grime.

"Mallory." Rachel knelt beside the bed and grabbed both of my hands in hers. They were ice cold. "There's a dead dude in the front yard . . ."

Engaged in Death

Stephanie Blackmoore

KENSINGTON PUBLISHING CORP.

http://www.kensingtonbooks.com

KENSINGTON BOOKS are published by

Kensington Publishing Corp.
119 West 40th Street
New York, NY 10018

All Kensington Titles, Imprints, and Distributed Lines are available at special quantity discounts for bulk purchases for sales promotions, premiums, fund-raising, and educational or institutional use. Special book excerpts or customized printings can also be created to fit specific needs. For details, write or phone the office of the Kensington special sales manager: Kensington Publishing Corp., 119 West 40th Street, New York, NY 10018, attn: Special Sales Department, Phone: 1-800-221-2647.

Kensington and the K logo Reg. U.S. Pat & TM Off.

ISBN-13: 978-1-4967-0478-8
ISBN-10: 1-4967-0478-9
First Kensington Mass Market Edition: July 2016

eISBN-13: 978-1-4967-0479-5
eISBN-10: 1-4967-0479-7
First Kensington Electronic Edition: July 2016

10 9 8 7 6 5 4 3 2 1

Printed in the United States of America

Chapter One

"I'm going to kill your mother," I whispered, meaning every word.

My fiancé, Keith, offered me an indulgent smile. His mother, Helene, had hijacked us again. I was ready to call off the whole damn wedding.

"You and me both, Mallory."

We were getting married in three short weeks. Keith, his mother, and I were at the country club where we were going to hold the reception, in the sleepy town of Port Quincy, Pennsylvania. I munched on fusty shrimp cocktail. The grandeur was decaying. We were going over the final details before the big day, and Helene, my soon-to-be-mother-in-law, was taking over, as usual. She'd spent the afternoon ordering people around and unraveling all of my work in the final hour.

I liked to plan things out. Some would say I had an unhealthy fascination with structure and order, arranging my life just so. In my twenty-nine years, I'd managed to plan my life with great precision. That was, until I ran into Hurricane Helene.

"This beef is too rare. Look at the blood when I cut into it. And this soup has too much sherry." Helene tossed her spoon onto her plate with a clatter. She glared at the small sample of food as if it were laced with poison. "I doubt you'll be able to fix this abomination of a meal before the wedding."

"I'm sorry, ma'am." The server whisked away the offending dishes. "I'll let the chef know."

Helene was dressed impeccably, as always, in one of her exquisite Chanel jackets. Pearls gleamed in her ears and diamond tennis bracelets sparkled on her bony wrists. Helene favored these and other signs of 1980s splendor: primary-color power suits, shoulder pads, and her signature gray Dutch boy haircut, always perfectly sprayed into place.

"Are you okay?" Keith rubbed my back. "You haven't eaten anything."

I touched his arm. "It's nerves, I guess. I'll definitely have some cake."

Just then, the manager of the country club rolled the cake into the ballroom. A bead of sweat ran down his nose and dropped onto the carpet. He glanced at Helene and quickened his pace. He set the cake before us, a perfect replica of the real thing, in three-tiered miniature. Pink sugar crystals glittered on a background of pale green marzipan.

"Everything will be ready. This will be a lovely wedding." He offered Helene a worried smile.

She sniffed in response as he cut small slivers of cake and positioned them on little china plates. "Just make sure my corrections are duly noted."

What Helene wanted, Helene got. Too bad I was the one paying for the wedding.

"Of course." The manager fled. He cast a massive

eye roll Helene's way. After an hour of this, I'd barely been able to suppress them myself.

"This looks incredible." My voice held a falsely cheery note, trying to smooth things over and make everything copacetic.

I tucked into the small slice of cake, which looked delicious. Never mind that Keith and I had picked devil's food with raspberry filling and Helene had nixed our choice.

"Wedding cake is white," she'd decreed. She immediately changed our cake to lemon chiffon with buttercream filling. After fighting with her over every detail, I was willing to concede.

"You did a great job with all of this." Keith gave my hand a squeeze. "You should be a wedding planner."

"Thanks." I returned his smile.

The truth was, though I loved to execute a plan, I was annoyed I'd carried out Helene's version of a perfect wedding. I'd actually had fun when I'd forgotten it was supposed to be my own wedding. I'd relished meeting with vendors and getting every detail just right. More than once over the past year of planning I'd fantasized about becoming a wedding planner, especially when things got hairy at my law firm. The only problem was, I felt like Helene's planner, not the bride. But that wasn't what mattered. *What matters is I'm marrying the love of my life in just a few weeks.*

"This cake is too dry. It crumbled to bits and pieces the instant I touched it with my fork." Helene got up to find the manager when he wasn't instantly at her beck and call.

"What happened?" I gestured around the empty ballroom with a helpless wave of my hand. "We wanted to get married at the courthouse, with a small reception on Mount Washington, overlooking the city. Or take up my mom and stepdad's offer and get married at their house in Florida. How did we end up here?"

"We can still elope." Keith's eyes twinkled.

Before I could ask if he was serious, his cell phone began to vibrate, dancing sideways across the white tablecloth. I glanced at the screen. Becca Cunningham, a first-year associate he worked with.

"Gotta take this. It's for the Emerson case." Keith stood and dropped a kiss on top of my head. He walked out to the country club's deck, overlooking the swollen Monongahela River, leaving me at the mercy of his mother.

I frowned. Keith and I were attorneys at different firms. I'd met all of the young attorneys he mentored, and I didn't trust Becca Cunningham. She was gushy and obsequious and had failed the bar twice. Ever since Keith made partner this past spring, she'd latched on to him and his cases. I suspected she'd made herself indispensable to avoid getting fired if she didn't pass the bar this summer on her final attempt.

I glanced out to the deck, where Keith was talking on the phone, animated and pacing in the July sunshine. A shadow passed behind me as Helene returned to the table.

"Watch your weight, dear. We wouldn't want you to stumble in the home stretch and undo all of your hard work. You need to fit into that dress." Helene snapped me back to reality. She didn't mean the "dear" part. Her eyes were all ice and daggers.

I had gotten out of shape from working long hours

at the firm and dining out. I'd recently slimmed back down to the size I'd been in college, thanks to all of the early-morning runs I'd been squeezing in these past three months. Still, I couldn't get rid of my stubborn little belly, a vestige of cortisol and stress and all-nighters at the firm, fueled by takeout and lattes.

My reply stuck in my dry throat, so I washed down the last bite of cake with a swig of champagne. "Don't worry, Helene. The dress will fit just fine." I seethed, but I was determined to be civil. *This is almost over. Three weeks, three weeks, three weeks.*

Helene's flinty eyes skipped over my now-empty plate to my stomach. She reached down and pinched my side through my thin cotton dress.

"Ouch!" I tilted back, hooking my chair's legs on the faded green and pink rose carpet, barely catching myself as I started to fall backward.

Helene threw up her bejeweled hands. "Just be careful. You need to look perfect, and I can tell you don't have an inch to spare."

Keith chose that moment to walk back in. His face fell. "Everything okay?"

"I was just complimenting Mallory on her discipline with her figure. She'll be a magnificent bride."

I didn't say anything but gave Keith the "let's get the hell out of here" stare. We wrapped things up and Helene moved in for her obligatory air kiss. She stalked out of the ballroom, leaving her trademark trail of Calèche in her wake. The aldehydic shards of her perfume seemed to hang in the air and pursue me after she'd gone, like an angry pack of hornets. I slumped back into my chair, air whooshing out of my lungs. I could feel the waiters at the country club relax.

"I really am going to kill her before the wedding. I'm sure of it."

"I apologize, Mall. She's out of control. But in a few weeks, we'll finally be married." We had left the country club and were safely in Keith's car. He leaned over the center console and squeezed my knee.

"I know. And that's what's important. She just commandeers everything."

Keith frowned and turned east, instead of toward the highway.

I took a deep breath. "I want to have a good relationship with your mother, and I'm trying. It's just . . . where are you going? This isn't the way to the nursing home. I thought we were going to visit Sylvia."

We were barely out of the confines of Port Quincy, heading in the opposite direction of the nursing home where Keith's grandma Sylvia lived, situated halfway between Port Quincy and Pittsburgh. No matter how crazy my schedule was, I stopped in to see Sylvia every other Sunday. I brought her a *National Enquirer* and little pastries from her favorite bakery. We ate and drank tea from an elaborate antique set from the grand old house she'd given up and gossiped about the reality TV show she was so fond of. Sylvia moved around her suite with surprising agility, dragging her oxygen tank behind her. She showed me articles she'd cut out of the newspaper and called people in from the hallway to chat with us.

Once in a while, I convinced Keith to join me. Sylvia claimed Helene had placed her in the Whispering Brook nursing home against her will and I was the only one who ever visited. I wasn't entirely convinced about her first claim, but I really was the only one who stopped in other than Helene's grudging biannual Thanksgiving and Christmas Eve visits and the few Sundays Keith accompanied me.

"You'll see where I'm going. It's a surprise." Keith had a mischievous smile. "We can see Sylvia next weekend."

My visit with Sylvia was off the table. I frowned and settled back into the buttery leather seat of his BMW. Sylvia was my only family left in western Pennsylvania, now that my mother, stepfather and sister moved to Pensacola three years ago. Sylvia wasn't technically my family yet, but she treated me like her own granddaughter. And unlike Helene, she was genuinely excited to have me join the family. There was no love lost between Sylvia and Helene. Since Sylvia was ninety-nine, she felt entitled to speak her mind. I tamped down a smile, remembering how Sylvia had gone on a diatribe about Helene just two weeks ago. Sylvia was pretty hard of hearing, so her criticisms had echoed down the halls of the nursing home. It was Sylvia who had told me I should trust my instincts and elope if I needed to call off this crazy wedding whirlwind.

"What?"

"Just thinking about Sylvia and how she's such a . . . piston. You never know what she's going to say."

"She loves you, Mallory. And I do too."

I rolled down the window and breathed in the fresh summer air. We made several turns and ended up far into the countryside, passing a rabbit warren of new housing developments cut into the hillsides, all with counterfeit names casting for a British air: Carrington Manor, Chichester Glen, Manchester Heights, though there was neither a manor nor glen in sight.

We turned into Windsor Meadows, which featured the biggest homes under construction of all the housing tracts. The development was about half finished, and we wended our way up a sharply sloping hill, past large new salmon and taupe-colored brick behemoths rising out of the mud, all sleek gables, peaks, and triangles. All vaguely alike. They sat close together on narrow lots, and new grass struggled to grow in front of them. Keith navigated a dead-end street and parked with a flourish in front of an empty lot, muddy and bare.

"Voilà!" He exited the BMW and rushed around to open my door.

"What is this?" Panic rose in my voice. "Why are we here?" This wasn't part of the plan. I fingered my watch and wondered if I should have called Sylvia to let her know we wouldn't be visiting today.

Keith's smile, which was threatening to crack his face, broke into pieces. "My mother feels bad about the friction between the two of you. She wanted to do something nice, so she purchased this lot as our wedding gift. We can build to suit as soon as we choose which house we want." The grin came back, triumphant.

"But . . ." I leaned against the car door, woozy and shocked. "We talked about this. I thought you wanted to stay in the city, close to work and close to our friends. We're more than an hour from Pittsburgh out here." I gestured around me, trailing off into silence. I didn't add, *out here, right under Helene's surgically enhanced nose.*

"I know what we talked about, but we'll be married, so we need to think of our future. We'll need a safer place for our future kids. I had such a great childhood in Port Quincy, away from all the craziness of the city." He frowned. "We thought you'd be happy with this."

"We? Which *we* are you talking about?" I couldn't keep my voice from shaking. "You and Helene? I would *never* choose this. I see this as a way for Helene to keep tabs on us, to control us and to turn us into Mr. and Mrs. Cul-de-sac."

Keith took a step back, crossing his arms. "What's wrong with being Mr. and Mrs. Cul-de-sac?"

I didn't reply.

"Wow. I guess I'm really off base. With your mom in Florida"—he pinched the furrow between his brows—"my mother can help out with the children once we have them. We have to be realistic."

I stared at him in shock. My mouth opened and shut like a beached fish gasping for breath. Living in a McMansion on the outskirts of Port Quincy was the last place on earth I wanted to be. If we were stuck in Helene's backyard, she could monitor us or, worse, direct our lives. I'd suffocate under the pressure. This wasn't part of the carefully calibrated plan for our future I'd envisioned. I felt ambushed.

"What about the commute?" I tried to keep my fury in check. I'd convince Keith with logic, if not emotion. "What about the fact you love living in the city? That I love it?" Despite growing up in the suburbs, I was a city girl now. I gazed beyond the edge of the housing development, where undulating green hills were dotted with black and white cows and brown horses. I couldn't imagine leaving our bustling city neighborhood for a pastoral retreat located ten miles past the boundary of a sane commute into town. "What about consulting me on major decisions?"

Keith began to sweat profusely and ran a hand through his thinning hair. "Do you honestly think you'll continue to work after we have children? Maybe at first, but c'mon, Mallory, are you really partner material? Do you even like practicing law? You could do something else. Something less stressful. Something you really want to do, when you figure that out. And you can do that from Port Quincy. I wasn't kidding about becoming a wedding planner."

The world began to spin. It was too hot, too humid, and too muggy. It was all too much. I closed my eyes against a wave of vertigo and slid down the car door, kneeling unceremoniously in the dust-covered road.

The ride back to the city was tense. We rode in silence until we reached our apartment building.

"My mother can sell the lot in no time if you're going to insist on being unhappy about her wedding gift. But let's not be hasty. You might realize it's a great idea and come around."

"I'm not going to 'come around' to this idea, Keith. I'm upset you'd make a big decision without even mentioning it. We're getting married in a few weeks, but sometimes it's like I don't even know you anymore."

We stopped at the mailbox in the lobby, and Keith extracted our mail, averting his eyes. "It's just pre-wedding jitters. Everything will be fine. I made a mistake. No, my mother made a mistake. You don't want to live out in Port Quincy. I get it. It was a bad gesture."

He handed me my portion of the mail, which

contained the usual bills and advertisements and a large brown padded envelope. He reddened as he separated his mail, shoving a glossy brochure for Windsor Meadows behind a letter. We began the torturously slow ascent to our apartment in the old brass elevator.

I sat at the dining room table and put my head in my hands, rubbing my temples to ease out the headache that had been building since we left Windsor Meadows. Keith rubbed my shoulders and, after initially tensing up, I felt the stress and misgivings begin to melt away.

"I love you. I want nothing more than for you to be my wife. We'll figure out where to live together. Everything will fall into place." He nuzzled my neck, making me laugh.

"It was a big shock. I thought it was a practical joke."

"Let me make you some tea." He looked at me with tenderness and concern as he padded into the kitchen.

While he fixed up the kettle, I turned my attention to the map spread out before me: a miniature model of the Port Quincy Country Club ballroom. I'd toiled over the seating chart as the last few RSVPs trickled in, trying to get it just right, with a focus bordering on obsessive-compulsive. I usually enjoyed this kind of puzzle, but it was an especially complicated task, not helped by the fact I didn't know many of the guests and their relationships to each other.

We had originally planned on thirty guests, just close friends and immediate family, but, thanks to Helene's decree, we'd be entertaining three hundred people, most of whom I'd be meeting for the first time. Things had long ago spiraled out of control and crossed the line into spectacle. There wasn't much of Keith's immediate family left, just Helene, Sylvia, and a few cousins from out of town. The guests were Helene's acquaintances from the upper echelon of Port Quincy society and distant relatives.

"Do you think Sylvia will make it to the wedding?" In addition to his father, Keith's other three grandparents were deceased, but Sylvia was still going strong. She was determined to attend the wedding, oxygen tank and all.

Keith chuckled and set down a mug of ginger tea. "If Sylvia has any say in it, she'll be there. She adores you." He leaned over for a kiss. "Besides, you can ask her yourself tomorrow." He returned to the galley kitchen.

I'd called Sylvia as soon as we were on the road and arranged to stop by to see her tomorrow to make up for missing our Sunday tea date. She'd been delighted and said she couldn't wait to discuss what had happened at the wedding tasting.

Everything will be okay. I examined the brown envelope. There was no return address, but the postmark was Port Quincy. Maybe it was an oversized wedding card. Gifts had already started to arrive, and a little village of boxes had colonized one corner of the apartment.

Keith's cell phone rang as I took my first sip of tea. I winced. It might be someone from work reporting on a weekend project. Maybe even the worrisome Becca Cunningham.

Stop it, Mallory. You're being irrational.

"Hello, Mother."

I could tell the call wasn't good.

"Oh, my God. When? Was she in pain? We'll be there soon. I love you too."

"What's wrong?" I set the mug down too hard, sloshing pale brown liquid over the sides. Hot tea smeared the carefully written names on the seating chart as it spread out in a soppy circle.

"Sylvia. She passed away half an hour ago. It must have been pretty soon after you talked to her. A nurse found her"—his voice broke—"in her bed. She was gone."

"Oh, Keith." I jumped up and hugged him, hard.

"I knew this day was coming, but I was sure she'd be here to see us get married." He crumpled into a chair, hunched over and deflated. Tears beaded in the corners of his dark blue eyes. "I should have listened to you and visited her today. Maybe we could have helped her."

I leaned down and embraced him. "There might not have been anything we could have done." I began to cry too, fat drops staining the brown envelope. "She said she had to get off the phone when I called because she had company. I'm sure they would have done something if they could have."

"Here." Keith handed me a box of tissues, knocking the big brown envelope to the floor. "What is that?" He began to pick it up, but I beat him to it.

"I'm not sure. There's no return address. Probably something wedding-related."

Keith handed me a silver letter opener as he answered his phone again.

"Yes, Mother. Of course I'll help you with the arrangements. We just need a few minutes to process."

Just like Helene. I sniffled back more tears. *She probably can't wait to put Sylvia into the ground.*

Shaking my head, I returned to the contents of the envelope. I wasn't sure what I was looking at. There were pictures, a whole stack of glossy five-by-sevens. The shots were grainy and dark. It appeared to be a person—no, make that two—in a car. My heart caught then accelerated. The car looked an awful lot like Keith's navy BMW. And one of the people looked an awful lot like Keith. I shuffled through the pictures, and the quality improved, as if the photographer had zoomed in and sharpened the focus. A blond, shining curtain of hair hid the woman's face. Her dark roots stood out in a severe line against her luminous hair. My throat started to constrict, and I flipped faster through the pile of photos.

"Babe, what's wrong?" Keith abandoned his phone and made his way across the room in slow motion.

The last photo was crystal clear. It showed Keith in the waning winter sunlight, the hood of his car encrusted in snow. In flagrante, with his mentee Becca Cunningham.

Chapter Two

Two days later, I still felt as if I were breathing under water. I was devastated by Keith's betrayal, but after sleeping for twelve hours, I slogged through the necessary tasks, starting with calling my mother, Carole, to tell her my engagement was over.

"But you'll end up a spinster." Her annoyance overrode concern. "You'll have no one left but divorced men."

I took in a sharp breath.

"And you'll run out of time to make me a grandma!" I pictured her leaping out of her chair in her cheery apple-green kitchen in Florida, wringing her dish towels and pacing a well-worn track in the linoleum. I put down the phone, hit my fist into my pillow, and then gingerly placed the phone back next to my ear. She was still going on, gathering steam.

"Just so you know," I interrupted, "I'm fine." This silenced her.

"Well, yes. How are *you* taking this, dear?" Her concern for me, once prompted, almost made me crack a smile.

"About time you asked her how she's coping," my stepfather said in the background. "Cut her some slack, Carole."

Thank you, Doug.

I enlisted my mom and my best friend, Olivia, to call all three hundred guests and tell them the wedding was off. Imagine my surprise when the Port Quincy Country Club informed me otherwise.

"Mrs. Helene Pierce said the reception is still booked," the manager said in a timid voice.

"Fat chance. You'll need the bride, and she won't be there."

I shut my cell phone off after the tenth call from Keith, the twentieth from Helene and the fifth from a man claiming to be Sylvia's lawyer. I refused to talk to any of them. No matter, since my mom and Olivia had the number at the grubby motel I was now hiding in. I'd told my secretary and the three partners I worked for I had a highly contagious disease and couldn't come to work. They were polite, but I could tell they'd already heard I'd cancelled the wedding. After those humiliating conversations, I sunk into a catatonic state, unable to get out of bed. I hadn't showered since I'd run off, and I'd been eating from the vending machine at the end of the hallway, watching reruns of *Married With Children* on TBS in the dark.

But today was Sylvia's funeral, according to the obituary in the Port Quincy *Eagle Herald.* If I could muster up the courage to get out of bed, I should show up and pay my final respects. Even if it meant facing Keith.

I thought back to the moment two days ago when

I had realized what the photographs in my hand revealed. After Keith crossed the room, he made a grab for them. I spilled the pile in a glossy fan at his feet. He picked up the photos, then recoiled and dropped them as if they'd burned him when he got a closer look.

"Mallory, it's not true. I don't know who sent these, but—"

"Save it, you jerk!" I pushed him away and ran to the bedroom closet, stuffing as much of my life as I could into the large suitcases that had been purchased for our honeymoon in Paris. My hands trembled so hard it was a wonder I packed anything. My wedding dress hung on the closet door, a giant, poufy confection of a ball gown, bulging against the garment bag encasing it. I wanted to tear it to pieces as if I were starring in a slasher film.

Keith stood open-mouthed in the doorway. "You can't go. You just can't. We have the wedding. It has to go on. We'll work things out. Just listen to reason!"

I charged toward him with the two suitcases, and he jumped out of the bedroom doorway when it was clear I was going to run him over.

"Don't talk to me. Don't touch me. I don't ever want to see you as long as I live," I hissed out in a single breath.

I bent to retrieve the photos. They might be useful someday. I crammed them into the brown envelope, bending some in the process.

"Mallory—"

"I can't believe I almost married you. Someone"— I waved the envelope—"just saved me from making the biggest mistake of my life. And if I knew who they were, I'd personally thank them."

With that, I flounced out, Keith hot on my heels. I pushed the elevator button, and he got in, cornering me.

"Just come to your senses and let me explain."

I grabbed the suitcases and whipped out of the elevator, leaving him trapped as the brass doors clanged shut. It was just the head start I needed. I banged down four flights of stairs to the basement, twisting my ankle in the process, and hopped out the back exit of the apartment building to crouch behind the Dumpster.

I was feeling pretty triumphant, with my adrenaline pumping, like a scorned Charlie's Angel. Then I realized I didn't have a getaway car. Keith and I rode downtown together each morning in his car. Until now, I hadn't needed a vehicle. I funneled every extra dime I made into paying off my law school loans, and I'd barely made a dent.

Swearing, I called a cab service and directed them to pick me up by the Dumpster.

"Just take me to a motel, any motel, out by the airport," I begged my cabby when he arrived half an hour later. I didn't want to run into Keith downtown or give him any clues as to my whereabouts.

So, here I was, two days later, licking my wounds in the cocoon of my rented room. The partners I worked for at the firm weren't happy I'd taken off Monday and today, fake contagious disease or not. News traveled fast around the legal world. I was sure Keith had gone in to work at his firm and his colleagues had ferreted out the news. Not to mention all of my coworkers whom my mother and Olivia had called, performing the grim task of disinviting them from the wedding.

The phone by the bed rang, and I sat up too quickly, hitting my forehead on the bedside lampshade. It was 11 AM.

"Pull it together, Mallory," I muttered as I picked up the receiver.

"I'm downstairs. Come help me bring up my stuff."

Sweet baby Jesus. It was my little sister.

"Rachel? What are you doing here?" My voice came out as a squeak.

"Mom told me everything. I was going to come to Pittsburgh and help you out before the wedding anyway. . . ."

My heart contracted at the W word.

". . . and the plane ticket was nonrefundable, so here I am. Come downstairs." She hung up, and I sank back into the pillows, stunned.

My quiet little refuge was over. *Thanks, Rachel.*

Two minutes later, I was awkwardly hugging my sister in the lobby. I hadn't made any special effort, so she and the desk clerk got to see me in my crusty, going-on-three-days jammies, the flannel magenta ones with the penguin-and-Christmas-tree pattern. My eyes were red and rheumy, my frizzy hair a rat's nest.

"It's July. Why are you wearing these?" Rachel held me out at arm's length, assessing me with her keen green eyes, her treacly fruit perfume nearly knocking me out. "You look like you've been hit by a truck."

"I didn't have time to pack season-appropriate clothing." I pulled back and gazed at my sister, aided by the mirror behind the front desk. Like she had any right to critique my outfit.

Rachel was seven years younger and nine inches taller. For her flight from Florida, she'd worn pink velour sweats with PUSSY CAT written across her shapely rear in cursive and a silver tank top that showed a healthy amount of midriff below and her round breasts above. A microscopic hoody tied around her narrow waist completed the outfit.

If you squinted hard enough, you could discern we were sisters, but we were very different. Rachel was tall and I was five-one. Rachel got the pretty almond-shaped green eyes; mine were big and brown. Rachel had wavy, honey-kissed hair, and mine was a nondescript sandy brown and impossibly curly when I didn't flat-iron it into submission. I alternated between slight and chubby, but Rachel had had the physique of a Victoria's Secret model since she'd turned fourteen.

We had the same raucous laugh and the same freckles, but that was about it. I was a people pleaser, having become an attorney to fulfill my mom's edict that one of us be a doctor or lawyer. I'd graduated from Carnegie Mellon a year early and gone straight through to law school at Georgetown. Rachel was a rabble-rouser, failing out of school and sporadically returning, doing whatever she pleased, showing up wherever the wind blew her, living her life with the greatest amount of chaos and consternation for our mother and stepdad as possible.

"Keith is a rat, but you're better off. Mom and Doug send their love." Rachel appeared genuinely concerned.

I'd managed to convince my parents not to fly up

by promising I'd come to Pensacola in a few weeks to heal. I'd asked my mom to tell Rachel not to come either, but she must not have gotten the memo.

"It's okay. Well, it's not okay, but someday it will be. Let's go to my room."

The desk clerk, a pimply kid of about twenty, was staring open-mouthed at my sister. In a minute, strings of saliva would be hanging down his chin.

"Could you help us?" Rachel cooed, gesturing to a pile of zebra-patterned luggage waiting by the entrance.

"I don't think he's a bellhop, Rach. Besides, how much stuff do you have?" I glanced back over to the automatic door for a closer look and did a double take.

"That's all yours?"

Rachel shrugged as the poor clerk snapped to attention. He loaded her gear onto a flimsy metal luggage cart, where it wavered and threatened to topple over, laden as it was with garish garment bags and suitcases. There was even a hatbox. A hatbox?

My sister wears hats?

With a flick of her purple fingernail, he followed us to the elevator and on to my room.

"Do you have any cash for a tip?" I don't know why I bothered to ask her.

She gazed at me, batting her eyelashes in contrition.

"Hold on." I fished a crumpled fiver out of my PJ pocket. "Here you go."

The clerk was still staring at Rachel as I shoved the cart into the hall and shut the door.

"He wasn't very helpful when I arrived here, as I recall."

Rachel slipped off her bejeweled platform flip-flops and plopped down onto the middle of the bed, stretching luxuriously like a cat.

"I've been calling your cell, but you didn't pick up. Now I know why." She leaned over and turned on my phone, which lit up with dozens of unheard messages.

"Give me that!" I quickly deleted the new messages from Keith and Helene.

Rachel grabbed the phone back and hit play.

"Ms. Shepard? This is Garrett Davies. I'm the executor of Sylvia Pierce's estate. I need to get in touch with you as soon as possible. Please call me back. This is the sixth message I've left."

"Sounds sexy." Rachel wiggled her eyebrows.

"I'm done with men. Forever." I reached for the phone and deleted the message. I didn't need it, since I had five others just like it.

"I know you feel that way now, but you'll be all right. These things just take time. Now, what do you have to eat?"

My eyes strayed to the trash can, overflowing with wrappers from the Snickers bars foraged from the vending machine down the hall, undoing the miles of runs I'd put in the last three months to prepare for that damn, cursed wedding.

"Umm . . ." A hot blush warmed my cheeks.

"Let's get you a shower, then go out to eat. You need real food, and frankly, this isn't healthy."

I smiled at my sister. The first genuine one to cross my face in a few days. Back when we were latchkey kids, I had been practically my sister's only caretaker, as our mom worked double time to get her decorating and staging business off the ground. While Mom was launching her career, I'd sat with Rachel after school, fixing her snacks and asking about her day. It felt odd but sweet to be fussed over by my little sister for a change.

"Actually, I need to get to a funeral. How'd you get here? Do you have a car?"

"I rented one for the next three weeks."

My eyes narrowed, the warm fuzzy feeling gone. "You rented one, or Mom and Doug did?"

It was my sister's turn to blush, and I had my answer. There was no way Rachel could afford to rent a car for three weeks on her hodgepodge of part-time jobs. Mom and my stepdad, Doug, had a soft spot for Rachel, funding her misadventures and paying to get her out of scrapes, though they didn't have a penny to spare now they were retired.

"Fine. Mind if I borrow it?"

"You can't. Only the person renting can drive it, but I can go to the funeral with you. Who died?" She said this with her characteristic bluntness as she reached for the remote.

"Sylvia. Ke—his grandmother." I couldn't even bear to say Keith's name. I feared I'd break out in hives.

"The really old one? Aw, she was the one you liked." Rachel got up to paw through one of her suitcases. "That sucks, Mall. Are you sure you're up for this? Keith and his mom are going to be there."

"I know. I'm going to hide in the back and wear my Jackie O sunglasses. We can sneak in after it starts. Helene cares too much about appearances to make a scene during a funeral. And he does whatever she wants, so he'll behave. With any luck, we'll just have to look at the backs of their heads."

I shuddered at the thought of even that minimal contact.

Rachel applied some red lipstick as if suiting up for battle. "We can pull this off. If you're really set on going."

"I owe it to Sylvia."

"I think I have something to wear to a funeral."

"Let's see if it's appropriate," I mumbled under my breath.

"What was that?" Rachel continued to dig through her suitcase.

"Nothing. Let's get ready."

We arrived at the Port Quincy First Presbyterian Church five minutes after the funeral began but, for us, right on schedule. My hair was sticking out in a corona around my head, thanks to the ride in Rachel's rented convertible Mini Cooper.

"I don't know why we had to leave the top down." I tried to flatten the hair I'd carefully straightened at the motel.

"The convertible was a free upgrade. It's summer. Make the most of it." Rachel slammed her door shut and ran her hands through her wavy, unscathed tresses. If anything, the wind had made her hair look even better, all beachy and tousled. She sashayed down the street to the church.

The wide oak doors were propped open, and we entered as discreetly as possible, sliding into a pew in the very last row. The minister was intoning away at the front of the church. I squinted and sat up a bit straighter, slipping my bug-eye sunglasses down my nose. As it turned out, I was grateful Rachel had overpacked. The hatbox had contained a pretty, wide-brimmed straw number, more appropriate for the Kentucky Derby than anything in western Pennsylvania. I'd pondered whether it would draw unwanted attention or help me shield my face. After the hair-ruining car ride, I was more than happy to hide under the hat.

"Sylvia McGavitt Smoot Pierce was a special woman. She touched the lives of everyone in this room. She was a daughter, a wife, a mother, a grandmother and a pillar in this community." The minister droned on with generic platitudes, doing little to convey what a remarkable woman Sylvia had been. I tried to pay attention to the bland eulogy but began to scan the room for my mortal enemies. I needed to plan a drama-free exit.

Bingo. Helene and Keith were ensconced in the front row. Helene sat ramrod straight in what looked like her impeccable, if ancient, black Halston suit and also a hat, but hers didn't seem silly like mine. Keith turned to listen to the minister, and I caught his profile. He looked awful. My heart twisted, and I gasped as a physical stab of pain radiated through my abdomen.

"You okay?"

I blinked madly to stave away the start of tears. Rachel put her arm around me and gave my shoulders a squeeze. Momentarily restored, I looked back at the man I had been ready to pledge my life to.

At this distance, Keith looked almost as ruined as I did. His usually handsome face was drawn and pale, the bags underneath his eyes puffy and purple-tinged. He looked all of his thirty-five years and then some. His shoulders were rounded, his usual bravado gone. It was hot in the packed church, and his thinning hair was pasted to his head in sticky strands. He was wilting.

He'd changed so much in the years I'd known him, but I hadn't noticed. I'd devoted all of my energy into my work at the law firm, days and nights and more days and nights, and I hadn't seen the embers of our love changing, cooling, and dying. It wasn't the same as it had been when I'd first met Keith. He'd been my mentor, a dashing young associate who'd made me laugh hysterically as we sat up all night going over depositions. We'd worked well as a team until he'd left for a neighboring law firm and a better chance at making partner. He had once been passionate and self-deprecating, and I realized, with a start, I hadn't seen that side of him in eons. These days, he was obsessed with making more money and took his mother's advice as gospel.

Keith had pursued partnership with zealous dedication and had been gone many evenings, driving me home and going back to his firm, returning in the morning for a quick shower. I hadn't suspected anything. It last snowed in March, so Keith's affair with Becca Cunningham had to have been going on for at least five months. Yet I had planned to marry this man in a few weeks.

The church had gone silent, and I looked up to see why. A mousy woman in her mid-forties, clad in a faded floral dress, had walked up to the pulpit. She removed the microphone and set it behind her. She extracted a pitch pipe from her pocket, blew a clear note, parted her thin lips, and began to sing "Ave Maria" a cappella. What emanated from her mouth was divine, ethereal, and transcendent. Her sweet soprano cut through my stupor, so strong it seemed to roll in waves to fill the immense church better than any organ ever could.

I began to sob. All of the emotion I'd been holding back bubbled over. I cried for my lost engagement, for Keith's betrayal, and for dear Sylvia. Rachel rubbed my back, and I didn't even blanch when she pulled a warm tissue, reeking of Britney Spears Fantasy, out of her bra and handed it to me.

I thought of how lovely Sylvia had been. She'd immediately taken me under her wing. She'd been a funny old battle ax, who'd earned the right over her ninety-nine years to say whatever was on her mind. She'd sworn like a sailor, played a mean game of canasta, and been my ally against Helene. My protector. I recalled our last visit at the Whispering Brook nursing home.

"Mallory, dear"—she'd held my hand in her knotted one—"I think you'll bring balance to this family."

I'd told her my concerns about Helene riding roughshod over our wedding and how it didn't feel like it was about my marriage to Keith anymore.

She'd chuckled. "Perhaps it's cold feet. It's good to listen to your instincts." Her lively blue eyes had glowed in her wrinkled face. She'd asked, "Hand me my laptop, will you, dear?" She had been hunting and pecking at the thing as I'd left, squinting through her reading glasses, her gnarled fingers surprisingly nimble. I couldn't believe that was the last time I'd see her.

The mousy woman stopped singing, and the spell she'd woven with her voice was broken. The power seemed to ebb out of her now, and she was just a plain woman again, walking away to take a seat in a pew. People stirred, as if they'd just woken up. The minister gave a final blessing, and Keith and the other pallbearers carried Sylvia's casket out of the church. I was due to walk down that same aisle with Keith as my husband, our marriage sealed. Instead, he was accompanying Sylvia's coffin.

"Duck down," I hissed, grabbing at Rachel's arm as discreetly as I could as Keith passed by. We should have left before the funeral ended.

"Cover your face," Rachel stage-whispered back, pulling my hat down over my jawline. My sister bent over double, pretending to look for something in her purse. I dared to glance up. Keith was scanning the pews, probably looking for me. I let out a sigh of relief as the casket disappeared out the door.

"We made it," I breathed, my hand over my pounding heart.

Rachel gathered her purse and began to fuss with its contents. She stood and pulled down her skirt. I shook my head, barely suppressing a smirk.

Rachel had indeed found something to wear to the funeral in her prodigious luggage. She was sporting a crushed black velvet dress, decorated with a smattering of iridescent sequins. It was an outfit suited for junior prom, not a funeral. And the length of her dress would be fine on a pre-teen, but it didn't quite cover enough of my sister's five-foot-ten frame. The edge of her thigh-high silk stockings peeked out from under the dress, complete with garter belt. I'd stared in disbelief when we left the motel room.

"Where were you planning to wear this dress when you packed?"

"The rehearsal dinner." She didn't blink.

Then again, my funeral outfit of a poorly ironed, lint-covered black suit, too tight across my Snickers-bloated midsection, was no better. The straw hat, good for hiding behind, didn't help. My getup telegraphed my mental state: rumpled and devastated. Rachel's outfit screamed a different message: hot, velvet sex. Which might have been why so many people were staring at us.

"We have to get out of here." I struggled to my feet and wavered on my uneven black heels. I was still a little out of it when I was getting ready, and I guess I hadn't noticed they were from two different pairs of shoes.

"Mallory, get over here," a voice commanded. *Crap. Too late.* Helene chastised me as if I were her naughty Yorkie and I'd just taken a poo on her rug. She must have realized I wasn't going to obey since she began to make her way over.

I panicked. Dawdlers blocked the side entrances, and a crowd of people slowly ambled out the church's wide back doors.

"C'mon." Rachel gave my hand a squeeze. "Excuse us. Sorry. Excuse us." She shimmied through the throng of funeral goers, gently shoving and pushing people out of the way. I held on to her hand as if it were a life preserver, stepping on toes and hurting feelings.

People gasped, "Excuse *you*!" and "Hold on, we're all trying to get out of here too."

I blushed at our rudeness, murmuring apologies,

but the situation was too dire for us to stay in the church.

We finally exited and spilled out onto the front stairs, where I ran smack into Keith.

"My God, why haven't you answered any of my calls? Darling, I've been so worried."

The pallbearers had placed Sylvia's coffin in the hearse, and I'd walked right into a trap. Keith reached for me, and I took an unsteady step back, rolling on my mismatched heels.

"Don't touch me." I took pleasure in Keith's wounded expression. I'd never wished to hurt him before, and I felt ill from all of the enmity bubbling up toward this man I'd almost married.

"There you are." Great, Helene was bringing up the rear. "We can work this out," Helene pleaded in a low voice.

A few people leaving the church looked at us with curiosity.

"There's nothing left to work out." I crossed my arms.

"You can't just cancel the wedding," Helene hissed. "Think of us." She gestured lamely toward Keith, who, to his credit, rolled his eyes and placed his hand on her arm. Helene looked like a cobra, her hair teased out over her ears, a tiny pillbox hat anchored on top with spiky bobby pins.

"Mother, this isn't the place for this discussion. We need to bury my grandmother. If Mallory doesn't want to talk to me"—he raised his eyes even with mine—"I understand, and I deserve it."

Helene looked as if she couldn't decide whom to strike, Keith or me. "Nonsense. You're still engaged to Keith, since you have his ring." Helene gave a haughty little jut of her chin, as if she were merely reminding me of the legal terms of a contract she wished to enforce.

Before we'd left the motel, Rachel had spotted the ring, winking merrily even in the low light, all three cushion-cut carats of it. "Are you going to give it back?" she'd asked.

"I don't want it anymore. I may as well." I refused to look at it.

Rachel had gingerly picked up the ring from the motel dresser and slipped it onto her pinky, the only finger it would fit. It was a honker. The first Christmas after Keith proposed, Rachel had grabbed my hand and yanked it up to her face for closer inspection. "Holy mackerel, you're an attorney in Pittsburgh, not a Kardashian! This is totally not your style."

I'd reddened and explained Sylvia offered Keith her petite antique ruby engagement ring, but Keith had demurred. Left to his own devices, he'd gone to a jeweler downtown in the Clark Building and plunked down enough money to buy a small house. I was embarrassed by its size, and I often turned the ring around so only the thin band showed, the heavy diamond biting into the soft flesh of my left palm. Just a few days ago, I couldn't wait to marry and switch to the thin, plain wedding band I'd selected.

I was eager to set Helene straight today, so I reached into my cavernous purse, where I'd thrown the ring before we left the motel. I scrabbled around for a few seconds until I felt it, the metal and stone cool against my fingertips.

"Then take it back!" I tossed it down the street as

a bride would her bouquet. It flew through the air in a gorgeous arc, flashing fire and brimstone, showering sparkles and rainbows as it fell. People on the sidewalk gasped, and the ring hit the pavement, making a pleasing plink, plink, plink as it skittered down the street. The monstrous diamond popped out of its delicate setting and rolled toward the gutter. It had never been sturdy or practical, just a pretty façade. Just like our engagement. I took great satisfaction in watching Keith chase after it.

"You'll never keep the house." Helene's face twisted with rage. Her low tones and concern about causing a scene were long gone. Her anger was so pure and hot, I staggered backward.

"Let's get the hell outta here." I grabbed Rachel's arm, pulling her back to the Mini Cooper.

Chapter Three

"Where to?" Rachel peeled away from the church, leaving a real strip of pungent rubber on the road.

"Two streets over."

"What? We need to get out of this place before Helene burns you at the stake." Rachel hunched over the steering wheel, relishing her role as getaway driver.

I grasped at the straw hat with one hand and clutched the car door with the other.

"I need to talk to Sylvia's lawyer. I've been ignoring him. And since I'm never setting foot in this godforsaken town again, I should get this over with." I didn't want to linger and planned on cutting ties with Port Quincy, Pennsylvania, for good that day.

"The guy with the sexy voice," Rachel said hopefully.

"Keep your panties on, Rach. This is business. Let's attend to it quickly and get back to Pittsburgh."

"I know your life sucks right now, but just try to have a little fun." My sister was touching up her mascara as she steered the Mini Cooper through narrow, yellow-bricked streets.

I ignored her last comment and directed her to the address Garrett Davies had left in one of his many voice mails. We parked in front of an art deco office building that had once been grand but was now dingy and climbed the three flights to his office. I pushed open a heavy door and entered a small waiting room, overcrowded with couches and end tables laden with neat stacks of *People, Prevention,* and *Better Homes and Gardens* magazines woefully out of date.

The attorney's assistant was an older woman with short burgundy hair. She was watching a small television behind her desk when we entered, out of breath from our climb up the stairs.

"We're here to see Garrett Davies. I'm Mallory Shepard, and this is my sister, Rachel. It's about Sylvia Pierce."

The curvy woman bustled over and settled us on a comfortable, threadbare tweed couch. "Yinz want some coffee or tea? Some pop or water?" Her western Pennsylvania accent was strong.

"No thank you." I offered her a polite smile. I didn't want to prolong this meeting.

"He can see you now, hon." She gestured for us to follow her.

"What did that witch Helene mean about you not keeping a house?" Rachel whispered as we were led down a shabby corridor. It was a far cry from the building my firm occupied, all chrome, glass, and gray marble.

"I have no clue. Maybe that's why he's been calling. Sylvia had a house, but no way would that involve me."

I stumbled as I entered Garrett Davies's office. Partly because my shoes didn't match and also because the man who rose to greet us was one of the most attractive I'd ever seen. He was about five years older than me and a foot taller, with dark brown, nearly black hair cropped close to his head. Lovely bright hazel eyes were framed with impossibly long lashes.

He shook hands with each of us, his grip strong and true, and motioned for us to take seats. He pulled a bursting file out of a squeaky metal filing cabinet.

"You're sisters." He glanced at Rachel and me.

I looked up, startled. Most people didn't see the resemblance.

"I'm sorry I didn't make an appointment." I tucked my shoes under my chair.

He turned his attention back to me and appeared immune to Rachel's outfit.

One point for him.

"I was wondering if you were ever going to return my calls." He didn't hide the peevish tone in his deep voice.

Never mind. Minus one point.

"I've been attending to some personal matters that are very pressing. I apologize." I also couldn't camouflage my annoyance and didn't sound apologetic.

"So I've heard. The wedding, the likes of which has never been seen in Port Quincy. It's big news around here when the town's favorite son is getting married. Congratulations," he added sarcastically, pulling papers out of the stuffed file.

Both my and Rachel's mouth hung open.

"Is there something wrong?" He looked genuinely perplexed.

He didn't know. I'd gotten plenty of stares during the fracas with Helene at the funeral and assumed word traveled fast around these parts. Everyone probably knew I was the jilted would-be bride. Heck, most of the people at Sylvia's funeral had probably just been disinvited from the wedding. But maybe not as many people knew as I thought, since Helene still had hopes I'd go through with it and marry her rat-bastard son.

"The wedding is off. I'm not getting married."

"Oh." He paused a beat and stared at me as if waiting for an explanation, then seemed to remember his manners. "I'm sorry."

"I'm not," I said, with a conviction that surprised me. "Please, let's get on with it. Why did you call?" The sooner we left, the better.

"First off, my condolences about Sylvia. She thought highly of you, obviously, as she left you her house."

"What house?" Rachel asked, at the same time as I said, "*The* house?"

Garrett laughed, his voice like silver bells. "Yes, *the* house. Thistle Park. And Sylvia was pretty wily. She predicted there'd be trouble if she willed it to you, rather than Helene or Keith Pierce, who were left the house in an earlier version of the will. She deeded it to you instead, two weeks ago. Just in time, too, but she couldn't have known that."

I chewed on this. Maybe that was why Sylvia had asked for her laptop as I was leaving the last time I saw her. The timing was right.

"You see, if she had just left it to you in her will—"

"I get it. I'm an attorney too."

"Sorry. I don't want to condescend." He raised his hands in mock surrender. "Well then, I won't explain it to you." His handsome mouth curled into a sneer.

"You can explain it to me." Rachel uncrossed and re-crossed her long, caramel legs. One lime-colored heel dangled from her right foot. Oh boy, it was *Basic Instinct* time, and my sis was doing her best Sharon Stone impersonation. "I'm not an attorney."

I shot her a frosty look. "Sylvia probably thought Helene and Keith would try to claim her will was invalid if she left me the house. That she made it under duress or was of unsound mind. Especially since she changed the will two weeks before she passed away, most likely right after I last saw her. But, if she deeded it to me, it's mine free and clear. It'll be much harder for Keith or Helene to contest it." *Sylvia was a genius.*

Garrett nodded his agreement, assessing me with shrewd eyes.

I frowned. "I'm flattered Sylvia wanted me to have her house. I just have no idea why. And until a few days ago"—the words hitched in my throat—"I was going to marry her grandson. Then the house would have been property I was bringing into the marriage, rather than property we received together."

Garrett made a noncommittal sound. "Who knows why she wanted you to have it. The deed transfer appeared today in the local legal paper. It's not like it was going to be a secret for long. They probably already know. The Pierces." He spat out the last bit, so I guessed he wasn't fond of Helene and Keith either. "Where do you practice?"

"Russell Carey. Complex litigation." It wasn't the most exciting work, with long hours, occasional all-nighters, hard-to-please clients, and years between victories. The cases representing banks and mortgage companies dragged on forever, but they appealed to my need for order. Any surprise rulings were appealed, making their way through the higher courts in slow and somewhat predictable fashion. I was good at it and it was a way to pay off my law school loans before the turn of the next century. I had spent six years at the firm and was determined to make partner.

Garrett Davies smirked. "As in class actions? So you play around with spreadsheets and do an occasional deposition. What are you, a junior associate? I'm impressed you know so much about small-time property transfers."

My cheeks burned and I stood, dropping my purse on the floor. He was obviously annoyed at my cutting him off earlier, but this was uncalled for.

"Thanks for your time." I bent down to shove the upended contents back into my bag.

"I'm sorry. That was rude. I don't get to work with big-city attorneys that often. I forgot my manners. Please, sit." He gazed at me with those hazel eyes, and my anger diffused a bit.

I sat with a huff.

Garrett rifled through the file on his desk. "Sylvia was working with the historian at the Port Quincy Historical Society, Tabitha Battles. She was going to donate some items from the house, but that will be your call now. She was also consulting with her real estate agent, Zachary Novak. She was trying to decide whether to sell the place. And if I may suggest—"

"Like I can stop you."

He sighed and ran a hand through his dark hair.

Against my better judgment, I checked out his left hand. No ring. *Half point.*

"I deserve that. I suggest you sell the house. Sylvia went into the nursing home half a decade ago, and the house is a disaster. Structurally sound, but a mess. I had the electricity and water turned on for you last week, per Sylvia's request, but I wouldn't want to live there."

Would Sylvia have told me about the house if we had stopped in to see her two days ago? If I'd been there, could I have saved her? *I'm sorry, Sylvia.*

"Mallory?" Rachel placed a hand gently on my arm.

I must have zoned out for too long. "If the house is in such bad shape, who'd want to buy it?"

"The land may be more valuable than the house. I know the fracking people were hassling Sylvia about granting a gas lease, but she wouldn't budge. She tried to set it up so you couldn't use the land for that purpose—it was her last request, in addition to you getting the house. Of course, being an attorney and all"—his tone was mocking—"you know she couldn't give you the house with that kind of restrictive covenant. But you should know her wishes, just the same."

"Fracking?" Rachel wrinkled her nose at the word. "What is that?"

"I'll explain it later." I was spent, my head spinning. The enormity of Sylvia's bequest was beginning to sink in. "Thanks for your time, Mr. Davies. If that's all, I think we'll be going." I rose, purse firmly in hand this time.

"One more thing." Garrett smirked, undoing my composure. "You'll need these." He reached into the accordion file and pulled out an enormous cluster of at least twenty keys looped around a metal ring big enough to fit over my wrist. He dangled them in front of me, in a taunting manner, and I plucked them roughly from his hand.

"What do these unlock?" I turned the keys over in my hands. Some were modern and others antique, giant copper skeleton keys with thistle handles oxidized to a mint green. There were even miniature silver and gold keys, so delicate I feared I'd bend them.

"I can't help you there, but I know this one"—he pointed to a conventional house key—"is for the front and back doors. Sylvia had the locks changed when she moved to the nursing home. This one"—he pointed to a worn brass key, blackened by time—"is for the shed out back. The rest of them? Could be doors within the house, cabinets, maybe jewelry boxes. You'll have fun exploring."

The weighty key ring made my new inheritance unavoidably real. I sank back to my chair for a moment, Rachel and Garrett staring at me.

"Thank you." I stood at last. "For arranging this for Sylvia."

Garrett Davies gave us a genuine smile for the first time. It nearly knocked me out. "Good luck." He shook my hand.

A frisson of electricity went through me as he let go, and I shivered.

"You're going to need it."

* * *

"What a jerk face." I couldn't get out of Garrett Davies's office fast enough, but running down three flights of stairs in mismatched heels wasn't the easiest thing to do.

"But I was right, he is hot. A teeny bit old but undeniably yummy." Rachel pulled down her dress, which was riding up dangerously toward her hips.

I snorted. "He's five years older than me, tops." I glanced in the car's side mirror, donning my sunglasses so I wouldn't see the damage the last few days had wrought on my face. And so my sister wouldn't see my growing exasperation with her.

"Right, like I said, he's kind of old. But still adorable. I'd date him."

I let my sister's comment pass. "Whatever. He's certainly not very charming." Though he *was* lovely to look at. Not that being attractive made him any less of a boor.

Rachel dismissed my last remark with a wave of her hand. "Let's go find your house." She started the rental, as excited as a child on Christmas morning.

"Sylvia's house." I couldn't envision it ever really being "my" house, especially if I wasn't going to keep it. "And Garrett Davies is right, not like I want to admit it. I'll have to sell it." No way could I hold on to a piece of property fettering me to my ex-fiancé and Port Quincy.

"It's still yours for now."

I directed my sister down a steep hill, away from Port Quincy's downtown, through a little valley and up another sharp incline. The charming turn-of-the-century office buildings thinned and transitioned to small houses, then larger ones. The houses closer to town had been chopped up into apartments, but soon we reached streets where stately Victorians lined the road, set back from wide emerald lawns devoid of dandelions. A landscaper tended a rose-bush in front of one house while another watered the lawn. We were clearly in the gentrified part of town.

"So, fracking. What is that?" Rachel drove the rental like Danica Patrick, ignoring the TWENTY-FIVE MILES PER HOUR signs liberally posted all over town. I clutched the door with white knuckles and said a silent prayer.

"It's a way of getting natural gas out of the ground. Hydraulic fracturing. You drill by pumping water and chemicals into the earth under lots of pressure, and it breaks the shale rock so the gas trapped inside bub-bles up. It's made a lot of people around here very rich, and it's generated a bunch of work for the law firm where I work."

"Chemicals?" Rachel wrinkled her nose. "That doesn't exactly sound safe."

"Maybe that's why Sylvia wouldn't allow it on her property. I wouldn't. But it's a much-needed source of income, especially in places like Port Quincy." We were about to miss our turn. "Take this left. Sycamore Street."

"You know where it is already?" Rachel accelerated the teeny Mini Cooper through a hard left turn.

My stomach swooped.

"Would it kill you to slow down? The house has been there for over a hundred years. It'll still be there when we arrive." I closed my eyes against her glare and counted to ten. "Back when Keith and I first got engaged, Sylvia offered us the house as a place to hold the wedding. We drove past it. You could barely see it from the street, the yard was so overgrown. Even from there, we could tell it was too far gone. We stayed in the car, and I didn't have the heart to tell Sylvia. We thought it would upset her too much. That was over a year ago." I shuddered, wondering how much further the house had deteriorated.

"I'm sure we can spruce it up. A little paint, polish the floors . . ."

"What do you mean by 'we,' Rachel? How long are you planning on staying?" I narrowed my eyes at my baby sister and thought of the copious luggage she'd brought with her. My heart plummeted.

"Before you called off the wedding, I thought I could apartment-sit for you and Keith while you were on your honeymoon. Then I'd try to get a job in Pittsburgh."

I chuckled. "Keith would never have gone for that." My laughter died in my throat. Why didn't she need to go back to her job at the bakery and her classes at Pensacola State?

"What about school? Aren't you enrolled this summer, to catch up? And what about your job?" A heavy feeling settled in my stomach, not helped by her erratic driving.

Rachel was suddenly very interested in the road and wouldn't glance over at me. She reached into her voluminous turquoise bag and donned her sunglasses.

"Promise you won't tell Mom and Doug. I dropped out. And gave the bakery my notice. It's nice living with them, but I think I need my freedom. It's time for a change."

"You didn't even finish the summer semester! After Mom and Doug paid your tuition." I shook my head.

At twenty-two, Rachel was still finding herself. Which would be fine if Mom and Doug didn't need to bail her out time and time again, sometimes literally. My parents adored Rachel, but they hadn't expected my sister to move back in once they retired. I often wondered if I played the part of the goody-good to Rachel's role as the wild child as an attempt to distinguish myself from her.

Before I could scold her further, the house loomed into view.

"There it is," I whispered, my voice softened in awe.

"Holy crap." Rachel slammed on the brakes.

"I'll say." I was momentarily distracted from my sister's job and school situation.

Sycamore dead-ended in front of Sylvia's house. Ah, here was where all of the dandelions were. They were chemically suppressed from the other well-maintained lawns, but here they bloomed in sunny profusion. The house was partly occluded by a stand of pine trees, thank goodness. A once-grand lawn flanked the house and stretched for acres behind it.

I got out of the car and treaded lightly up the path of herringbone bricks, crushing the stems poking through. Weeds reached through the path to tickle my ankles and calves. Rachel caught up with me, trailing her long nails in the thigh-high meadow that had overtaken the grass.

There it stood. The brick walls had once been white but were now a blistering gray, faded and flaking from years of neglect. It was three stories high, with a shingled mansard roof, a central brick tower, and a front porch composed of a series of arches. A porte cochere sagged off to the right, the roof threatening to cave in. The whole thing was decked out in crumbling trim ornate enough for Liberace's jumpsuit.

"What are those, pineapples?" Rachel pointed at the gingerbread roofline, where each corner of the house was adorned with a cone-shaped object, anchoring the house to the sky.

"I think they're thistles. That's the name of this place, right? Thistle Park."

Rachel started to laugh. "Isn't that fancy." She adopted her best British accent. "We can be the duchesses of Thistle Park."

I didn't laugh. I was closer to tears. *Sylvia, I can't take this on. Did you really mean for me to have this house?*

We pressed on until we were directly in front of the beast. A straggly clump of lilac bushes threatened to climb onto the porch, and fat bumblebees, the size of baby hummingbirds, buzzed around the bushes, then my neck and ears, making me dizzy. The place had decayed even more in the year since I'd seen it from the street. It was a beautiful, moldering pile of rubble.

"This place is way past dumpy." All of Rachel's former excitement had subsided.

"It's bordering on condemnation, more like it. Although, Garrett did say it's structurally sound."

"And it's ginormous." Rachel pushed up her sunglasses and took a step back, then another, and craned her head. "This place has so much potential."

Her keen green eyes gleamed with schemes and plans, and just like that, she was excited again.

"You can tell it was amazing once. But it's so far gone. Let's not get ahead of ourselves until we've seen the inside." Even Rachel's enthusiasm couldn't surmount my growing sense of dread.

"After you." Rachel solemnly gestured me forward.

I gingerly climbed the front stairs. The three front steps were stone, but they had bowed gently with the passage of many feet, approximating a crooked kind of smile. Forest-green paint peeled away from the wooden porch floor in narrow curly sheets. The wood felt pliant and rotten beneath me, and petunias grew out of a hole in the porch's corner. I removed the colossal key ring from my purse, the different metals jingling like a discordant wind chime. I selected the simple key that would open the house, according to Garrett. The door swung open with no resistance, and we stepped in, holding our breaths. Turned out that was a good thing, as the place reeked of ammonia.

We were greeted with hushed darkness in the entrance hall, and I trailed my fingers over the walls with my fingertips until I connected with a light switch. The hallway chandelier sprang to life, the old wiring emitting a perceptible whine.

"Whoa!" This time, I was the one exclaiming and, for once, Rachel was silent. The inside was as ornate and in as bad a state as the outside. We were surrounded by dark paneled wood, the varnish blackened and crusted over. The scuffed floors were covered with threadbare rugs and led to a grand staircase, probably once flanked by two thistle finials as big as my head. Only one of the two thistles remained. The house seemed to let out a sigh. I shivered.

"Kind of creepy." I rubbed the goose bumps sprouting on my forearms.

We combed each room, pulling back heavy drapes, stirring up dust and letting in sunlight through streaky windows.

"Was that a bird?" A small, black winged creature fluttered out from the dusty brocade, narrowly missing my sister.

"I think it's a bat!" I ducked as it escaped out an open transom window. "Great, we need rabies shots just to live here."

Pictures in sepia stared at us from the walls. They featured women under parasols, shielding their delicate skin, attended by men with comical mustaches and little bow ties. Few smiled. The faded, busy botanical wallpaper was interrupted by ghostly, vibrant rectangles where paintings had once hung. Heavy brass sconces hung from the walls, crooked and candle-less. Silverfish scuttled across the floor in the lone bathroom, and the air was heavy and humid. Every nook, cranny, and shelf was filled with decorative glass, now dusty and dull.

We pushed and jimmied swollen pocket doors that resisted our meddling and felt as if they hadn't been cajoled out of their tracks for years. From the second-floor landing, I could see a carriage house, a greenhouse with nearly every pane of glass shattered, a weedy tennis court, and a large shed, listing to the right. Two statues of angels in flight, one of them missing a wing, the other her arm, presided over an overrun garden, choked with hydrangeas, irises, and day lilies. The garden took over a large swath of the backyard, which stretched far back to a copse of trees and a gazebo. The seven bedrooms on the second floor were as old-fashioned and lavish as the downstairs and also as neglected. We couldn't even open the door sealing off the third floor. None of the keys on the key ring worked.

"Good. That'll give you an excuse to see Garrett Davies again," Rachel said coyly. "Maybe he has the key."

"I don't think we need to see him again." I kicked up little piles of dust as we descended from the third-floor landing. "Although it might be worth it to pick his brain."

Rachel and I marveled at the contents of the house. It was a control freak's nightmare.

"Are you okay?"

"Mm-hm." I sank into one of the parlor's lumpy couches, suppressing thoughts of the dust that would coat the backside of my black suit. "Just overwhelmed. I'm screwed, Rach. No one will want to buy this place."

My sister hitched up her shoulders in response.

That bad, huh. I picked at some thread unraveling from the couch and shut my eyes against my new reality. I thought of the apartment I'd so recently shared with Keith, where things were sparse and neat, everything in its proper place. Then I pictured the man who lived there and ground the heels of my hands into my eyes to burn out the vision of him. When I opened them, I was still at Thistle Park, surrounded by the ruined splendor of times past.

And all of this moldy decadence was overpowered by a sour stench. By now, our eyes and noses were running freely.

"This smell is intense." Rachel was breathing through a tissue held over her nose and mouth.

My eyes were tearing and I spoke with my nose pinched shut. "Cat pee," I announced in a nasal voice.

"Geez!" Rachel stood up. "What was that?"

It was the likely source of the smell, a streak of black, white, and orange. A slim calico hissed at us, darting down the hall to the back of the house. I ran after the small cat in time to see it jump onto the kitchen sink and out the open window to the back porch.

"More windows left open." I followed the cat out to the back porch. The calico was guarding a cardboard box, and from the mewling emanating from it, I guessed what was in it.

"A kitten." Bowls of fresh water and kibble stood nearby.

"Looks like someone is feeding them." Rachel shied back as the calico headed toward her. "Do you think it's safe to pet it? The cat could have rabies."

I laughed. "You sound like Mom." I bent down to let the cat smell my hand in a gesture of good faith.

The little calico shied away at first, then came back to sniff me.

"She's friendly, at least." I reached out to pet her.

The calico erupted into an outsized purr, surprisingly loud since she was so tiny. Her kitten sat up curiously. It looked like a fluffy little apricot.

"I don't think they should stay outside. Even if someone's been feeding them."

"I guess not," Rachel agreed reluctantly.

The calico looked at my sister hopefully as she

rammed her head against my hand, rubbing and purring.

"We can air this place out and get them some litter boxes, and you can move out of that motel. You can't stay there forever."

I muttered a noncommittal reply as we moved the mama cat and her kitten inside. The calico looked at me uncertainly when I picked her up, but she seemed fine when Rachel moved the box with her kitten.

Just then, a horrible noise like a dying bagpipe clanged through the house.

"What was that?" Rachel looked down as if the sound had come from our new furry friends.

"The doorbell?" We settled the cats with their provisions in the kitchen and trooped down the long hallway to open the front door.

"Howdy, ladies." Our visitor grabbed my hand before I had a chance to properly take him in. He kissed it with a flourish.

I retracted my hand from his sweaty octopus grip. He repeated the performance with Rachel. My sister giggled and gave me the side eye, as if to say, *This should be good.*

"I'm Shane Hartley of Lonestar Energy. Which one of you lovelies is Miss Mallory Shepard?"

"I am." I didn't want to admit my identity to this joker.

"I saw your car out yonder." He jerked his chin toward our rental. "I wanted to introduce myself and set up a meeting with you." He extracted a business card from the back pocket of his jeans and handed it over.

I reluctantly accepted the moist card and noted its star and Texas insignia.

I narrowed my eyes and gave him a thorough once-over. He was short, about five six. He was aided in the height department by a pair of heeled cowboy boots, and he wore tight, faded jeans and a red plaid shirt. A round belly hung over a big belt buckle, standing out from the rest of his slight frame. His jolly face was lined and heavily tanned beneath his ten-gallon hat. The years of sunshine made him look older, but I guessed he was about forty. His drawl definitely placed him from the heart of Texas, yet he seemed to be overdoing it for a folksy affect. My sophomore roommate had been from Dallas, and she hadn't laid it on this thick. I glanced at his card again. It had numbers for offices in Houston, Texas, and Port Quincy, Pennsylvania.

"Nice to meet you, Mr. Hartley. What can I do for you?" There was a black pickup truck in the driveway, with a man in the passenger seat and another squeezed in the backseat. The truck bed was loaded with yellow instruments and tripods.

"I see you're a woman who doesn't beat around the bush." He looked past my shoulder, as if expecting to be invited in. No way was I showing this house of horrors to any callers.

"I just heard you're the new owner of this here piece of property, and I wanted to tell you about all of the exciting opportunities Lonestar Energy can offer you. If you can spare an hour sometime this week and mosey on down to my office, we're prepared to make you an offer for a gas lease beyond your wildest dreams."

I frowned, remembering what Garrett had said about Sylvia's wishes regarding fracking and drilling on her property.

"I don't think so." My good manners bubbled to the top. "I mean, no thank you, that won't be necessary."

Shane Hartley looked as if I'd knocked the wind out of him. He rocked back and forth in his boots and rubbed his hands together, ready to dig in for the hard sell. The rotten porch swayed softly with each of his movements. "Now, ma'am—"

Ooh, big mistake. I might be turning thirty this fall, but I hated being called ma'am. I needed to get this guy off Sylvia's porch immediately.

"No, thanks. I don't think it would be appropriate to drill on this land. Nothing you can say will change my mind." I crossed my arms and tried to stand firm, but I felt myself wavering.

Shane Hartley began to laugh. "Now see here, little lady. Why do you think you know whether it's appropriate to drill here or not? You have plenty of land and you'd barely notice we were here. It'd be very lucrative. I'm not sure you have the funds to tend to this house, but we can make that possible. Why don't you come on down and hear what we have to offer—"

"She said she isn't interested." Rachel leaned over Mr. Hartley.

"Yeah. Sylvia Pierce left me this house and property, and it's my understanding she didn't want any fracking at her childhood home. I'm going to respect her wishes. And"—I took a step toward him, emboldened—"I don't believe it's any of your business how I finance the renovation of this house or what my plans are."

Shane Hartley threw up his hands. He gave us

some space and moved from the porch to the walkway. "Fine. But between you and me, I'm not sure how long this piece of land will be yours, ma'am, if you catch my drift."

"Excuse me?" I whispered, struggling to keep my voice under control. It didn't escape my notice he'd placed extra emphasis on the "ma'am" part. *Perfect. This guy can already figure out how to get my goat.*

"Word through the grapevine," he drawled, "is there were some discrepancies about how Miss Sylvia bequeathed you this place. Rumor is, this house is supposed to belong to Helene and Keith Pierce. They're smart people, ma'am, especially that Keith. He's an attorney. There are valuable things in this house that belong to the Pierce family, not some interloper, and I have a feeling when this is all straightened out, it won't be your decision about what to do with this parcel."

Rachel told me later I let out a shrill little shriek before I lunged down the stairs, but I don't remember since it happened so fast. When it was over, I'd pushed little Shane Hartley so hard he'd landed in the high grass. He tumbled over in an exaggerated pratfall as if he were an NBA player falling to draw a foul.

As the wrath left my body in waves, it was replaced by a sense of alarm. Hartley was lying on the ground shaking and made no move to get up. Could I be prosecuted for assault? I was about to go help him when my anger percolated again as I realized he was trembling with laughter.

"Shoot, girl, you are something else!" He stood in one fluid, cat-like movement, rubbing his tailbone.

The men in the truck were cackling too. The lace curtains of the nearest neighbor snapped shut.

Awesome. I had an audience.

Rachel left the porch and stood imperiously over Shane Hartley. She had more than a few inches on him, especially in her four-inch heels. "Get out of here right now, before we call the police for trespassing. You're not wanted."

Mr. Hartley smirked, picked up his hat, and placed it on his head. He was still chuckling as he got into the black pickup, blew us a kiss, and drove away.

"Thanks, Rach." I was still shaking when Shane Hartley drove off.

Rachel slung her arm around my shoulders. "Anytime, Mall."

"What a warm welcome," I joked in an unsteady voice. "I hope everyone in this place is as friendly."

We tried to salvage what was left of the day. I checked out of the motel by the airport, and we barely jammed all of our stuff into the Mini Cooper, making two trips to accommodate Rachel's stuff. We unloaded our luggage and made a trip to Target to buy sheets, snacks, litter boxes, and a few other provisions. When we returned, the house didn't seem as creepy, just stinky and dusty and sad. We feasted on Port Quincy's finest pizza and Oreo cookies for dessert. I wasn't anywhere close to feeling normal, but it was a start.

"At least you have your appetite back." Rachel gestured to the bag of cookies we'd just kicked.

"Baby steps." I gave her a small smile.

I was happy to be out of the motel and bade my sister good night as I closed the door to the bedroom I'd chosen. I put the new sheets on the florid but tarnished brass bed and fell asleep thirty seconds later.

The day's events must have lodged in my subconscious because my dreams were disturbing and shockingly vivid. A fire in this house and a woman screaming. I tried to find her but couldn't pick the right key to open the door. None of them fit. I was choking on the fumes. A hand reached out to save me. It was Sylvia.

"Thank goodness." I hugged her, engulfed in thick black smoke. "What do you want me to do with your house?" Her embrace grew stronger, and I tried to pull away. I realized I wasn't hugging Sylvia, but Helene. She wouldn't let me go and squeezed ever tighter, like a boa constrictor. I tried to scream, but my throat filled with ash. Keith stood to the side, just beyond the curtain of smoke. He shook his head with disapproval and refused to intervene. It was too late. Helene had almost crushed the last breath from my lungs.

"Mallory, wake up." Rachel was shaking my shoulders.

I must have been having a nightmare. I struggled to sit up, but the mattress had sunk in overnight.

I rolled back into the deep divot in the bed, pulling the sheet over my head to staunch the weak light coming through the window. I checked my watch with one open eye. "It's only six a.m. I can sleep a whole extra hour and still make it to work on time. Leave me alone."

"There's something you need to see. Right now."

I detected a slight edge of panic in Rachel's voice and flung off the sheet covering my head.

"What is it? What's so important this early?" I was

groggy and grumpy. I'm not a morning person, and today would be my first day back at work since my life blew up. I wanted to hide under the covers as long as possible. I wasn't eager to test-drive Thistle Park's plumbing this morning either, as there was no way to shower, only a claw-foot tub encrusted in grime.

"Mallory." Rachel knelt beside the bed and grabbed both of my hands in hers. They were ice cold. "There's a dead dude in the front yard."

Chapter Four

"Tell me again."

The Port Quincy chief of police was staring me down, trying to break me. I searched my sleepy brain for any nuggets of wisdom from my criminal procedure class in law school. I wanted to go all Fifth Amendment on his ass and end this interview but ultimately decided it'd be better to play nice. So, I rubbed my eyes with the cuff of my penguin pajamas and recounted the events of last night and this morning for the umpteenth time. It was strange. The more I repeated myself, the less certain I was.

"We came back from the motel, bought some sheets and snacks, unpacked and ordered a pizza. We went to bed around ten. We didn't leave any lights on. I swear there were no dead people on the lawn when we fell asleep. My sister woke me around six this morning and told me about . . . him." I delivered this monologue in a monotone, because it was hard to impart enthusiasm when you'd been saying the same thing for hours.

"Him" being one Shane Hartley, the man I'd argued

with and pushed. A man my sister had threatened a mere twelve hours before he'd turned up dead in front of Sylvia's house, now my house, the back of his head bludgeoned.

The interview had started soon after the sun rose. We sat in what we'd been calling the breakfast room, and the morning rays bathed us in buttery, diffuse sunlight. Three hours later, the room was no longer pleasant but sour and stuffy. I was also dying in my flannel sleepwear, which I hadn't been permitted to change out of. I hoped the cops liked me sweaty.

"Maybe he was killed somewhere else and brought here?" Rachel looked marginally more comfortable in her shorts and silk robe.

"No way. Your grass is soaked with blood," Chief Truman shot her down. "Someone definitely bashed his head in right here, and he bled out in your petunias—"

My stomach plunged.

"—and expired in your front yard. You okay, Miss Shepard?"

I stood and covered my mouth with my hand.

"My sister's a little squeamish."

"Just today." I was still ruing the loss of that extra hour of sleep, even though I now had worse things to worry about. I swallowed and sunk back into my seat.

"Maybe you need to eat something," Truman's sidekick, Officer Faith Hendricks, gently said.

They were an odd pair. Truman was tall and imposing, with a stern, disapproving expression. He had a big gut and salt-and-pepper hair that was thinning at the crown. He was handsome in a craggy, avuncular kind of way. Although I'd never met him before this morning, he looked vaguely familiar.

Faith was gorgeous, with creamy milkmaid good looks and a sunny smile. Her caramel ponytail bounced behind her as she nodded, eagerly encouraging me and my sister to spill our guts and further incriminate ourselves. Faith couldn't have been a day over twenty-five, but her enthusiasm made up for lack of experience. Both Truman and Faith peered at me with genuine concern, which was the nicest they'd been so far this morning.

"I made us Pop-Tarts for breakfast, but I dropped them when I saw him," Rachel chimed in.

"I figured so," Truman said drily.

I would never eat another Pop-Tart so long as I lived. I shut my eyes and replayed the morning's events in the dreadful reel running on repeat in my head.

I'd run down the stairs, Rachel on my heels, as soon as I'd processed what she said. Sure enough, there had been a dead man in the front yard. A whole ten feet from the front door. He had been on his back, staring up at the pale morning sky. His face had leered in death, a thin trickle of blood running out of the corner of his mouth, which was rigored into a skeleton smile. His right hand had been awash in rusty stuff, as if he'd touched his head before he expired. It was Shane Hartley. And right in front of him had lain two fresh cherry Pop-Tarts, broken into pieces.

I'd stared at him in silence for a full fifteen seconds.

"Why are those there?" I'd finally asked, pointing to the breakfast pastries and not the dead man. It had seemed like a fair question, though, looking back, a better one might have been, "Did you hear anything last night?"

"I was going to wake you with breakfast in bed since it's your first day back. I wondered if we got the paper, which is dumb, because no one's lived here for years, but it was early and I was out of it. I opened the door and saw him, and it was still pretty dark, so I walked over to figure out who was lying there and if they needed help. When I realized who it was, I panicked and dropped the Pop-Tarts," Rachel had prattled on in a rush before she'd begun to cry.

I'd gently steered my sister around so we couldn't see Mr. Hartley's body. "It's okay, Rach. Not really okay, but we have to do something."

"I can make more Pop-Tarts."

"We could do that." I'd pulled her up the porch steps. "But I was thinking maybe we should call the police."

"Oh, right, of course." Once we had gotten back inside, the door shut firmly behind us, we'd snapped out of it and done a pretty good job of dealing with the body on the lawn. The police had arrived about five minutes after we'd called 911. We'd been here ever since, hunkered down around the old oak table in this octagonal room, drinking cold coffee with Port Quincy's finest man and woman in blue.

"Tell me again."

"Just like she said," Rachel began. "We—"

"Nope, we've told you enough," I interrupted. "We're not going to change our story."

"Your story?" Chief Truman perked up.

Oops, bad choice of words.

"Our truthful accounting of what happened. Do we need a lawyer?"

The chief smirked. "I thought you are a lawyer."

I flinched. "I am, but I don't practice criminal

defense, and I don't know anything about murder investigations. Are we suspects?"

Rachel tensed up next to me. I grabbed her hand under the table and gave it a reassuring squeeze. No matter what, I wasn't going to let them incriminate my little sister or me.

"Neither of you appear to have been in a struggle," Faith said slowly.

Rachel relaxed.

"Now hold on." Truman shot Faith a dirty look and leaned closer to us across the table. "Ma'am, a man was murdered right here at Thistle Park while you and your sister were admittedly on the premises. What I can't wrap my head around is your claim neither of you heard a peep last night."

Geez, what was with the ma'ams flying around this town? I obviously needed better wrinkle cream. I didn't know what pissed me off more, the fact I was a possible murder suspect or that I'd just been called ma'am again.

"I did have a nightmare sometime before Rachel woke me. Someone was screaming in my dream. Or at least I thought it was a dream at the time."

Duh. Why hadn't I made that connection until now?

"What time was that?" Faith sat up straighter, her pen poised over her little notebook, the picture of an eager student.

"I don't know," I stammered, sounding defensive.

Chief Truman and Faith exchanged knowing glances.

I rushed in to fill their disappointed silence. "I feel awful about what happened. I really do. That poor man. But we didn't have anything to do with it." I couldn't wait for Shane Hartley to leave yesterday, but that didn't mean I had been hoping for his demise.

"Oh, come on," Rachel said wearily. "I don't want to speak ill of the dead, but the guy was a class-A jerk. I'm sure he had lots of enemies."

Faith gave her a disapproving glare.

"And no matter who killed him, it's awfully convenient he ended up dead on my—Sylvia's—front lawn." I took a swig of water and tried to set the glass neatly on the table. My hands shook so badly I splashed most of the water out of the glass. This earned another portentous look between Truman and Faith.

"True, but we have several witnesses who saw you get into a physical altercation with the victim yesterday." Chief Truman was barely able to contain his glee, as if he'd just laid down a royal flush.

How in the heck does he know that?

"Why would you try to hide that from me?" He cracked his first smile of the day, a real Cheshire special.

Crap. A trickle of sweat ran down my back. *Stupid, stupid. You always shut up, and you always get a criminal defense attorney when you talk to the police.* Though I didn't practice criminal law, I'd had a few occasions to advise my clients to clam up in the event authorities questioned them. And I *had* watched *The Wire.* And here I was, digging myself a bigger hole, thanks to my teeny-tiny lie of omission. I just couldn't bring myself to tell them I'd shoved Shane Hartley hours before he was murdered. It was time to shut up for real, even though Rachel and I hadn't done anything.

"He wouldn't leave." Rachel pushed back from the

table. "Honest. He was threatening *us,* not the other way around."

I nodded, my lips pursed. I'd Krazy Glue my mouth shut if I had to.

Then I quickly abandoned my internal promise to stay quiet in less than a nanosecond. "He said something was wrong with the way Sylvia left me the house and that it would be Helene and Keith Pierce's property soon enough."

That revelation raised two sets of eyebrows. Ultimately, Truman and Faith said nothing. They stuck to their previously successful tactic of waiting for me to stick my foot firmly into my yapping mouth. I chewed on my lower lip to keep from talking. Rachel stirred her spoon around in her cup, the metal making a grating noise against the bone china, her coffee long gone.

"We also heard about an altercation you had with the Pierces after Sylvia's funeral." Faith smirked. "Do you have a problem controlling your temper, Mallory?"

I managed a sip of water, trying to play it cool. It took every ounce of control to keep my hand from shaking. I used the time my drink bought me to wonder how they'd found out so quickly. Did gossip really spread this fast in a small town?

"So what?" I finally ventured. The truth should be good enough. "Helene Pierce is crazy."

"We know," Faith said, surprising me. "I'd just like to hear your side."

It was possible they'd heard about these incidents before Hartley's death had even been called in to the police. I was impressed and worried, but I was no murderer. Then it dawned on me. Faith and Truman had popped up from the table several times during our interrogation to field phone calls. Their colleagues must have been gathering intel and relaying the information to them.

"He had no business being back here while it was dark. I told him to buzz off, and I meant it. I admit I pushed him, but he deserved it. He threatened me. It wasn't like he came back here in the middle of the night to strike a business deal."

Faith glanced at Chief Truman, wordlessly asking for permission. "Actually, that's precisely why he came back here."

"How do you know that? It's not like you can ask him now." The words left my lips before I realized how insensitive I sounded.

"Because he drew up an offer letter for this property. Not to lease it, but to buy it outright. A pretty big offer based on the number of zeros. He was probably going to slip it in the mail slot since you'd rebuffed him. Let the money talk for him."

"How much?" Rachel's eyes were shining. She'd been quiet for a while, a much savvier suspect than I was. But at the mention of money, she perked right up and leaned toward the cops, abandoning her nervous ritual with the spoon and cup.

"We can't tell exactly. The note was soaked with blood. Some of the ink smeared, but we're talking high six figures."

I gulped. Good thing I hadn't had a Pop-Tart after all.

"The surveyors who were with Shane Hartley told our colleagues at the station the same version of events as you did, and that's what matters for now," Chief Truman said. "That is, I don't have enough information to take you for a little ride downtown. We're done here. Thank you for the coffee."

Truman and Faith stood to go.

I faded back into my chair with relief.

"Oh, ladies?" Truman barked.

"Yes?" My voice was a squeak.

He wasn't finished with me just yet.

"You two be careful. You might think about installing an alarm system. We'll be in touch."

"That's it?" I'd wanted them gone all morning, and now I didn't want them to leave.

"What about the body?" Rachel's eyes darted in the direction of the front yard.

"Gone." The chief glanced at his watch. He was done with us. "Impounded his truck too. You'll need to cut down the crime tape and you might want to hose off the grass, but that's it."

Faith touched my arm lightly. "You hear anything, give us a call."

They handed us their cards and waltzed out of the breakfast room.

"What's that smell?" Faith asked the chief.

"Cat piss," he whispered back, but not quiet enough for me to miss.

Rachel flopped back with relief as soon as the front door shut. We hadn't even bothered to show Truman and Faith out. We were safe, for now.

"I thought they might arrest us." Rachel flashed me a shaky smile.

"Me too. But for what? I certainly wasn't marauding around last night, confronting trespassers. And I was so exhausted, I wouldn't have noticed a murder going on right under my window. Which is apparently what happened." A shiver trilled up my back.

Someone had been killed just below me. Had the murderer even realized Rachel and I were inside? We'd parked the Mini around the back of the house and turned off all the lights, so it wouldn't have been obvious.

"Who wanted Shane Hartley dead?" I wondered.

"Like I said, he was a jerk, so I bet there are a lot of people in this town who wanted to off him." Rachel's hand flew to her mouth.

"No worries, Rach. I'm sorry he's dead too. No one deserves to be murdered, especially that way. But that doesn't change the fact he was a complete Neanderthal for the whole five minutes we talked to him."

I glanced at my cell phone, its red light flashing malevolently like a dragon's eye. Work beckoned, but I turned it over, dismissing it for the moment. Whatever was happening at the firm could wait.

"Let's go take care of the front yard." The thought of Shane Hartley's blood drying on the grass made me ill.

It took us a while to find the right key to the shed, extricate an old hose from a tangle of rusty tools and yard implements, and find a spigot on the side of the house. We worked in silence, jittery and pensive. The hose barely stretched around the porch, and water sprayed out in arcs from hundreds of pinprick holes in the rotten canvas. Mini rainbows shimmered in the mist from the hose, and I chose to focus on them instead of my grim task.

Rachel turned away as the weak spray hit the bloody grass. Out of the corner of my eye, it ran red, then pink and finally absorbed into the ground, leaving a sodden puddle. We gathered the yellow crime tape and had just finished scrunching it into a slick plastic ball when a gray sedan pulled into the pocked driveway, pausing in front of the sagging porte cochere. Two women climbed out of the car.

"Smart choice. I wouldn't park under that thing either." My voice was calm and welcoming in an attempt to mask the tension of the day.

Rachel grabbed the crime tape and tried to throw it over the side of the porch, but the slippery yellow plastic unspooled and fell in a pile at her feet.

"Are we here at a bad time?" The shorter, plumper woman stared at the tape, transfixed. She nearly dropped the large foil-covered bowl she carried. Her eyes trailed over to the wet patch of grass, as if she expected to see a body neatly outlined in chalk, or even Shane Hartley's cooling corpse.

"No, we're fine." I threw the yellow plastic inside, where the waiting calico pounced on it before I shut the door. I dried my hands on my pajama bottoms. I hadn't had a chance to change. I glanced at Rachel, happy to see she was covered up, albeit in a slinky but firmly tied silk robe and shorts.

"I'm not sure where the morning went." I lamely gestured at our sleepwear.

Before I became too preoccupied with my appearance, my attention switched to our visitors. The first woman was short like me and almost as wide as she was tall. Her blond hair was teased into an honest-to-goodness beehive. Her voluminous top was dotted Swiss, with little green circles on a white background, which she had paired with tomato-red pedal pushers, ones that perfectly matched her red cat's-eye glasses. She looked like a cheery box of Krispy Kremes.

"I'm Beverly Mitchell. You can call me Bev. We're the official Port Quincy Welcome Wagon."

Bev pumped my hand, her numerous thick band rings tickling my palm. She thrust the heavy, cold glass bowl into my arms so she could shake hands with my sister.

I turned to the meeker woman mincing up the bowed porch stairs. She was tall and willowy, but all of her height was wasted, as she hunched forward like she wanted to disappear. Her floral housedress was faded and pilled. She looked through a curtain of lank, dull brown hair, which had escaped her clip. Her eyes, myopic and magnified behind large wire frames, darted right and left. She finally reached us and awkwardly handed Rachel a basket of muffins but didn't offer her hand.

Where have I seen her before?

"You're the singer from Sylvia's funeral," I blurted out.

The woman nearly jumped out of her sandals. She said nothing, neither confirming nor denying it.

"Your voice is amazing." I tried to not scare her any further. "Are you a professional singer?" That seemed to have gotten through to her.

"I just sing for church." She shrugged. "I'm the receptionist at my dad's auto body shop. I was going to be an opera singer"—she gulped and looked down—"but that ship has sailed."

"I'm Mallory Shepard, and this is my sister, Rachel." I cradled the heavy bowl in my left arm and reached out to shake her hand.

The woman took a step back, leaving my hand hovering awkwardly in the air.

"You inherited Sylvia Pierce's house." She gave me an appraising look but didn't seem to notice my extended hand.

"In a way." *How did she know?* "Does everyone know everyone else's business in Port Quincy?" I blurted out.

The woman released a peal of genuine laughter, and this time she held out her hand and consented to a weak handshake, her hand cold and papery. But the laugh was real and warm and rich and full, like her singing voice.

"I'm Yvette Tannenbaum. Excuse my poor manners. My husband told me about what happened here last night. A real murder in Port Quincy. It's just a little . . . unsettling." The laughter in her voice died out.

"Y-*vette*," Bev tsk-tsked her friend. "No one is supposed to know about that yet. Although, you're right." She gave me a pointed look. "Everyone is in everyone else's business here. No one can keep a secret."

Rachel and I exchanged glances. "So everybody in town knows someone was murdered here?"

Yvette shook her head. "Not yet. My husband, Bart, is the mayor, so the police alerted him immediately."

"But I'm sure most people will know soon enough. It'll be in the *Eagle Herald*. Things like this just don't happen in Port Quincy. . . ." Bev's gaze strayed over to the patch of wet grass. "Is that where he passed?"

"That's where we found him." Rachel refused to look.

Bev trembled but seemed to steel herself. "I know it's not right to say, but I can think of about a hundred people who are rejoicing now that Shane Hartley's dead."

"I wouldn't talk like that, Bev." Yvette leaned

against the railing. "Especially since you're one of those hundred people." She looked a little faint.

Rachel seemed ready to catch her if the whole thing snapped off and, from the looks of the rotted porch rail, it just might.

Bev glared at her friend. "You know I wouldn't hurt a flea. Even if that flea was a rotten, no-good snake oil salesman and a land-ruining son-of-a-you-know-what."

"Chief Truman seems to think Rachel and I are somehow implicated, which is ridiculous. Especially if Mr. Hartley had so many enemies."

Rachel snorted next to me in agreement.

"Well, his wife is a decent human being," Bev sniffed. "How she'll manage with the baby due so soon, I don't know." She clucked her tongue.

"That poor woman," Yvette addressed the porch floor. "She didn't deserve this."

My heart wrenched. Even if Shane Hartley wasn't well liked in Port Quincy, he was a real person, not just a caricature. My heart did a flop for his wife and unborn child.

Yvette peered at her hands, twisting her gold wedding ring around and around. "I hope you don't mind me asking. I don't want to seem ghoulish. Were you here when it happened?" She peered up through her curtain of hair. "Did you hear the struggle?"

Rachel swallowed. "We were here, but we were sleeping. We didn't hear a thing."

"I don't think the police believe us." I shifted the heavy bowl in my arms. The bottom was cut glass, and the weight of it had already pressed patterns into the skin on my arms, little acorns, berries and sheaves of wheat. "They just left after questioning us all morning. That's why we're still in our pajamas."

"You can keep that, honey." Bev proudly gestured to the large dish and deftly changed the subject. "The glass, in addition to the zucchini casserole. It's McGavitt glass, made here in Port Quincy. Right in the factory owned by Sylvia's family. And don't worry, the zucchini's from the farmers' market. I didn't grow it."

I tried to lift the heavy dish to get a better look. "You don't say. Thank you." I hoped we liked Bev's zucchini casserole, because we'd be eating it for weeks. I didn't delve into her odd remark about not growing the veggies herself. *What is with these people?*

Bev snorted. "You don't know anything about Thistle Park, do you?" She gestured around the grounds, the gems in her costume jewelry glistening on her fingers like Jolly Rancher candies. "Sylvia tried to keep things just as they were when the house was built. It's like you're living in a little bit of preserved history."

"Something like that," I mumbled. I had been a history major in college and was fascinated by the house, but that didn't mean I reveled in the mess inside. "Sylvia told me about Thistle Park, but only because she wanted to escape from the nursing home and move back in. I'm trying to figure out what to do with this house and how best to carry out her wishes." There had been no love lost between Shane Hartley and Sylvia, according to Garrett. How would she have felt knowing he had been murdered on her property?

"So you're staying?" Yvette glanced around the beat-up porch.

You're crazy, her eyes said for her.

Rachel, however, peered at me with hope in her eyes.

"I don't know. This place could be lovely, but it'd take a lot of sweat equity and money to even get it to the point where I can sell it. It's barely livable. And after what happened . . . I don't feel safe here."

"Honey, believe it or not, this town is safe. You don't need to worry about a thing. That's why Yvette and I came over today. You can ask us for anything. We're just so excited you two girls moved in, even if it's temporary." Bev gave us an encouraging smile. "People are real friendly here in Port Quincy. You'll see."

Yvette stood from her railing perch. "It was nice to meet you. I need to get going, but do let us know if you need anything."

Bev pulled out a card that read, "Port Quincy's finest seamstress" with her cell number. She pressed the card in my hand before she swooped in for an impulsive hug, all soft and bosomy and smelling of cinnamon. I was barely able to hold on to the casserole. Bev's impromptu hug made me long for my mom far away in Florida. Had I made a mistake deciding to move into Thistle Park? Bev and Yvette began their descent down the bowed porch stairs.

"I hope I'm not being rude." Yvette looked back. "But I heard about you calling off your wedding. Breaking things off with Keith Pierce and his mother. That was the right thing to do. You dodged a real bullet there."

I shivered as Yvette followed Bev back to her gray Toyota. I agreed with her but didn't appreciate her metaphor. I'd come too close to murder weapons lately to feel comfortable even hearing them mentioned, thank you very much.

"I'm not sure Febreze is meant for hundred-year-old rugs."

Rachel doused another fragile rug with lavender-scented odor remover.

"Maybe we should use vinegar or baking soda."

I sat on an uncomfortable, fraying horsehair couch, staring at my cell phone, willing it to self-destruct. When Rachel and I had entered the kitchen to put away Bev's casserole and Yvette's muffins, the device had been buzzing like an irritated mosquito. Apparently finding a dead body in front of one's newly inherited mansion wasn't a good enough excuse to call off work at my law firm.

Especially since I'd taken the previous two days off to go to a funeral, lick my wounds, and avoid Keith downtown. I'd slipped off to go to the bathroom this morning while Chief Truman and Officer Hendricks were grilling Rachel and e-mailed my best friend, Olivia, at the firm. I tried to describe the discovery of the dead body in the least alarming way possible as I tapped away on the miniature keys and explained why I wouldn't be coming in to work again. All in the time it took to pee.

My e-mail to Olivia only made my phone hum more fervently. I finally called back Alan Brinkman, the partner who gave me most of my work, and instead of hello was greeted with, "Will you be taking tomorrow off for some other person's convenient death, Mallory?"

"I think I can manage to come in." I tried to laugh off his officious tone. "Although, these things do tend to happen in threes." I promised Alan I'd be in tomorrow. I'd have to face the partners' ire and the associates' whispers and avoid Keith, who worked in the building next door.

"What do they want from me?" I grumbled to Rachel. "I can't possibly concentrate and bill clients if I'm wondering why and how Shane Hartley ended up dead right under my nose." Before this week, I'd spent more time at the office than usual, banking hours to make up for the time I'd take off for my honeymoon. That would no longer be a problem.

"You need a new job." Rachel moved into the adjoining library to spray another rug. "You can't work next door to Keith's office building and avoid him every day. Or that Becca Cunningham."

"But why do *I* need to find a new job? Keith and his tartlet should leave town."

Rachel stopped spraying and gave me a look. "Because you're overworked. You're burned out. Even before this happened."

"I'm one year away from making partner. I can't quit now." It was true. I wasn't sure what I was going to do after I made partner, but the goal was within my sights, and I'd put in too much work to abandon it now. And work was the only thing going well right now. I needed to hold on to it like a life preserver.

My sister snorted. "You've been drinking the Russell Carey Kool-Aid a little too long."

Stung by her assessment, I turned around and closed my eyes, wishing away my new reality, but when I opened them, I was still in Sylvia's dilapidated house. A house I would need to sell, fast, before its upkeep drained what little savings I had. I pictured restoring the house to its original glory and felt a pang. Would I really want to sell it then? A crazy thought percolated up from the recesses of my brain. *What if I keep the house? What if I turn it into a B and B and hold weddings here?* I shook my head as if chasing away a gnat, dismissing the idea as a passing moment of insanity. I opened my eyes and turned back to my sister.

"I'm sorry," Rachel said grudgingly, putting down the spray bottle.

"It's okay. I just don't want to even think about my career on top of this house. I need to sell it and I have no idea how I'll get the money to fix it up. Although . . ."

"What?"

"If I could just get a refund for the damn wedding reception, it would be enough to do some renovations."

"They still won't let you out of it?" Rachel gasped.

"Nope." I retrieved my purse and unfurled the ratty contract I'd been carrying around like a bad luck charm. I spread it out on the ottoman, and Rachel skimmed it page by page.

"I'm no attorney, but this looks pretty iron-clad. You missed the date to cancel the wedding by a week."

"And they know it. No one at the country club will return my calls."

"Couldn't you file a lawsuit to try to get it back?" Rachel squinted harder at the contract, as if she could bully it into releasing me.

"It wouldn't be successful. Besides, I made it in good faith. I never imagined I wouldn't be getting married. It's not the country club's fault Keith can't keep it in his pants." It was the first joke I'd made about Keith, and Rachel erupted into a gale of laughter. I warmed, genuinely thankful I hadn't married Keith. No matter what happened, I was better off. Heck, maybe in a few months I'd even be laughing about it. But I needed my reception deposit back.

I decided to beg for it in person. So, I left Rachel at Sylvia's house and walked the mile to the country club. I sat outside the manager's office, offering his assistant a tight-lipped smile as I tapped my foot on the faded plaid carpet. I wished I'd saved my engagement ring to pawn, as satisfying as it had been to toss it down the street.

"He's very busy." The doe-eyed girl blinked her false lashes at me. "Maybe you could leave him a message."

"I'll wait. He hasn't returned any of my calls."

Her eyes grew big. "You're the woman who's been calling about the cancellation?"

"Miss Shepard, what a pleasant surprise." Mr. Haines, the manager, burst out of his office, white hair greased into place, blinding dentures flashing his trademark grin. He was happy, all right. He had all of my money for a wedding reception that wouldn't be happening. I cursed myself again for agreeing to pay for it. Keith had purchased that silly ring, and I'd thought I'd have some measure of control over the wedding if the bride's side of the family, aka me, paid for it. I'd been wrong about that too, since Helene had taken over within hours of our engagement. The last time I'd seen Mr. Haines, he'd nervously brought us a sample of wedding cake to try, and his fear of Helene had been palpable. Today he was doing a poor job of acting contrite as he settled me in a chair facing his desk.

"I'm here to see if you'll reconsider about the deposit. Perhaps you could find another event to take the place of the reception. I'll do everything in my power to mitigate this—"

"That won't be necessary." His chompers gleamed. "It would be too much of a hardship for us to try to reimburse you. I'm truly sorry about your broken engagement." He rocked in his leather chair, the springs whining, his face a failed mask of concern. "But you knew this when you made your deposit, Miss Shepard. This is contracts one oh one." His small, smug smile quivered at the corners of his thin lips.

I'd been to a few events at the Port Quincy Country Club before Helene had strong-armed us into choosing it for the reception. They served the same fare for each event: over-and-undercooked prime rib, stringy chicken and tepid hors d'oeuvres. It wouldn't be much of a loss to shelve my wedding. But I had signed the contract and, per the cancellation clause, it was too late to get out of it.

"Fine then." I stood and gathered my bag. I flung it over my shoulder a bit too forcefully, as it crashed into the crystal dish on the edge of his desk, scattering butterscotch candies everywhere like tan Ping-Pong balls. "The reception will go on."

He blanched, his ruddy face draining to a pale grayish green, as his windfall slipped away. "Don't you consider it a bit tactless to celebrate that day? The show doesn't always have to go on."

"If I'm paying for it, it does. Get ready for a party like you've never seen before."

I hightailed it back to Thistle Park in record time, anger fueling my legs.

"I guess that didn't go so well," Rachel assessed, as I flopped back onto the couch, sweaty and agitated.

"I didn't get the deposit back, but that's to be expected." I filled her in on my unsuccessful showdown with the manger. "Looks like I'll be planning another wedding—I just need to find a bride to take over the reception in two weeks' time." Keith's suggestion that I become a wedding planner had come to fruition— just not how I'd expected. My fantasy of throwing a wedding in Sylvia's house, beautifully restored with the money from my deposit, wasn't going to happen. But if I could find a bride, I'd be throwing her a wedding on the same day I was to be married.

Rachel opened her mouth to say something, then set down her spray bottle, alert. "Someone's in the backyard."

I peeled myself off the couch and followed my sister to the back porch.

"Can we help you?" I asked the slight girl lying on her stomach in the backyard.

"Shh." The girl stuck her hand under the porch. "I almost caught him."

Rachel and I obeyed her and stood in silence, as if bewitched.

The girl called to something under the porch stairs, sweet and low. Her voice grew louder and more pleading. "Here, little guy. C'*mere*, little kitty."

The calico was pressed against the now-shut kitchen window, meowing and watching the girl, her tail swishing with impatience.

"Oh no. We didn't get all of the kittens," I whispered to Rachel.

The girl glowered at me.

"Sorry."

A tiny black kitten tottered out from under the porch, toward the girl and the tuna in her hand. At the last second, he realized this was an ambush and scampered left. I reached down and scooped him up as he ran by the porch.

"Gotcha!" I cradled the runt in my arms. The calico meowed louder through the glass, and the girl followed us inside.

"There, little kitty." I deposited him on the floor with his fluff-ball sibling. The calico cat grabbed her prodigal kitten by the scruff of his neck, dropped him in the box, and began tending to him.

"I was worried about him," the girl explained, as if it were perfectly natural we'd found her in the backyard playing kitten pied piper. "He always runs off." She glanced at the apricot kitten. "Now they're both okay."

"You've been feeding them." A statement, rather than a question.

The girl stood and faced us, a deep bloom of pink obliterating her freckles. She looked like a little Goth elf. She was about twelve or thirteen and had thin, gangly legs and a heart-shaped face. Her dyed blue-black hair was gathered into a messy ponytail, but her roots were blond, as were her eyebrows. Her skin was so translucent her violet veins showed through, and she had the biggest hazel eyes I'd ever seen, a little Cupid's-bow mouth, and a changeling manner. She was already a few inches taller than me, which wasn't a hard feat to attain.

She opened her mouth to reveal magenta-banded braces. "I had to! The mom cat had kittens about two months ago, and she needed food. My dad won't let me get a cat, and when I told my grandma about the kittens, she promised we could bring them to the animal rescue. Until she changed her mind." She frowned. "She said I shouldn't really be coming over here, that it's dangerous since Miss Sylvia left. But the little black kitten is always wandering off, and I was scared he'd get separated. Besides, I want to be a veterinarian when I grow up, and this is good practice." She'd started off panicked and apologetic, but by the end of her explanation, she was haughty and sure of her convictions.

"I'm not mad. Thanks for taking care of them." I tried to get the girl to look me in the eyes.

Finally, she did. "Are you going to keep them?" She fiddled with an earring.

Rachel and I exchanged glances. My mom had refused to let us have a pet during the lean years after our dad left. When she'd married Doug, he'd brought two pugs into our family. Keith hadn't wanted pets, and our apartment hadn't allowed them. I'd never had a cat, but I'd always wanted one. I just hadn't counted on three at once.

But I had already decided to keep them, my heart melting every time the calico diligently tended to the apricot kitten and now its jet sibling.

"Of course we'll keep them." I offered the girl a smile. "This is more their home than mine, and"—I shuddered—"I think the calico already took care of that nest of mice in the dining room credenza."

"Do you promise they'll be inside cats?" The girl's pale blond eyebrows, so incongruous with the blue-black hair, tented together over the bridge of her nose in concern.

"I promise." I suppressed a smile.

The girl's elfin face relaxed. "When did you guys move in? It's been empty forever."

"Last night." Had she heard about the murder? "I'm Mallory and this is my sister, Rachel."

"I'm Summer." She offered a surprisingly firm handshake for someone so young.

I grinned at the incongruity of her sunny name and her dark appearance. With her inky hair, she seemed an unlikely candidate to have that name.

"I've never been in the house." Summer turned around in a slow circle. "What is this room?"

"The butler's pantry, we think," Rachel said.

We were in a narrow vestibule connecting the kitchen and the dining room. China, crystal, and boxes of silver cutlery were neatly stacked on shelves reaching up to the ceiling.

Summer's eyes lit up. "I've never seen a butler's pantry. I used to say hello to Miss Sylvia in her garden, and she'd let me pick flowers. But that was a long time ago. Like, when I was really little. I'm thirteen now. Did you know we're neighbors? My backyard connects with yours."

"And you've been looking after the cats for how long?"

"She had kittens in May, and I brought her the box. I'm not technically allowed to come over here, but I needed to help her. I sneak—I mean, I come over here every few days."

I tried not to let her see my smile.

"Do you have any pets?" Rachel asked.

"My dad won't let me get one," Summer groaned. "He says he's allergic, but I don't believe him."

Now that he was done chowing down on moistened kibble, the little black kitten she'd found under the porch twined his way around her ankles. His outsized purr filled the room. This kitten was in love.

"Tell you what, Summer. You can take the kitty home, and if your parents won't let you keep it, you can bring it right back." I reached out to give the black kitten a pat.

"It's just my dad. And my grandpa and grandma. And thanks," she whispered. "I've always wanted a cat."

"Do you need a box? Or kitten food?"

"Nah. He'll let me carry him. He's a he, by the way. And I already have some more of that under my bed." She gestured to the bag on the floor.

"One more thing, Summer. You weren't here last night, were you?" *Please let her not have been here when Shane Hartley was murdered.*

"No way." Summer looked solemn. Her hazel eyes grew as wide as saucers. "I *was* here yesterday, but I left before it got dark. Why?"

I wasn't quite sure I believed her.

"No reason. You can come over anytime. Just make sure you tell your dad and your grandparents." I was sure everyone in Port Quincy knew about Shane Hartley's untimely demise by now, and if her father and grandparents knew she was here, they wouldn't be too happy.

"I promise." And with that, she gave us that massive grin, with a bright flash of magenta braces. She began to walk back to her house, cooing to her little kitten as she made her way toward the garden, navigating around the broken angel statues and through the waist-high weeds.

Chapter Five

It had been a long day. Tomorrow would be my first day back at work since I'd called off my engagement, learned of Sylvia's death, inherited a house, and slept through a murder. Rachel and I triple-checked each window and door before we retired for what would be a fitful night of sleep. I woke up every hour, mistaking each creak and sigh from the old house for a murder possibly under way.

Rachel had a similar night's sleep, judging from the puffy bags she sported beneath her eyes. When I got to Pittsburgh, I started my workday with a trek to the back entrance to avoid running into Keith or Becca Cunningham out front. I'd added myself to Rachel's auto rental policy and driven the Mini Cooper, parking in a distant lot, not daring to use the subterranean parking shared with Keith's firm.

I hid in my office most of the day. My best friend, Olivia, brought me lunch, and I scanned the halls each time before I ventured out. I felt other associates' eyes bore into the back of my head, and trails of whispers, both real and imagined, followed me down the hall. One young first-year, a noted gossip, craned her neck out of her door in anticipation of my visit to the bathroom. She drew her head back in with a little squeak when I came into view.

Thankfully my secretary snapped, "What are you looking at?" as the girl shut her office door.

My cheeks burned. I felt as if I were performing a collegiate walk of shame, but I'd done nothing wrong. I doubted Keith felt the same way one building over.

The day was largely wasted, as I didn't feel I could fairly bill clients for my distracted, patchy work. I spent more time figuring out how to find a bride to take over my reception than I spent on real work.

Olivia and I brainstormed about my unwanted wedding reception over lunch in my office. I needed to find someone to donate the shindig to in a hurry.

"Why not hold a fund-raiser for a charity?" Olivia suggested. "Or you could try to find someone who can't afford a wedding."

"That was my thought too, but how would I go about finding them? Put out an ad in the paper or on Craigslist? Besides, who'd be ready to get married in less than three weeks?"

"That's just it. You did all the prep work. Everything's set up. You have all of the favors and decorations. All the country club has to do is prepare the food and drinks and serve them."

"I guess. The favors are actually at Keith's apartment, but who'd want my specific wedding, er, Helene's idea of a wedding? And if I found a bride, how could I quickly customize my reception into a wedding she'd want?"

But it was worth a shot. I turned to my computer

and nervously licked my lips, gearing up to write the strangest Craigslist ad ever.

"Free wedding or evening event available at the Port Quincy Country Club, date non-negotiable," Olivia read over my shoulder.

I typed up the rest of the ad quickly, feeling raw and exposed, even though I hadn't included my identity. But enough people in Port Quincy had been uninvited to the wedding it wouldn't be hard to figure out I was the author of the post. And here I was, advertising that my engagement and would-be marriage had blown up in my face. Still, if I could find a bride or a group to use the event space and food, I'd be doing some good and making lemonade out of decidedly sour lemons. I took a deep breath.

"I hope this works." I closed my eyes and clicked submit.

"Bravo!" Olivia gave me a high five.

I should have felt good about creating the post, but my stomach twisted into a hard, sharp knot.

The commute back to Port Quincy didn't help. I jockeyed with other harried country-dwellers eager to get home after a long day in the city, cutting each other off at eighty miles per hour.

"What are you doing here?" It came out kind of brusque, but I couldn't help myself.

I was in no mood to deal with surprises now I was back at Thistle Park, but Garrett Davies sat on the top step of the porch, with murder in his eyes. A squealing, mewling shoebox pocked with ragged air holes fidgeted beside him, containing what I guessed was one angry kitten. It took a few beats to connect the dots. The fact that Garrett looked delicious in his navy suit didn't help. His tie was loosened and his top button was undone. He cocked one eyebrow in a question, inviting me to say something. His eyes narrowed. *Summer's eyes.*

"*You're* Summer's dad?"

"Yes, Mallory, I'm Summer's dad. I like to be included in decisions about whether my daughter is allowed to have a pet or not. And since you and my daughter failed to consult me, I'll let you know belatedly what my decision is. No pets." He stood and handed me the box. I tore off the top, and the kitten popped his furry jet head out. He blinked in the sunlight and scrabbled out, clinging to my neck.

"It's okay, buddy." I rubbed his downy head. "We'll take you back. You don't ever have to see this mean man again."

He began to purr, no worse for wear.

Garrett rolled his eyes. "You sound just like Summer. I'm not mean, just sensible. Summer's thirteen, and she can barely keep her room clean. How is she going to take care of a cat? Plus, I'm allergic."

"So I've heard. Although . . ."

"What?"

I walked up to Garrett and, before he could refuse, handed him the kitten.

He sighed and accepted the little black ball of fluff. He halfheartedly petted him, getting cat hair on his suit. "It's okay, Jeeves. You'll be happier here with your mama cat and fellow kitten."

I laughed. "Summer named him Jeeves?"

"Yes. She talked nonstop about this place and how you have a butler's pantry. So he's Jeeves. But feel free to change it." Petting the kitten seemed to soften him. "Sorry to dump this on you, but I really can't have a cat."

"You seem just fine." My voice was soft and low. I'd meant that he seemed to deal well with Jeeves, but it came out sounding like I was talking about how hot he was.

"What?" He looked up sharply.

"You're not sneezing. And look, he's kneading you, and the scratches aren't even getting red. I don't think you're really allergic."

Garrett frowned and looked at the little kitten. "I guess not." He still sounded doubtful. "Come to think of it, my father told me I was allergic every time I asked for a pet growing up. Maybe it was just a tactic." He smiled briefly. "I still don't know if Summer can handle a cat. I'm really busy with work, and I can't saddle my parents with this. It wouldn't be fair. I'm a single parent, and they do so much for Summer as it is."

"But she's already taken care of three cats." I was secretly pleased he'd affirmed what Summer said yesterday. There was no Mrs. Davies in the picture. "She figured out the cat was going to have kittens, brought her a box to have them in, and made sure they had food and water. She even noticed Jeeves ran away and found him."

He sighed. "Summer did a good job with them. Now I know where her allowance has been going. I just wish she hadn't disobeyed her grandparents and me by coming over here. Until Sylvia deeded it to you, it was vacant, and now with Shane Hartley's murder, it makes me crazy knowing my daughter was here by herself."

Shane Hartley's murder had taken over the entire

front page of the Port Quincy *Eagle Herald* and even gotten a small mention in the Pittsburgh papers. The articles mentioned Hartley was chief of operations for Lonestar Energy and had left behind a pregnant wife, but they didn't mention what a divisive figure he'd been in Port Quincy. I was thankful I wasn't a suspect in print, but it was futile to hope no one would find out. Thistle Park was now infamous. This wouldn't help when I tried to sell the house.

"Summer wasn't entirely truthful, but she did help the cats. She wants to be a veterinarian."

Garrett perked up. "She told you that? Good, because veterinarians don't usually dye their hair black or purposely dress in rags. I hope she grows out of this phase."

I smiled. "I'm sure there are some veterinarians with dyed-black hair out there. And you've got nothing to worry about. She's a great kid."

He stared at me for a second, petting Jeeves, who seemed quite content to be settled in his arms.

"There's another reason for my visit. I finally found Tabitha Battles's card. And Zachary Novak's. Tabitha's at the historical society and Zach was Sylvia's real estate agent. If you want to proceed according to Sylvia's requests, they'd be the people to talk to. Oh, and the number for Sylvia's handyman, Will Prentiss. He used to cut the grass a few times a year, clean the gutters, and check on the house."

He cradled Jeeves with his left hand and handed me the two cards and a Post-it note with his right. Our fingers brushed.

The contact flustered me and somehow he dropped the cards. We both bent to pick them up, our movements mirrored.

"Ow!" I cried out as our skulls connected.

"I'm so sorry." Garrett set Jeeves on the porch and cradled my forehead in his hands. "Stand still."

Stars flashed and I felt a bit woozy, but he held me upright. His large hands rifled gently through my hair, undoing my bun, my hair slipping through his fingers. Then he stopped and inhaled sharply.

"Yup, you're going to have a giant bump." He tipped my chin up, peering intently into my eyes. He smelled of spearmint and oranges, and I held fast to his arm to keep from swooning. "You can see, right?"

I nodded, looking down. I had to break the intensity of his gaze. "Can you?"

"Oh, yes." His voice was husky.

I reached up and touched the top of his head, making him wince. "You'll have a bump too. I'm such a klutz." It was true. I had always been a bit ungainly, and since moving into Sylvia's house, I had the bruises to prove it. I was always running into heavy pieces of furniture and tripping over threadbare rugs. Tears began to form in my eyes from the pain throbbing in my head.

"It's my fault." He brushed away a drop that had made its way to the tip of my chin.

"Hello there," Rachel purred, opening the front door. "I thought I heard someone out here." Her eyes went wide when she saw us standing so close. She picked up Jeeves and nestled the kitten by her chest, which was on full display, peeking out of a red tank top I recognized as mine, and a plaid bra, mine as well. It wasn't meant to be a push-up, but that's what happened when you put D cups in a B-cup bra.

"Are you bringing the kitten back?" She looked at

Garrett with interest, probably putting two and two together as I had and realizing he was Summer's father.

Garrett and I jumped back, releasing each other.

"Actually, I'm taking Jeeves home." He picked up the box from the porch. "Mallory made a good case. Summer will be ecstatic. It's about time she got a pet."

I laughed and could have hugged him. I shook my aching head, as if clearing water out of my ears. *Whoa, what? I just got out of a six-year relationship with a man I was about to marry.*

He took Jeeves from Rachel, seemingly immune to her charms. "Have a great night, ladies." He gently deposited the kitten in the box and closed the lid. He headed for the backyard connecting the properties, following the same meandering path Summer had, whistling a tune.

Rachel peered at Garrett's retreating form with a look of confusion. She wasn't used to men being impervious to her seduction techniques. She wheeled around to stare at me. "Wow, Mallory, that man is totally smitten."

"What?" I emerged from a private reverie, my hand on my head.

Rachel smirked. "And it looks like you are too."

That night, I had vivid dreams, but instead of murder on the front lawn, they involved naughty things with a certain neighbor, Garrett Davies. I woke up hot and flushed. I felt a bit different. In the grogginess of early morning, I couldn't put my finger on it. By the time I descended the grand staircase to grab some breakfast, I'd pinpointed the change in my mood. I felt optimistic. A smidge less bleak.

But I swore off men. Especially lawyers. Especially from Port Quincy, Pennsylvania. *Look what it brought me last time.* Nothing but pain and recrimination. I wasn't even finished mourning my engagement to Keith. What were the five stages of grief? I was stuck on the anger stage. The "strangle Keith" part and the "slash Becca Cunningham's tires" part. Still, Garrett Davies made me smile and, for now, that was enough.

"You seem better."

I loaded a bagel into the Sputnik-era chrome toaster. I smiled at my sister. She was playing with the orange kitten on the worn black and white checked floor, waving a feathered toy. The kitten was going nuts while the calico looked on.

"I do feel a little better."

"You know, it's never too early. I think you need to start getting back in the swing of things." She looked up as the kitten leaped through the air. "Maybe with Garrett Davies."

My smile vanished. Was I that transparent, or did Rachel have some kind of psychic sister superpower?

"I'm not rebounding with Garrett Davies after a broken engagement and a six-year relationship!" My face grew warm, and I picked up the kitten and nuzzled her, hiding my cheeks, which were probably glowing crimson.

"So my hunch was right." Rachel nodded sagely. "You like him so much you don't want to ruin it by making it a rebound."

"He's a jerk, and he's our neighbor, and there are about ten thousand other reasons I can come up with why I wouldn't date him." But he had taken back

Jeeves, so he wasn't truly a jerk. And he did have meltingly beautiful hazel eyes.

"We'll see." Rachel's mouth curved into a simper.

"Have a good day, Rach."

I drove off for Pittsburgh, waiting for the dread to build. It was my second day back to work, and although I'd managed to avoid Keith and Becca yesterday, it was only a matter of time before I ran into the cheater and his accomplice.

But my hopeful feelings soared, and it made work slightly more bearable. The whispers about the cancelled wedding, the pitying glances, and the gazes cutting away from mine stung a bit less. People probably thought I'd gone on meds, the change in my mood was so complete. It ticked me off in my feminist soul that it took interest in another man to make me feel less adrift.

"Are you ready to venture out?" Olivia asked at lunchtime. She floated the idea tentatively, as if I were a healed leper leaving the colony for the first time in a dozen years. Her dark brown eyes squinted with concern beneath her bangs.

We'd been fast friends since the first day I met her seven years ago, when we'd been nervous summer associates. She had warned me about getting involved with Keith, a senior associate, when I was working for the firm as a law student, but I'd brushed her off. When my engagement ended, I'd gotten a big hug instead of an "I told you so," and Olivia had done most of the work to undo my elaborate wedding plans. She was my rock.

"I believe I am." I rubbed the egg-sized bump on

my head like a good-luck talisman. I smiled, thinking of Garrett walking off into the sunset with Jeeves.

"What are you grinning about? You look like you've got a secret."

"No secrets. I'm finally settling into Sylvia's house. I'm actually glad Rachel's here. And the people in Port Quincy are all right. I don't think I'll be murdered in my sleep."

Olivia blew her thick black bangs off her forehead, eyeing me. She didn't press me about it.

"And, I'm starting to feel okay about what happened with Keith. Lucky, even. I'm better off without him."

"That's the spirit." Olivia held up her hand for a high five.

"Now I just need to find a bride and revise my wedding."

Before Olivia arrived at my office I'd checked my personal email. I'd had a surprising ten inquiries about my "free wedding" giveaway. But none of the requests would work. Several brides desperately wanted a wedding at the country club, but wouldn't be able to use the space on the appointed date. They wanted to know if I'd had any success negotiating using the country club space at a later date. The Port Quincy Dalmatian Rescue League was interested in taking over the event for a fundraiser, and they wanted to feature their pooches. A quick call to Mr. Haines, the country club manager, nixed that idea.

"There can be no animals on the premises, Miss Shepard. Good luck finding a group to take over your reception." I could hear the condescension in his voice, and could picture his sneer curving around his blinding dentures. I hung up before I said something I regretted. I filled Olivia in on my phone call with Mr. Haines, and all of the requests to use the reception that wouldn't quite work.

"You know," Olivia said cautiously, "it might be time to haul out the big guns. This would make a great story."

"Like for the newspaper?" I squeaked, dropping my purse in alarm.

"I guess you're not ready for that."

The two of us made our way out of my office. I didn't want to broadcast my failure of a wedding so publicly, but I was bound and determined to find a bride to take over the reception. I just had to find that bride without humiliating myself any further.

The elevator stopped its smooth descent and we crossed the marble lobby and exited revolving doors into the humid day. We headed for our favorite restaurant, a hole-in-the-wall that served delicious Indian food, a safe block away. A rivulet of sweat traced my spine, gluing my silk shirt to my back. I hid behind my sunglasses, glancing around for any signs of Keith or Becca.

A woman exited the identical chrome and glass skyscraper next door. She looked right then left and tentatively ventured out. She spotted me at the edge of her vision, dropping the bag she was carrying. Papers flew out of the overstuffed satchel, and she froze. Her eyes darted over as she finally scrambled to retrieve her documents. As she leaned over, her dark roots contrasted with shining blond hair, Heather Locklear–style, circa *Melrose Place*.

"Becca Cunningham," spat out Olivia.

"I'm not hungry anymore." My legs turned to jelly, and bile rose in my throat. I stood rooted to the ground, my feet useless as I clung to Olivia's arm.

"Wait, Mallory!" Becca stuffed sheaves of paper into her cranberry shoulder bag. It was identical to the one I carried. Keith had given me the soft leather attaché for Christmas. My head spun. Had he gifted her the very same present? Keith was nothing if not efficient. Becca advanced toward us, abandoning the rest of her papers to the sidewalk, where they were picked up in the slight breeze before wafting into traffic like giant, rectangular snowflakes. "Please, I need to talk to you. I want to tell you—"

She didn't get to tell me what was so pressing, because Olivia grabbed me by the elbow and wrenched me around in an about-face.

I left my stomach on the sidewalk, along with my dignity, as we power walked back to our building and zoomed up in the elevator. I wasn't sure which was worse. Running into the woman Keith had been cheating with, or the look of panic in her eyes. I didn't really hate Becca Cunningham. *She* hadn't gotten down on one knee and offered her fidelity to me. Keith had.

Olivia grabbed us sandwiches from the firm cafeteria and forced me to choke down a few bites while we hunkered in my office. My newfound courage was gone. Pleasant thoughts of Garrett Davies evaporated, replaced with visions of me skulking about in shadows, never venturing out for fear of seeing my ex or his paramour.

"I wonder what she was going to tell you." Olivia sat primly in one of the blond wooden chairs that faced my desk. "Surely not apologizing. It's a little late for that."

"I need a new job." My sister's advice had been spot-on. "And that was just her. If I ran into Keith, I'm not sure what I'd do."

"You didn't do anything wrong. You didn't cheat."

There was a knock at the door, which opened before I could invite the person in. My secretary hung back, as if she'd been running interference, on her way to warn me. She gave me an apologetic shrug before she continued down the hall.

"Mallory." Alan Brinkman, the partner who gave me the majority of my work, was about fifty, with rheumy eyes, a graying comb-over, and a snappish manner. He was always dressed in perfectly pressed suits, well taken care of by his wife. The long hours and the stress of working for Russell Carey for more than twenty-five years had taken their toll on him. He was cold and dismissive with associates and petty and obstructive with opposing counsel. I'd sacrificed many evenings pulling all-nighters for Alan, and though he was a bear to work for, he gave me plenty of assignments, real experience, and good reviews. And that was what counted around here.

Olivia jumped up, taking her tuna sandwich with her. "See you later." She gave me a sympathetic look as she closed the door behind her.

"What can I do for you, Alan?" The chirpy tone in my voice was fake, and the corners of my mouth quivered with the effort of maintaining a plastic grin. I was already on thin ice for taking off three days this week, legitimate reasons be damned. Alan might like my work product, but he didn't tolerate personal crises interfering with the practice of law. And it was odd he'd decided to swing by my office. He usually summoned me to his with a curt bark on the phone.

"I want to know what's going on with the investigation into Shane Hartley's death." It was the same tactic he used when cross-examining witnesses. No exchanging pleasantries with Alan. He went straight for the jugular. It was a technique I was trying to hone, but I didn't appreciate being on the receiving end.

"Pardon me?" I tried to stall and gather my thoughts for this interrogation.

"Lonestar Energy is one of this firm's biggest clients. I was very upset to hear my star associate was involved with a client's death." Alan's left eye began to twitch in unison with the pulsating vein now standing out above his right temple.

Uh-oh.

Alan was about to go nuclear. I'd only seen him this agitated once, and it was right before he threw his Penn Law class of 1989 paperweight at his secretary. She'd taken it in stride, but the firm had decided it would be better to give her a nice payoff so we could all pretend he hadn't almost decapitated her.

I gulped some air and tried to still my nervous hands. I would have been ecstatic to hear Alan call me his star associate just a week ago, but now I was sweating. "Involved? I wasn't *involved* in Hartley's death. I just inherited my, um . . ." Here, I stalled, not sure what to call Sylvia. "My future grandmother-in-law's house. The first night I spent there, he was murdered. I barely knew him, and I had no reason to want him dead."

Alan loomed over my desk, all six feet of him. His stale coffee breath mingled with his aftershave. I recoiled and tried not to roll my chair back.

"You were seen arguing with him the day before he died. Are you a suspect in Shane Hartley's murder?"

Good question. Am I?

The answer was maybe. Unofficially. But that was none of Alan's damn business. Had the firm been in contact with the Port Quincy police? How did he know I'd argued with Hartley?

I leaned forward, my face three inches from his. "Do you really think I spend my time prowling small towns and bashing in the skulls of people I've just met?" I laughed, but it came out wrong, all strangled and high-pitched, like a muffled sneeze.

Alan's face relaxed. He rubbed his twitching eye. "It just looks bad. Some of these lawsuits we're defending on behalf of Lonestar have reached a delicate stage."

"You mean they're about to settle."

"To put it bluntly, yes. Shane Hartley, as head of operations for Lonestar here in Pennsylvania, was an indispensable part of that process."

"Maybe that's why he was murdered. Someone didn't want a settlement to go through. Or maybe it was a threat against Lonestar."

A look of annoyance returned to Alan's worn face. "Just help the police do their job, and you do yours. I know you're going through some blips in your personal life, but you need to focus on your work and keep your hours up."

Blips? That was one way of putting it.

"Yes, Alan," I said, all obsequious and obedient.

I sagged when he left my office. The door snapped shut.

"Oh crap." I couldn't have the firm scrutinizing my work or questioning my involvement in Shane Hartley's death. I needed my job, and I wanted to keep my head down and turn in good work so I could make partner.

Then again, I'd done nothing wrong. If the firm was poking around in my business, I'd poke right back. I opened Russell Carey's internal document system on my computer. Searches for *Lonestar Energy* and *Shane Hartley* yielded over three thousand documents. It seemed like half of Port Quincy was suing Lonestar. The majority of the claims alleged Lonestar miscalculated gas royalties, poisoned animals, overfilled noxious retention ponds, and turned a blind eye to wastewater leaks. There were a few wrongful death cases from workplace accidents and gas explosions. Russell Carey was very busy defending Lonestar.

I stopped billing for the cases I should have been focusing on and lost the rest of the afternoon. I read all about the trouble Lonestar Energy got into and how my colleagues at Russell Carey LLP got them out of it.

Saturday arrived, and after I'd lived at Thistle Park for five days, the house was still an utter disaster. It would probably be that way for weeks, if not months. Even if I fixed up the place, it'd cost a fortune just to maintain it. Though the enormity of the task weighed on me and brought out my inner neurotic control freak, I was charmed by this odd, hulking mansion.

Since Alan's visit yesterday, I'd been daydreaming of opening the mansion as a B and B. I imagined treating guests to a Gilded Age trip back in time and planning weddings that would be held in the lush restored garden out back. My mind wandered to the old cookbooks in the kitchen, which had beckoned to me from day one. I pictured serving food inspired by the dishes cooked here long ago. I used to love cooking before I started practicing law, but these days I never seemed to find the time.

Today we were having company, and I was appalled by the state of the house, as if it had fallen into disrepair under my watch. I woke up before dawn and attempted to make a dent in the squalor, or at least show I'd tried.

"Appearances," I said to myself. "Watch out, or you'll turn into Helene."

Rachel slept while I cleaned. I hummed a tune as the calico and her apricot kitten watched me polish the dark wood in the back hall. I hoped the lemon-scented oil would overpower the lingering smell of mustiness and cat pee.

The hallway featured several large mirrors, the glass now hazy with age, spotting my reflection with gold flecks. Cobwebs adorned the chandelier above, and desiccated spiders hung upside-down, like the rusted-out, inverted skeletons of old, broken umbrellas. I stood on tiptoe and batted them with a broom. I spent hours polishing, mopping, and sweeping, working out the stress of the week on the woodwork while I sweated in the humid air.

The hallway seemed to be filled with the ghosts of the family that had lived at Thistle Park. I felt watched, but not in a bad way. A large oil portrait of a woman at the far end of the hallway caught my eye. There weren't many paintings left in the house. Most of the walls had oval and rectangle-shaped patches of vibrant wallpaper, once preserved behind the pictures.

I moved closer. The woman in the portrait stared at me with what, at first, seemed to be an imperious glare. Her pretty mouth was set in a hard line. Her visage was dimmed by lacquer that had aged and grown dull, but I could still make out the mischievous gleam in her dark brown eyes. They danced with mirth, as if she found my predicament amusing.

"Whatever. You can stop smirking at me. This place probably wasn't a dump when you lived here."

I grabbed a rag and polished the tarnished nameplate affixed to the bottom of the heavy gilt frame. "Evelyn McGavitt," I read aloud.

"She was Sylvia's mother."

"Geez!" I dropped the wood polish with a splatter and whirled around to confront a tidy, willowy woman a few years older than me, with a smooth cap of startlingly red hair. It was too vivid not to have come from a bottle. She had unsettling gimlet eyes, and she was wearing a wool skirt and riding boots, despite the July heat.

"I'm sorry I startled you. The doorbell must be broken. I rang and knocked for a good five minutes, then I let myself in since the door was unlocked. Thistle Park is so enormous, it must be hard to hear what's going on in the front hall."

"That's okay." I smiled over my initial shock. "You must be Tabitha Battles. Thanks for meeting me on a Saturday."

I'd made appointments with Tabitha from the historical society and Zachary Novak, Sylvia's Realtor. I hoped they could fill me in on Sylvia's plans for the house. I had apparently lost track of time in my mania to clean.

"Who did you say she was?" I gestured to the smirking lady in the painting and wiped my hands free of furniture polish.

"The painting is of Sylvia's mother, Evelyn McGavitt. It's a little overwhelming. I can tell you about the history of this house and the people who lived in it." She paused. "But just so I'm clear about my intentions, Sylvia was considering donating several items to the historical society. Nothing permanent, just loans for long-term display. It's your decision now, of course, and I don't want to pressure you."

I appreciated her honesty and forthrightness. "Sure. Let's go into the front room—er, the parlor, I guess, and we can get started."

Rachel was awake and met us in the formal room.

"I made scones and cheese straws yesterday." She plopped down a silver tray laden with treats. "I used recipes from one of the old cookbooks in the kitchen, with some modern substitutions. We don't have lard, for instance."

I beamed at my sister. For once, we were thinking on the same page. We dug into the food after Rachel and Tabitha were introduced.

"Delicious." Tabitha was right. Rachel's scones were amazing.

I gave my sister an appraising look. She smiled back with a flush of pride.

"You know," Tabitha said, "if you choose to renovate this place, it would make a great bed-and-breakfast."

Rachel's eyes widened with excitement. "That's what I told Mallory."

I took another bite to avoid talking. Last night, when I returned from my disastrous day at work, Rachel had practically drawn up a business plan. She wanted to help me renovate Sylvia's house and, according to her, once we got the attic unlocked, we could live on the third floor and run the bottom two floors as an inn. I didn't tell her I'd envisioned the same plan—because my thoughts were mere daydreams—but Rachel actually thought we could pull it off.

I'd thought of one of my favorite places on earth, a little B and B where Keith had proposed to me, nestled in the Blue Ridge Mountains. It was owned by a kind, capable woman. I remembered thinking during our stay she had a wonderful life, running her own business and meeting new people. Could I really pull that off, here? In Sylvia's house?

"You'd still have enough space to live here." Tabitha's eyes shone, unknowingly echoing Rachel's suggestions and my daydream. "And you could hold events. Parties and weddings . . ."

That was the one kind of event I kept blocking from my mind. I'd begin to picture a marriage ceremony in the gazebo out back, then mentally shut down.

Rachel jumped in, saving us from an awkward silence. "I'll get us coffee."

Just then a knock sounded at the door.

"That'll be Zachary Novak," I said as I moved toward the hall.

Tabitha's face crumpled.

Rachel returned with a pot of coffee, a pitcher of water, and delicate teacups, all balanced on another silver tray. Zachary Novak nearly had a heart attack when he saw my sister. I was wearing dark jeans and a button-down ruffled top, presentable enough for this business meeting, though now reeking of lemon oil. I refused to dress up on the weekends, my only respite from the heels, suits, and dresses I wore at the firm. Rachel, however, was wearing a flirty sundress and high wedges that laced around her calves. Her eyes widened when she saw him, and she set down the drinks in a hurry.

"Call me Zach." He held my sister's hand a beat too long.

Tabitha's eyes appeared to twitch, but maybe she was blinking out some dust. There was enough floating around.

Like most men, Zach was captivated by Rachel. And he was just her type: tall, built, and blond, with startlingly blue eyes and a strong jaw. He flashed her a special smile as he sat across from her. I tamped down a fleeting thought that maybe now she'd never look twice at Garrett Davies.

The four of us sat in wingback chairs around a small table, feasting on Rachel's scones and drinking coffee out of real Wedgwood cups. The floor was bare, as Rachel and I had carefully rolled up the rugs last night and left them on the back porch. We didn't need to asphyxiate our guests with eau de cat piss.

"Garrett Davies told me Sylvia was working with both of you to decide what to do with this place." I straightened the pen and notepad in front of me. "I want to know what her intentions were so I can make a decision."

Zach jumped in. "Sylvia was considering selling Thistle Park. She was worried the house was too far gone and that most buyers would only be interested in the land, either to build houses on these five acres, or to drill for shale gas. So I was exploring whether there were any buyers who wanted to renovate the house or at least not use the land for fracking."

"Were you successful?"

"Yes and no. You can't really sell with that kind of covenant attached, to make someone promise not to do something with the land. It's zoned to allow drilling. The house was never officially on the market, but there were some inquiries. A large family was interested, especially considering Sylvia was willing to sell it cheaply. But . . . they took one look inside and got the heck out of here."

I choked on a sip of coffee, politely coughing it off.

"But you've already made great strides."

"Sylvia would be pleased." Tabitha looked around the now neat room.

"I know you want to honor Sylvia's wishes," Zach pressed on, "but if you don't try to find the perfect buyer, this land will be snapped up in a heartbeat. Someone will develop it and build twenty houses. Or you could keep the house and lease the land for drilling. The money would fund renovations."

"Why do the gas companies want this particular piece of land?" Rachel practically simpered, batting her mascaraed lashes at Zach.

I stifled a giggle. Surely Rachel was joking with him. Wasn't she?

"No one else in this neighborhood will allow Lonestar to drill. This is their last chance." Zach addressed Rachel, his mouth curving in a slow smile.

"But you can't really tear this place down," Tabitha interjected. "It's basically a historical landmark. It was designed by a famous architect."

"No, it's not. Official historical status was never applied for or granted for Thistle Park." Zach sat back smugly and Tabitha fumed. The two squared off, glaring at each other over their teacups and cheese straws.

My sister coolly assessed Tabitha.

"It *should* be a historical landmark. And Sylvia was looking into that process. This house is very important to Port Quincy." Tabitha's eyes got a faraway look. "Sylvia preserved it over the years for a reason. If you stay here, you'll be celebrating that history."

I gulped a slug of coffee and grimaced. I wasn't sure I wanted to stay here. Would I be beholden to keep this place exactly as it was? I was fascinated by the idea of Thistle Park as living history, and I loved watching period piece dramas on TV, but that didn't mean I wanted to live in one, especially now that I didn't have the money to restore it.

Zach set down his teacup with a sharp clatter. "Sylvia didn't mention anything about seeking historical status. I'd know. My grandmother worked here, and my father was practically raised with Keith's father. Although I wasn't ever close to Keith, Sylvia has been very good to my family, and she treated me like her own flesh and blood. She told me everything." His cool blue gaze crackled with anger.

Tabitha rolled her eyes and studied her cloth napkin with undue seriousness.

Zach turned to me. "I was taking all of Sylvia's concerns into account, and I'll do the same for you. Some people in Port Quincy might tell you it's your responsibility to take all of this on"—he glanced around at the chaos that was Thistle Park—"but think about what's best for you. I predict that will be selling. Although, with a murder here, it'll be hard to find a family willing to move in." Thank goodness he hadn't brought up Shane Hartley by name.

"One thing I am certain about, while I own it, is I'm not comfortable with drilling here. Especially since Sylvia was against it." I wiped a crumb of scone away.

"Fair enough." Zach gave an easy smile, slipping back into sales mode. "If you decide to sell, I'll be happy to help." He beamed at Rachel as well.

Tabitha doled out an icy glare to Zach. "Sylvia was considering donating the house to the historical society. The McGavitt family built this house, and their glass factory was the heart and soul of Port Quincy. We'd love to have the house, but I don't expect you to donate it. Sylvia wasn't even sure how she felt about that. She felt the house was a living thing and should have a family in it and not be a sterile museum. Perhaps that's why she gave it to you, Mallory, for you to live here."

Phew. At least if I kept this place, I wouldn't need to keep everything the same, like a time capsule.

"The McGavitt family," I said slowly. "That was Sylvia's middle name."

"That's right. Sylvia's grandfather was a glass baron. We have an exhibit about the family. I'd love to show it to you if you'll stop in to the historical society." Tabitha included my sister in her warm invitation, but Rachel didn't seem to be biting.

What is with her?

"It'd be helpful to include some pieces from the house," Tabitha concluded her pitch.

"Sure. Take whatever." The house was filled with endless knickknacks, and damned if I knew whether they were valuable or not. It was like living in a crystal flea market.

Tabitha's jaw dropped. "We don't want much. Some photographs, and we'll make copies and return the originals to you. Some glass, of course, since the family decorated with pieces from their factory."

"Seriously, take what you like. I'm sure it'd be better if some things were on display at the historical society, instead of in this mess of a house."

Tabitha beamed, her sharp features softening. We set up a time next weekend to choose items for her exhibit. The four of us made small talk while we finished our coffee.

Zach glanced at his watch. "Well, it's time for me to go. I have an open house. Nice to meet you." He gave Rachel a special smile. "See you around, Tabby-cat." He smirked as he navigated the heavy furniture on his way out.

"Only three people on this planet are allowed to call me that, and he's not one of them," Tabitha spat as soon as the front door thudded shut. "Not anymore, at least."

These two obviously had a history. I raised my eyebrows and looked at Rachel to silently confer, but she wasn't paying attention. She sat up tall in her chair, her eyes following Zach down the path and back to his car. Tabitha didn't seem to miss that.

"I should get going too." Her smile was tight.

"Thanks for meeting with us."

She returned the sentiment with a real smile this time. "The pleasure is mine. Sylvia made the right decision, leaving Thistle Park to you. Keith and Helene Pierce would have sold to the highest bidder. You'll do her proud, no matter what you decide."

Tabitha's impassioned good-bye caused my eyes to prickle.

Rachel finally came back to life, a predatory gleam in her pretty eyes. "You're not still seeing Zach, are you?"

My mouth nearly dropped open. "Rachel," I hissed.

"No, it's okay." Tabitha looked at Rachel head-on. "I'm not seeing him anymore. He's all yours. Just be careful. Zach is a handful."

"I can take care of myself, thanks."

"I have no doubt about that." Tabitha was a consummate professional. She bade us good-bye again and I walked her to the door.

I returned to my sister, about to chastise her for her rudeness, but she cut me off.

"It's raining men here in Port Quincy. Who would have ever guessed?"

Chapter Six

The next day, I resumed cleaning, with Rachel's help. She bopped around the house in tiny running shorts and a tank top, singing aloud with her iPod, mopping the wooden floors and alternatively dancing with the handle.

I'd flung open all of the windows and was dusting the myriad of trinkets, vases, and glass all around the house, but I was creating more of a mess than before. The fluffy orange kitten studied the dust motes spiraling lazily through the sunlight.

About twenty minutes in, I sat down.

C'mon. I don't have time for this.

"You need a break," Rachel sang out from the hallway, twirling her mop around like a dance partner. "It's the heat."

It was true. There was no air-conditioning at Thistle Park, and we'd already blown the fuses trying to hook up half a dozen fans.

"Okay." I allowed my baby sis to let me off the hook, when I was the one who'd demanded we clean today. "If you insist."

I rifled through the stack of documents I'd printed Friday night before I left the firm. They were complaints and pleadings from Lonestar Energy's many lawsuits, brought by families living in Port Quincy. If you believed the plaintiffs' claims, Lonestar's fracking hadn't left the land or water unscathed. Just glancing through the documents, I could think of a dozen families that wouldn't mind if Shane Hartley or any other Lonestar executive met an untimely death. Chief Truman and Faith Hendricks probably knew this as well, which gave me some measure of comfort. I couldn't really be a suspect. This was all a hideous coincidence.

I leaned back onto the funny-shaped piece of furniture that Tabitha had called a fainting couch. I'd just rest my eyes for a minute.

I smelled her first. A whiff of strawberry bubble gum. My eyes fluttered open. A grin, all metal and magenta braces, and the source of the strawberry breath came into view. Then a smattering of freckles and those elfin hazel eyes. Hovering two inches from my face.

"Summer." I sat up, nearly colliding with her as I had with her father.

"See, she's not dead." Rachel returned to her mopping.

Summer laughed, shifting Jeeves from one arm to the other. She'd brought the little black fluff ball back, hopefully for a visit, and he seemed content to nestle in her arms. He sported a navy harness encrusted in rhinestones. Summer unhooked her kitten and he trotted into the hallway, meowing in search of his sister and calico mama.

"Did your dad take you shopping for supplies?" I

sat up, rubbing my eyes. The thought of Garrett and Summer selecting things for this spoiled little kitten brought a smile to my face.

"Oh yeah." Summer perched on an ottoman. "He even feeds Jeeves from the table, and I'm the one who has to tell him not to. My grandpa said Dad's reinforcing bad habits."

The calico and Jeeves's sister kitten came over, eager to sniff him and welcome him back.

"Dad's only letting me keep Jeeves if I promise to dye my hair back to blond by the time school starts." Summer brought her long ponytail of dull, inky hair in front of her face, crossing her eyes to look at the ends. They were split and the texture of straw.

"Honey"—Rachel moved over to inspect her hair—"you'll never get this blond again. Your hair will melt before you lighten it. Or worse, turn as orange as that kitten."

"That's what my grandma said, but Dad won't budge."

"You know"—I considered Summer—"you'd look really good with a pixie cut. And your roots are just about long enough."

"A pixie cut?" Summer frowned. "Like Tinker Bell?"

"Like a young Mia Farrow." We'd finally gotten the Internet hooked up, so I flipped open my laptop. I typed in a search and swiveled it around when I found a 1970s picture of the actress. "See?"

Rachel jumped up and made a beeline down the hall.

"She's so pretty." It was as if Summer couldn't believe she could ever look as lovely.

Rachel returned brandishing a pair of scissors and a towel. "You're way prettier than her." Rachel did an experimental clip on one of her own wavy strands. "These are just sharp enough. What do you think, Summer? Are you ready for a haircut?"

I began to get nervous. "I don't know about this. Your dad might kill me, and we've just gotten over kitten-gate." I moved closer to Summer, hovering in a protective stance. I pictured Garrett sitting on the porch, glowering, replacing the sunny, sexy Garrett who'd lately occupied my mind.

"Dad will be super happy to see the dyed part gone." Summer sat on the tasseled ottoman, tucked the towel around her neck, and sat up straight. Her voice was full of confidence, but she steeled herself with her eyes closed, as if undergoing a dental exam. "Besides, if he's mad, I'll tell just him it was your idea." She opened her eyes and giggled.

"I like this kid." Rachel undid Summer's ponytail and fluffed out the dull, black hair.

"You're really sure?" I bit my lip. "We could make a quick call to your dad or your grandparents."

"Positive." Summer looked more relaxed as Rachel combed gently through her fried hair. She squeezed her eyes tight again when Rachel thwacked off most of it with one cut.

"Can I look?" Summer paled when she opened an eye and spied the artificially raven tresses pooled around her on the floor.

"Not yet." Rachel stuck the tip of her tongue out in concentration.

I fluttered around the ottoman, praying Rachel knew what she was doing.

"You're pretty good at this," I said a few minutes later.

Summer sagged with relief.

"I had a six-month stint at Custom Cuts in Florida." Rachel trimmed Summer's hair ever closer. "I could do this in my sleep." She shot me an *I-told-you-so* look.

Fifteen minutes later, I marveled fully at Rachel's handiwork. Summer looked lovely and ethereal, her hair a shining cap cut close to her scalp. The cut freed her, and the girl she was shone through without all the jarring dyed black hair.

"Ta-da," Rachel cried, as I handed Summer an old pewter hand mirror.

Summer looked as if she'd cry, and Rachel's eyes went wide.

"I look so . . . *nice.*" A giant, cheek-splitting grin erupted on Summer's face. "Thank you!" She jumped up and hugged Rachel and me together, pulling my sister down into her embrace, which was surprisingly strong for such a reedy girl.

"You're welcome, sweetie." Rachel sent me a relieved look.

Summer picked up the mirror again and stared at her reflection in awe, running her hands over her nearly shorn head. Then she set it down, grabbed the broom leaning against the window, and began to sweep her hair into a tidy pile.

"Can I help you guys clean? My dad said you could use a hand. Jeeves can hang out with his mom and sister."

Score another point for Garrett. I smiled. "We'd love your help, but wouldn't you rather be out with your friends?"

"My best friend, Jocelyn, is at summer camp in New Hampshire." Summer scowled. "And my other friend, Phoebe, goes to live with her dad in Maryland in the summer 'cause her parents are divorced. It's just me and my grandparents and my dad."

"And Jeeves."

"And Jeeves." She brightened. "What did you name his mom and sister?"

Oh crap. "Um, the mom is Whiskey—"

"And the kitten is Soda." Rachel picked up the little orange kitten, making me regret our choices. We'd settled on those names when the cats managed to knock over an ancient bottle of liquor during their play.

"Cool." Summer looked fondly at the reunited cat family. "So, how can I help?"

"We can roll up the rest of the rugs and take them to the back porch," I suggested. "Then finish mopping."

It truly was a three-person job. We'd dealt with the rugs in the parlor so we could meet with Tabitha and Zach, but there were more to deal with in the dining room. We needed to move the heavy wooden furniture, or at least raise the table and chair legs high enough to slide the tattered rugs out from under them. After pricing how much it would cost to clean genuine hundred-year-old rugs, I wasn't sure if they'd live to see another day. They could air out on the back porch for the time being.

"Are you sure you're up for this?" I asked Summer, my question garbled as I hooked the collar of my T-shirt over my nose.

"If I can clean cat litter, I can do this." Her voice was nasal and high since she held her nose.

Rachel and I heaved up each leg of the dining room table in turn, and four times Summer pulled the rug's corners out from under them.

"Yuck." Rachel rolled the pungent wool into a cylinder. Rachel and Summer each grabbed an end, and I took the middle, balancing the heavy rug on my shoulder. We tried to make our way past the pocket door, which was stuck halfway shut.

"This door is so annoying." I jammed my shoulder against it as I shimmied through with the carpet. We made it to the back porch and threw the offending rug on top of the pile from the parlor.

"Whew." Summer wiped the sweat from her brow. "Let's do another one."

"We need to un-jimmy this door." I frowned as we returned to the house. "It would be easier if we could carry things through the dining room."

Rachel and I each grabbed a side of the pocket door and rocked it back and forth, trying to jam it back into its track.

"Be careful," I called out as Summer moved in to help us. "Rachel, Summer's dad will kill us if she gets hurt." At that moment, the door popped out of its track and hung, barely stable, all cattywampus from its frame.

"Geez Louise." I tried to steady the door, which had half fallen on my sister.

"Thanks." She propped it up in a less precarious position.

The three of us eased the door out of the frame and slid it onto the floor, sweating and grunting as we positioned the heavy wooden slab.

"What is that?" Summer peered into the empty pocket door track.

"A piece of paper." I plucked the item from the ground. "It must have made the door stick."

It was folded into quarters, and was so old it almost cracked along each crease.

"It looks like it says something." Summer peered over my shoulder.

"Let me see!" Rachel tried to snatch the delicate onionskin paper out of my hand.

"Hold on." I whirled around to protect the find. "We can all look at it."

With shaking hands, I smoothed the paper out on the dining room table, all discolored and brittle. Fine, spidery cursive filled the page:

My Dearest Heart,
   I have discovered your plans. You will never find the paintings, as I have hidden them from you. I do this out of love and concern, so you may avoid the gravest of mistakes.
   Yours always,

Here the note stopped, the delicate stationary torn in half.

"Who in the heck wrote this?" I asked, at the same time as Summer cried out, "There are hidden paintings somewhere in this house!"

"So the rumor is true." Tabitha took a sip of wine and leaned across the table, her gimlet eyes shining.

"If you believe this." I gestured to the note spread out on the tablecloth. I'd called Tabitha as soon as Summer left. If anyone would know about hidden paintings at Thistle Park, it would be the town historian. Helene and Keith were also likely candidates, but I sure as hell wasn't going to ask them.

Tabitha could barely contain her excitement. She'd invited Rachel and me to dinner and asked us to bring the note.

"I can't go," Rachel had said airily as she blotted her lipstick and arranged her hair in a messy bun in the only bathroom. She pouted her lips in the gilded mirror and gave her reflection a practice pucker.

"Why not? And why are you dressed like that?"

Rachel was wearing what, for her, constituted a demure dress. It was baby blue and almost skimmed the tops of her knees. She'd traded her usual high heels for modest espadrille wedges, and her nails, for once, weren't a shocking color but were a delicate shell pink. The only concession to her usual come-hither look was the top of the dress, unbuttoned rather low.

I'd changed from my cleaning garb into a jean skirt and linen tank top and hoped a nice jacket would dress it up enough for dinner. I was ready to go in twenty minutes, after I tamed my hair and applied a bit of mascara and lip gloss, while Rachel calmly reached for her cosmetics bag and spread out the contents of a mall makeup kiosk in the small bathroom. How she managed to look fresh and dewy and young under all of that makeup mystified me. It was like old times back when I was in high school, when Rachel's complicated ablutions and beauty routines already took twice as long as mine, even though she was still in middle school.

"I have a date." She whirled around. "Tell Tabitha I can't come to dinner because I have plans with Zach."

"You can tell her yourself. And I doubt she cares who Zach sees." I didn't think this was true, though, recalling Tabitha's shrewd appraisal of Rachel and Zach's banter yesterday. It seemed she cared very much.

"Nope. She'll be annoyed. Are these earrings too much?" Rachel swished her head back and forth, and the sparkly blue bulbs jangled and flashed.

"Try some studs if you're going to wear your hair up. Are you going out with Zach to annoy Tabitha or because you genuinely like him?" I sank onto the prim love seat across from the pedestal sink and the claw-foot tub. Furniture in a bathroom? Why not.

"Because I like him, silly." Rachel screwed in a pair of diamond studs.

"Are those mine?" I jumped up quickly and took a deep breath of something familiar. "You're wearing my perfume too?" I recoiled as the scent of Coco Mademoiselle nearly knocked me over.

"Just a spray."

Try a gallon. As long as I could remember, Rachel had been sneaking clothing, jewelry, makeup, and perfume out of my room like a seasoned thief. It would take weeks before I noticed anything was missing, and by then, Rachel had usually lost the fruits of her pilfering.

"Can I borrow them?" Rachel stood and returned to the mirror, holding the other stud in her hand, poised over her ear. At least her expression reflected back in the mirror was suitably sheepish.

"Tell you what, you can have them both. Keith gave me the perfume, and I don't think I can ever let it touch my skin again. I'd probably burst into flames. Maybe it will give you better luck. And Helene gave me those earrings"—I shuddered—"so you're welcome to them too. We should have them exorcised

before you wear them, though." My sister might as
well enjoy them, since I'd be happy to have them out
of my possession.

Rachel beamed and threw her arms around me,
enveloping me in the cloying scent. Still, I held on to
my sister tight. Whether she was a kleptomaniac or
not, I didn't want to let go.

A horn sounded in front of the house.

"Gotta go." Rachel skipped from the bathroom.

"Wait, where's your date tonight?"

But Rachel was already gone. I hoped she wouldn't
parade Zach around the same restaurant where I was
meeting Tabitha.

So far, so good. Almost every table at Pellegrino's
was filled, but none held my sister and Zach. And
while the tables were close to each other, the collective chatter and soft piped-in Muzak offered us some
measure of privacy. The lighting was low and the
tables were lit by small candles. Wall sconces glowed
along each wall, and potted plants and small trees
were strategically placed between deep mahogany
booths and intimate tables. I could barely see the
other diners' faces, let alone hear what they were
talking about. But, I couldn't relax. This would be
just the kind of place Zach might take Rachel on a
first date. There weren't a lot of restaurants in Port
Quincy, and the night was still young.

"Earth to Mallory." Tabitha gave a kind smile.

I laughed. "Sorry, please start over. Could there
really be paintings hidden in the house? There aren't
many left on the walls."

"There's a local legend that some important

paintings disappeared right around the time there was a fire at Thistle Park, back in nineteen thirty-four. It started in the dining room, where the paintings were rumored to have hung. No one was ever certain if the paintings were stolen or if they went up in flames. The whole room was destroyed."

"Why wouldn't people just assume they were burned? Before we found this note, that is."

Tabitha squinted at the brittle paper, as if it'd explain its cryptic message. "If the accounts are true, Sylvia's mother, Evelyn, was beside herself. She claimed the paintings had been moved from the dining room wall before the fire started. No one could corroborate her story, since the fire was so destructive. They thought she was hysterical." Tabitha paused for a sip of wine.

"So, what happened? The house obviously didn't burn down." I'd never heard this tale from Sylvia. Then again, it had happened a good seventy-five years before I'd met her.

"They managed to contain the fire and save the rest of the house, but the dining room and kitchen were basically gone. And even worse, Evelyn ran back into the house, muttering about the paintings. It made sense she'd try to save them, since they were the most valuable things left at the time. It was the Depression, and they'd sold off the rest of their art collection to keep the factory going. Evelyn didn't make it. She died of smoke inhalation. Sylvia's father, Charles, almost died as well, trying to pull her out."

"How awful. And even more awful for Sylvia, to lose her mother like that." I grabbed my third roll of the evening and took a bite of the heavenly crusty stuff.

Tabitha frowned. "She didn't know at first. She'd eloped the evening before with Thistle Park's gardener, Albert Smoot. It took weeks for her to receive the news her childhood home had almost burned down and that her mother perished in the fire."

"I've never heard this story," I said slowly. "And I thought Keith's grandfather was an attorney, not a gardener?"

"He was. Keith's grandfather was her second husband. Sylvia came back home three months after the fire and her elopement. Her first husband, Albert, had died. She never left Thistle Park again."

We munched in silence for a few moments.

"Poor Sylvia." I wiped my mouth with my napkin. "She once jokingly called the house her penance, but I didn't pry, and now I understand."

"She probably felt guilty for running off on the eve of her mother's death."

"So, maybe these paintings burned in the fire, or maybe they were rescued right before. And if Sylvia's mother was desperate to get back into a burning building—"

"Then maybe she hid them!" Tabitha finished triumphantly.

"It wasn't worth risking her life over some paintings." I couldn't fathom reentering a burning building to claim any possession.

"It was the Depression."

"Were they really that hard up? Wasn't the glass factory still going?"

Tabitha nodded. "McGavitt Glass didn't officially

close until the nineteen-sixties, but Port Quincy and the factory never fully recovered. Until now, with the fracking."

"Which Sylvia was opposed to."

"Not everyone is. My parents, for instance, were able to retire when they leased to Lonestar. Drilling has created hundreds of jobs in this town, and some would say it's completely revitalized Port Quincy. But yes," Tabitha laughed, "Sylvia made her opinions known. Shane Hartley was a regular visitor of hers, badgering her to grant him a drilling lease. She got him blacklisted from the nursing home."

"When was this?" Maybe it was connected to his untimely death. Although, I didn't want to connect those dots. Could Hartley have visited Sylvia at the nursing home on the day of her death? Or had Sylvia hired someone to take care of him, and they finished the job after she passed away? *Don't be silly. Sylvia was no killer.*

"I'm not sure." Tabitha puckered her brow. "I know because I was there when it happened. I can check my planner if you'd like."

"That isn't necessary." Truman and Faith were probably working like mad to find Shane Hartley's murderer.

I fished around the basket for more of the tasty warm bread. Carbs were my downfall, and now that I didn't have to squeeze into a tiny-waisted wedding gown, I couldn't stop myself. There was nothing left but a cloth napkin and some crumbs. "Sorry. I devoured all the bread!"

Tabitha smiled at the empty basket and took another sip from her glass. "Please, eat up." She ate delicately, pondering each forkful of her salad, her bright red hair glowing in the dim light, her neck long and thin. She reminded me of a flamingo. "Still, the most logical conclusion about the paintings is that they burned in the fire."

"Unless Evelyn hid them somewhere no one has ever thought to look." I picked up the brittle note.

"And they're right under your nose, hidden in the house." Tabitha's eyes sparkled as the waiter delivered our dishes.

"What were the paintings that hung in the dining room?" I speared eggplant Parmesan with my fork and plopped it into my mouth.

"I have no idea. This was all just speculation. Until now." Tabitha held the tiny piece of yellowed paper to the light.

"So this is it." Zach plucked the note from Tabitha's hand.

"Hey!" She twisted around in her chair to reach for the leaf of paper.

"Rachel was just telling me about your discovery." Zach scrutinized the note.

"Fancy seeing you here." I glared at my sister.

Rachel gave me a barely perceptible shrug and cut her eyes toward Tabitha.

Zach frowned. "Do Helene and Keith Pierce know about this?"

"I hope not!"

Zach's pretty surfer-boy mouth turned down at the corners. "I could see them making trouble for you if they knew there were valuable things in the house, more valuable than old silver, glass, and furniture. They'll try to get into that house faster than you can guess."

He was right. Maybe it was time to install a security

system, like Chief Truman had suggested. This time, its purpose would be to keep out Keith and Helene, not a prospective murderer.

"You're right. Thanks for the warning."

"You bet." Zach tipped an imaginary cap toward Tabitha and steered Rachel with his hand on the small of her back.

"Enjoy your dinner." Rachel threw Tabitha a false smile, her eyes glowing with triumph.

"Likewise." Tabitha didn't conceal her annoyance.

"Zach," I called out more harshly than I meant to.

Several patrons swiveled their heads in our direction.

"The note." I toned my voice down a fraction. "You still have it."

"Oh." He flushed, gently depositing the frail scrap of paper into my outstretched palm, like a priest bestowing communion. "My mistake."

The next day, after work, I was relieved to get home. I was getting back into the swing of things at the firm. I was burrowing back into my cases, pleasing Alan with my work and racking up billable hours, but I was also distracted. I wanted to nose around Thistle Park for evidence of the hidden paintings.

"You know this place better than I do," I murmured to Whiskey, setting my purse down in the hallway. I picked her up and she began to purr. "Have you seen any valuable paintings around here?"

Rachel had left me a voice mail about getting her nails done. Thank goodness Port Quincy was small so my sister could walk everywhere while I drove the rental to Pittsburgh and back each day. "Looks like we're all alone, kitty cat. Let's go fix a snack before we explore." I carried the calico through the front hall. Soda, the kitten, trotted behind us, her tiny orange legs churning to keep up.

We never made it to the kitchen. The skin at the base of my neck prickled first. Then a small rustle came from the dining room to my left. Whiskey stiffened in my arms, and she began to softly hiss. Soda ran up the stairs. Steeling myself, I peeked around the now-defunct pocket door into the room.

Keith was jiggling the heavy mahogany breakfront away from the wall. Several silver picture frames toppled off the top and onto the floor. He was so focused on his snooping he hadn't noticed me. As he peered behind the breakfront, I grabbed a tiny teal glass bird from the credenza beside me, some of the McGavitt Glass Company's best work. I set Whiskey on the floor, wound back, and threw the glass as hard as I could at my ex-fiancé's balding head.

My aim was usually pretty crappy, but anger must have sharpened it.

"What the hell!" Keith jumped when the glass bird flew past his ear and connected with the dull rose damask wallpaper, missing him by mere inches. It shattered into smithereens, the glass shards all glittery like topazes on the hardwood floor.

"Looking for something, Keith?" I was still trembling. Whiskey settled next to me, resuming her hissing.

"You could have killed me." Keith stepped away, his hands in the air, as if I were aiming a gun at him.

I smiled coolly. "You're trespassing. This is *my* house, remember? Sylvia gave it to me. My aim won't be so poor next time." I picked up another glass animal from the credenza menagerie, this time an ornately cut pink elephant. I palmed it like a baseball, ready to wind up and throw.

"I just came in to see . . . how the cats were doing. This little guy in particular," he improvised poorly. "He was Sylvia's favorite. I wanted to make sure the ferals were being fed."

"Nice concern, but I'm not buying it. I've been living here for a week. And Sylvia hasn't lived here for years. No one seemed to care there were strays on the property all the time your grandma was in the nursing home."

"She always had cats at the house when I was growing up." Keith relaxed a little. "I didn't know you'd actually moved in. I didn't think this place was livable." He smirked and looked around. "Well, now I see he's okay, I'll be going."

"It's a she, Keith. Calicoes are always girls." I said a silent thank you to Summer for that tidbit of knowledge. She'd make a wonderful veterinarian. "And you never cared about this place. Tell me why you're really here."

Keith blinked stupidly. Sweat darkened the collar of his once-crisp blue shirt. Drops of perspiration dotted the yellow silk tie I'd given him. Once, I'd been wildly in love with him, but now the sight of him nearly turned my stomach.

"I wanted to see how you're doing. Especially since someone was murdered here. I know you've been hiding from me downtown. I've been looking for you where you used to have lunch with Olivia. Your secretary won't patch my calls through, but you can't hide forever. We need to talk like civilized adults about what happened."

"What happened?" I was trembling. Live, rage-fueled wires lit up my nerves. "You cheated on me three weeks before our wedding, that's what happened. Now get the hell out of here."

"This *is* my family's house." His eyes were flat. "I still can't figure out why Grandma Sylvia left it to you and not her real family. Especially . . ." His eyes trailed to the empty spaces on the walls, confirming my suspicion he now knew about the paintings.

"I was more family to Sylvia than you were these last few years. What were you looking for?"

Keith answered me with silence, so I pulled my phone out of my suit pocket and began to dial.

"Who are you calling?" He licked his lips, which he always did when he was nervous.

"The police." I took a step back, my finger hovering over the send button.

"I'm leaving, I'm leaving!" He wiggled past me into the hallway.

I couldn't believe I'd been within a hairbreadth of marrying this deceptive man.

"How did you get in?" I followed close behind.

He stopped, his forehead creasing into a half-dozen lines.

"This." He dug into his pocket. With a sigh of regret, he held up a house key, identical to the one on my key ring.

I snatched it out of his hand and offered him a grim smile. Then I handed the key back to him.

"The locks will be changed within the hour. Keep

that as a memento to remember the last time you ever set foot in your grandma's house. My house now."

True to my word, I called Will Prentiss, Sylvia's handyman. He arrived within the hour. His name seemed familiar to me, and I wondered if I'd read it within the many Lonestar complaints and filings that now comprised my bedtime reading most nights.

He parked his truck in front of the house. He was an affable-looking middle-aged man, with sandy hair and kind brown eyes and a sunburned face. He wore work boots and walked with a barely perceptible limp, his right foot hitching up a little higher with each step than his left. Though it was hot, he wore long cargo pants and a long-sleeved T-shirt that reached to his wrists. There was a shiny patch of skin visible on the right side of his neck above his collarbone.

"Good to finally meet you." His red face cracked open with a smile. He seemed shy and couldn't quite meet my eyes, but he was genial and upbeat. He turned around and surveyed the mangy yard.

"Been a while since someone cut the grass."

I hid my embarrassment. "I've been kind of busy. We'll get around to it eventually."

He laughed. "That's what I'm here for. I did that kind of thing for Sylvia, both when she lived here and when she went to the home. Hard to keep up with a big house like this, but I kept things from getting too outta hand. So, you're having trouble with your locks?"

"I'm having trouble keeping certain people out."

"Helene Pierce? Or Keith?"

I burst out laughing. "How did you guess? Just Keith, but I wouldn't be surprised to find Helene trespassing too."

He nodded. "She couldn't wait for Miss Sylvia to pass on to get her hands on this place."

"Why is that?" Suspicion curdled the smile right off my face.

"All the antiques, I suppose. And Helene probably would've leased the land for drilling, or sold it off, because she never passed up an opportunity to make money. Though I don't recommend fracking on your property." Will ran his hand uneasily through his hair.

"That's definitely not going to happen now. In addition to changing the outside locks, I could also use your help with the attic. It's locked and none of my keys work." I wanted to change the subject and stop talking about the Pierces. My blood pressure was rising just from recalling Keith's unannounced visit.

Will frowned. "There should be a key in the door to the third floor. It's been a while, but the last time I was here, it was there."

Rachel came home from her manicure and made us all some lemonade while Will oiled and changed the many locks on the doors and windows of Thistle Park.

"And now we'll check out the third floor." He took a long pull from his lemonade. Mint leaves swirled among the ice cubes, fresh and fragrant from the wild garden out back.

The three of us trooped up the steep servants' stairs to the third floor. Rachel and I paused, panting, a few steps below Will as he worked in the small landing. He'd climbed the stairs twice as fast, despite his limp.

"I swear the key was in the door this winter." He picked the lock.

"Maybe the paintings are hidden up here," I whispered to Rachel.

"Paintings?" Will snorted. "That old legend? You're more likely to find a pot of gold at the end of a rainbow than any paintings hidden here."

Apparently my whispers hadn't been quiet enough. "What do you know about them?"

"Miss Sylvia used to talk about growing up during the Depression and how her parents sold off all the good art. She married her father's attorney to keep from losing this place after her parents died." Will was referencing Sylvia's second marriage. "If there'd been some valuable paintings here, she would have found them. She needed the money."

Within minutes, the lock "popped" and Will pushed the creaky door open.

"Hm." He stepped into the attic.

"Hm what?" Rachel eagerly moved past him and into the space. It was big, more a proper third floor than an attic. The front part seemed to be divided up just as the floor below, with large rooms leading off a narrow hallway. The back section was parceled into smaller rooms, some barely bigger than a closet. The ceilings were less ornate than downstairs, with no molding or gilded murals, unless you counted the water stains from the leaky roof. But the space wasn't what had elicited Will's response.

"It was locked from the outside, but someone's been here recently."

I followed Will's eyes down the hall. A trail of footprints marred the heavy dust, so thick it looked as if they'd been made in snow. I shivered. Perhaps our trespasser was still here.

"Don't walk in them," I cautioned Rachel, who was advancing toward the back hallway. "I'm calling the police for real this time."

Chapter Seven

"Trouble seems to find you, Miss Shepard." Chief Truman shook his head at the footprints in the dust, as if I had somehow conjured them expressly to annoy him.

"This town seems to be full of trouble." I narrowed my eyes at him. "I lived in Pittsburgh and was never threatened nor woken up to a corpse outside my window. Not until I came to good old Port Quincy. I thought small towns were supposed to be safe."

The chief's nostrils flared.

"Lemonade?" Rachel appeared at his side with a sweaty glass.

"Don't mind if I do." He settled kinder eyes on my sister.

"Do you think this has anything to do with Shane Hartley's murder?" Faith Hendricks was walking the length of the hallway, snapping pictures before we disturbed the dust.

"I'm not sure," he admitted wearily, "but probably not. Everyone knew this place was abandoned. Anyone could have been up here."

"Someone has the key to the third floor," Will piped up. "I come in here a few times a year for maintenance, and it's always been in the lock. I didn't even bother going in."

"And whoever has the key used it very recently." Faith returned with her camera. "Come take a look. I'm done with my pictures. Just don't touch anything else."

Chief Truman, Rachel, Will, and I gingerly stepped around the footprint trail to reach the far bedroom at the end of the hall. It was cramped, with a severely sloping ceiling to accommodate the lines of the mansard roof above. The sheets on the single iron bed looked mussed and recently used. There was a bottle of cheap chardonnay on the floor, half drunk, and the remnants of crackers and cheese on a china plate I recognized from a set in the butler's pantry. There were a few scented candles set on saucers, burned to the wick. And some mouse droppings.

"Ew." Rachel wrinkled her nose.

"You know what this is," I seethed. "Someone's love nest."

"Probably teenagers." The chief shook his head dismissively.

"No way. Brie and chardonnay? Teenagers would leave behind Doritos and Milwaukee's Best."

Rachel nodded, seemingly impressed with my assessment.

"This couple is older."

And I know just who it is. I rubbed my eyes, trying to flush out the mental image of Keith and Becca Cunningham scampering around this very bedroom.

"Meow." Soda the kitten had found her way up the

stairs and cried plaintively at my feet. I picked her up and snuggled her soft orange fur.

"You think you know who it is?" Chief Truman cocked his head, examining my expression.

"Keith Pierce and Becca Cunningham." I scratched Soda underneath her chin. "I caught Keith creeping around here this afternoon. Looking for something. Of course, he had a key to his grandma's house. I stupidly didn't think about that until he showed me. That's why I asked Will to change the locks."

Truman sighed. "I hate to break it to you, but you inherited this place a week ago, and before then Keith Pierce wasn't trespassing. I'm sure Sylvia gave him a key. Do you have any reason to think he's been here since last week, after this place was deeded over to you?"

"No." I shook my head in defeat. "But I bet he was meeting his girlfriend here before he found out Sylvia left me the place."

Faith and my sister politely turned their eyes away from mine as I reluctantly mentioned Keith's cheating, but Truman just stared at me.

Keith and Becca could have met in any hotel in Pittsburgh. There was no reason for them to come all the way out to Thistle Park. And a week ago, the rumor that some valuable paintings might be stowed in the house hadn't been revived. I wanted to kick myself for discussing it with Tabitha out in the open at Pellegrino's. I frowned, wondering just how discreet Tabitha and Zach were.

"I've been here while Mallory was at work. I would've known if someone had come into the house," Rachel added.

"Just the same, I'll follow up with Mr. Pierce. I'll make it clear he'd better not trespass again," Truman promised.

Faith carefully wrapped the wine, the plate, and the food remnants in a brown paper evidence bag.

"Thanks, Chief Truman." I sank into a spare wooden chair. What I wouldn't give to be there when he set Keith straight. "How's Shane Hartley's murder investigation going?"

The chief grunted. "You're no longer officially a suspect, so that's good."

"Tell that to my employer," I muttered.

"I did, numerous times."

"What?" I sat up sharply, digging my spine into the hard wood. The firm was aware I had been here the night Shane died, but I didn't actually think they'd questioned the Port Quincy police in any great detail.

"Russell Carey is very thorough." Truman gave me a pitying look. "I assured them you're no longer a suspect. Congratulations, I believe you. I don't think you, or you"—he glanced at Rachel—"murdered Shane Hartley."

"Who are the suspects?" I was still trying to calm down after hearing my law firm had contacted the Port Quincy police to suss out whether I had murdered one of their clients.

"We can't share any details about our investigation." Faith sounded bleak.

Wouldn't, or *couldn't* share, because they had nothing? I recalled the dozens of lawsuits filed against Lonestar Energy and all of the angry former workers and families who'd allowed drilling on their property, only to see it turn out badly. Anyone could have killed Shane Hartley, but I was no longer a suspect.

I decided to take what I could get and call it a day.

Rachel and I slept well that night, secure in the house, all of the locks employed to keep would-be murderers and trespassers at bay. Extra sleep didn't help me focus at work, though. I'd been an exemplary associate right up until the day I found out about Keith and Becca. Turning in excellent work, pleasing partners and clients alike, all while hitting my billable hours requirements, with a (sometimes admittedly fake) smile on my face. Now I was officially slipping, my attention drawn back to Port Quincy and Thistle Park, lost paintings, murdered gas executives, and an ever-elusive bride to take over my reception.

Interest in my Craigslist ad had died down, and I was considering Olivia's suggestion to pitch my reception to the newspaper as a features story, but something held me back. It was one thing that half of the town knew me as Keith Pierce's cuckolded, would-be-wife, but seeing the tale in print was another story. Unfortunately, I didn't have the luxury of hiding from the media. As I left work, my cell rang, the number unfamiliar.

"Mallory Shepard?"

"Yes?"

"This is Denise Gregory, features editor at the *Eagle Standard*. Are you the author of the Craigslist post offering up a wedding?"

I tripped on a crack in the sidewalk outside of my building and caromed into a man hurrying by.

"Sorry," I muttered, collecting myself, my nerves bathed in ice. "Yes, I did write that ad."

"Wonderful. I wanted to know if you'd found anyone to take your offer and get a comment from you about your wedding and this act of charity. It must have been quite an ordeal standing up to the Pierces." The editor said this last bit in a breathy tone, gossipy and fake-chummy.

"Um, no comment." I clicked my phone off, feeling guilty about having hung up on her, but I couldn't talk about the cancelled wedding as a retort to Keith and Helene, even if it would net me a bride to take over the reception.

After work, I stopped at Thistle Park, gathered up Whiskey and Soda in their new carriers, and trooped off to the Port Quincy veterinarian. Summer and her grandma had taken Jeeves for a checkup yesterday, and Summer had called to report his clean bill of health. It was a gentle hint that I should take in my two cats. Luckily, the vet had a cancellation and could fit me in.

I sat in a squeaky vinyl waiting room chair, the carriers on either side of me. The office was empty, all but me and the front desk attendant. A dog barked in one of the examination rooms. I closed my eyes as I petted the cats through the tops of their carriers, planning the rest of the evening so I could catch up on work. The front door tinkled behind me.

"How fortuitous to run into you." The voice sent chills up my spine. A second later, the sharp fizz of Calèche reached my nostrils, poisoning the air and warning me too late. Baxter the Yorkie seemed to recognize me. He strained at his leash, front paws flailing in the air. Whiskey wasn't too happy about the dog encroaching on her space and hissed.

"Helene." I stood and tried to sound as cold and commanding as she did. It didn't work and came out as a meek croak.

"I wasn't sure how to reach you, since you won't deign to speak to me or my son." Helene's mouth was set in a harsh line of disapproval, a look she'd seldom strayed from in the years I'd known her.

I stared at her incredulously. "Keith was trespassing. I don't need to be civil when I find someone has broken into *my* house." Bull's-eye.

Helene blinked and seemed to shake for a moment in her nude pumps. "I wouldn't be so sure of that." Her hiss was barely above a whisper. She took a step closer, squaring her skinny shoulders beneath her shoulder pads.

Baxter whined and twisted, trying to lick my hand. Next to Sylvia, Baxter was the only other family member of Keith's I'd ever liked, and it killed me I couldn't bend down to scratch behind his little white ears.

"It was going to be a surprise, but I may as well tell you." Helene's voice dropped softer still. "I'm suing you. And I'm going to win."

A mixture of fear and rage bubbled up. "So, freaking sue me, already!" I brought the young man manning the check-in desk to his feet. "Bring it on!"

My bravado didn't match my actual feelings. I couldn't afford a lawsuit on top of squirreling away money to renovate Sylvia's house and keeping up with my law school loans. My heart began to beat at a faster clip. Could Helene hear it or see it knocking against my rib cage through my thin blouse?

"Everything in that house, including those paintings, had better be exactly the way you found them." Helene delivered this threat in a near screech. She jabbed one French-manicured finger in the air, punctuating each word.

It was my turn to whisper, my suspicions about Keith's visit confirmed. "How did you know about the paintings?"

"Port Quincy is a small town. One you could never hope to understand." Helene shook her head pityingly, and I took a step back, moving in front of my cats.

"It's you who doesn't understand much. You never appreciated Sylvia, and you tried to bully her out of the only home she'd ever known."

The receptionist was really getting into our tiff, and I was giving him more fodder. Baxter whimpered, and I tried to tone it down for his sake.

"Try to remember Thistle Park was never yours," I said quietly. "It isn't even your family. You married into it."

Helene offered me a wide smile, so big her bridgework appeared. "Marry into the family?" She tilted her head, considering my choice of words. "You, my dear, didn't even manage that."

She picked up Baxter, turned on her heel, and minced out, the door bouncing shut behind her.

I threw it open and shouted after her, "I dumped Keith, not the other way around!" It was too late. I was treated to her smile in the rearview mirror of her Cadillac as she drove off, leaving me coughing in a cloud of exhaust.

* * *

I was unsettled from my run-in with Helene. After the kitties received clean bills of health, I returned home to hunker down at the kitchen table. I plugged away at my laptop, making little mistakes as I caught up on work until the wee hours of the morning. I soldiered on at work the next day, stopping to eat lunch with Olivia in my office.

"You need to take a break." Olivia tucked a strand of her long black hair behind her ear. "Promise you'll take off the time you set aside for"—here, she paused—"your honeymoon."

"I can't take time off." I paced in front of my office window, overlooking the aptly named Point, where the Allegheny and Monongahela Rivers joined to form the Ohio. A pigeon fluttered outside my window, trying to alight on the ledge, but the sharp, rusty spikes erected at the base kept it from landing. *Why do you want in here so badly when all I want to do is get out?*

"Alan's already mad I took time off for my broken engagement, Sylvia's funeral, and the murder investigation on my damn front lawn. No more time off. It doesn't matter I'm on track to bill over two thousand hours this year. Besides, I can't risk this job. Especially if Helene's not bluffing. I'll need to pay for an attorney. Unless you want to represent me?"

Olivia shook her head. "In a pinch, but I don't do estate work, and neither do you. Or I'd suggest you represent yourself."

"A woman who is her own lawyer has a fool for a client." I sat heavily in my chair.

"Well, there's one good thing about all of this." Olivia tucked into her burger and fries. "I starved myself to fit into that stupid sea-foam bridesmaid's dress, no offense. Now I can celebrate and eat whatever I want, and you can celebrate the fact you didn't marry that cheating bastard."

"I'll toast to that." I clinked my paper coffee cup with hers. I only managed to eat half of the limp salad before Olivia left. I was still on my lunch hour, so I could investigate some non-work issues. I unlocked my computer and searched for the firm's Lonestar documents again and filtered them for the name of Sylvia's handyman, Will Prentiss.

Jackpot.

William B. Prentiss had sued Lonestar Energy this past winter for negligence related to an accident on his farm. I cringed, reading the complaint, which spelled out in detail how an explosion had injured Will. He had been examining his well, which had stopped producing water. A pocket of methane had ignited and exploded, burning Will's right side. He had been airlifted to a hospital in Pittsburgh, where he'd spent a month recuperating. For a while, it hadn't seemed like he'd make it. I read Will's horrific deposition, trying to stay detached as I heard his friendly voice in my head. I recalled the shiny patch of skin on the right side of his neck, his limp, and his long sleeves and pants in the summer heat.

The other documents included long depositions from Will's mother and his doctors on the plaintiff's side and various Lonestar employees, including Shane Hartley, for the defense. Shane came off just as pushy and arrogant in his testimony as he had on

Sylvia's porch. He insinuated over and over again that Will was a smoker, ergo he'd had a hand in what Shane deemed "an unfortunate accident." He was a skilled witness for Lonestar, casting doubt as to whether the gas leak was even Lonestar's fault, as the company didn't have any drilling operations on the Prentisses' land, just the next farm over.

Still, this case would probably never go to trial. Lonestar wouldn't take the chance a jury would award Will a big payout. Having met him and experienced his gentle charm, I knew he'd definitely elicit sympathy. Why hadn't the case settled already? Could Will have killed Shane Hartley? He certainly had reason to hate Lonestar, and even Shane, after the suit had dragged on. Will's mother had been reduced to tears during her deposition.

I was startled by a rap on my office door. Closed doors were frowned upon at Russell Carey, but I needed a heads-up. Will Prentiss's case documents were still displayed on the monitor. I locked my computer screen and croaked, "Come in," expecting it to be my assistant. It wasn't.

"Alan, what brings you here?" I instantly brightened, feigning enthusiasm and verve.

"Am I interrupting your lunch?"

"I was just about finished." I sequestered the half-eaten salad behind a pile of discovery requests.

"I'll get right to the point. I'm here to discuss one of the firm's clients, Helene Pierce."

My salad congealed in the bottom of my stomach. The firm managed some of her investments, but I didn't really think of her as a client.

"We've handled a lot of business for the Pierces over the years."

I bobbed my head in assent, but didn't trust myself to reply.

Alan, of course, knew about my broken engagement and relationship to the Pierces, as he'd alluded to my "personal problems." He towered over me, probably waiting for me to jump in and fill the silence. I stayed quiet for once.

"Why don't you fill me in about the Pierces' artwork that may be . . . temporarily in your possession, so we can solve this little mess?"

Giving me just enough rope to hang myself. "I inherited Sylvia Pierce's house. Actually, she deeded it to me, free and clear. Helene Pierce is furious it wasn't willed to her. That's really all that's going on. I'm not sure any artwork exists. Or how the Pierces, with all due respect, have anything to do with me or my work here."

"You have your senior associate promotion review later this summer, to see if you're more partner material, or just counsel." Alan's face was devoid of emotion. "Or"—he narrowed his tired eyes—"if you'd be better off working somewhere else."

I clenched my teeth so hard I feared they'd crack. I couldn't believe he'd gone there.

"Yes," I whispered, a glint of fear replacing my ire.

"I'm not saying you need to capitulate to Helene Pierce, but the Pierces are upstanding members of the community, with a long history in western Pennsylvania. As you know"—here, he smirked—"Keith Pierce used to be an attorney here, and his father before him. The Pierces have a right to know if there are valuable things in that house and what's going on, until this is all straightened out."

I gave Alan a stony smile and willed my beating heart to slow down. "A woman was treated badly by her daughter-in-law and grandson. She gave her house to someone who actually gave a damn about her. Now they want the house back. It's too late. They don't deserve to know anything about anything, much less have a right to paw through *my house*." I tried to focus on a spot above Alan's head. If I dared look in his eyes, I feared I'd leap across the desk and claw them out of his skull.

"I can see I've upset you. I just don't see why you'd oppose a woman who is a business associate with Lonestar Energy, a client that generates fifteen percent of our firm's profits. I can't fathom why someone who wants to be a partner at Russell Carey would even think about doing that. Do you have any idea what will happen if the Pierces take you to court over this? You have a good shot of making partner *someday*, but frankly, that might need to be taken off the table unless I see some cooperation."

The wheels were churning in my head, which was still recovering from his ambush. *What did he say before his thinly veiled threats? Helene has a business relationship with Lonestar Energy?*

My phone mercifully began to ring.

"I have to take this." I glowered at Alan, one hand on the phone.

He sighed and moved away from my desk. "Think about your career here, Mallory." He shut the door behind him.

I glanced at the phone. It was Olivia. I let it ring.

I swiveled my chair to face the window. A window I'd rarely looked out of in the six years I'd toiled here, trying to prove myself. Far below me, on the pavement, men and women went about their day, carrying out errands, rushing to appointments, and greeting each other. Hundreds of feet above them, I began to panic. Helene's retribution worked fast.

Chapter Eight

I fled Russell Carey minutes after Alan left, racing back home to Port Quincy.

Awesome. I'm starting to think of this place as home. It was turning into more of a home than Pittsburgh, as the quirky little town was beginning to grow on me. Whenever I saw Yvette Tannenbaum outside her father's auto body shop, she gave a friendly wave, and Bev Mitchell stopped to chat when I ran into her at the grocery store. It was a charming town with a slower pace of living I could actually get used to. I was committed to staying until I unraveled the mystery of the paintings, until I sold Sylvia's house, and until I found a bride to take over my wedding reception. Shane Hartley's murder was another matter. I'd leave that to Faith and Chief Truman.

"Why are you home so early?" Rachel's apron was covered with floured handprints. The kitchen was a baking explosion. A smell both spicy and sweet wafted from the oven. My stomach growled with approval.

"Tough day at work." I gave her a look that pled, *Please don't ask me to explain.*

Rachel poured me a glass of milk and cut me a hefty piece of spice cake, fresh and warm from the oven.

"This is what you did for me when I had a bad day at school, remember?"

I remembered. The role reversal hit me hard. When had this happened? When I'd first heard my sister was in town, I'd worried it would be the status quo: me bailing her out of messes, taking care of her, and making sure she didn't get into trouble. We'd be back to the days when our father had just walked out. But instead Rachel was my rock, while my carefully orchestrated life was going up in flames.

"Thanks." I dabbed at my milk moustache. "Let's try to find out if the rumor about the paintings is true. I've been getting some pressure at work about Helene."

"Helene?" Rachel stopped cleaning and wheeled around. "What does she have to do with your work?"

"Alan, the partner I work for, visited me today." I drew a figure eight over and over again in a little puddle of milk on the old table. "It seems Helene and Lonestar have some type of business agreement, but I can't tell what it is. I searched for any documents the firm has that might relate to those two."

"What did you find?"

"Tons of Lonestar stuff, but the three docs that mentioned Helene were password protected."

"I'm still confused. I get that Helene wants to get her hands on those paintings, if they exist, but what's that have to do with Lonestar Energy?"

"I'm not sure, but Helene is using the firm to threaten me, and if anyone's going to find the paintings, I want it to be us."

"Then what are we waiting for?"

We spent the next three hours combing every inch of Thistle Park. We shined flashlights behind heavy furniture, inched into crawl spaces in the basement, and even dared to venture into the coal cellar. We opened trunks, cabinets, and the belly of the big grandfather clock with its disapproving man-in-the-moon face. We unleashed moths and dust and learned where all of the keys on the key ring fit. I took particular care in the dining room, since that's where Keith had been looking. I found an antique pistol that looked like it hadn't been fired in decades and dropped it into a heavy vase next to the fireplace for safekeeping.

"Just because they hung here once," Rachel panted, helping me move the heavy credenza back in place, "doesn't mean they were hidden here."

"I'm beginning to doubt this legend, that note notwithstanding." The note with no signature was tacked onto the refrigerator. "It could be real, but someone found the paintings before the dining room and kitchen burned and Sylvia and the gardener ran off."

Rachel shrugged, and we continued our search. We ended on the third floor. After Will and the police had left the other day, we'd explored it briefly, but it was much more sparsely furnished than the lower two floors. Today, Whiskey and Soda accompanied us.

"This isn't a kitty toilet," I reminded them as they nosed around.

"I think I'll tackle that room." Rachel gestured down the hall to the love nest. I hadn't entered it after the police left, and we'd left it even dustier than when we'd found it, thanks to Faith's attempt to take fingerprints.

"You're the best." I gave my sister's arm a squeeze. "I'm so glad you're here."

Rachel beamed and set off down the hallway, with a trash bag to eradicate all traces of trespassing lovers from the small chamber. I was still convinced it had been Keith and Becca. I briefly closed my eyes against that thought, then slowly walked around the third floor, peeking into empty wardrobes and ducking the sloping ceilings.

"I'm glad there's another bathroom." I turned on the faucet, which ran brown, then clear.

Rachel returned and shook her head with wonder. "All of these bedrooms, and we thought there was only one bathroom. This'll make it way easier to turn this place into a B and B. This floor is huge. We, I mean you, could comfortably live up here and rent out the other two floors."

"Not gonna happen, Rach. I'd love to." My voice was weighed down with regret. I didn't admit I'd been daydreaming the same thing. It wouldn't help me focus at work if I pined away for an escape plan that was impossible. I had to be practical. "I don't have the time, or the money, especially since I can't get my wedding deposit back." Case closed.

I left the hall to inspect the final bedroom. This one held a few boxes and a large trunk. The other bedrooms were similarly sparse with thin metal beds and small dressers. "Servants quarters," Chief Truman had mused.

"Maybe they're in here." My voice held no real conviction. The trunk was large, but not big enough for framed paintings. I flipped open the creaky lid, the leather straps disintegrating at my touch. It contained clothes that were more than a century old, by the looks of them.

"Ooh, this is gorgeous." Rachel sighed with delight, grabbing a creamy lace dress. She held it up to herself and performed a twirl.

"They were teeny back then." The dress would only cover Rachel's mid-calf. It might fit me since I was short, but only if I wore an actual corset to whittle my waist down to nothing. Spanx weren't gonna cut it.

I dug out a small bound leather book.

"Let me see!" Rachel slipped into little-sister mode. She used her height to her advantage and plucked the book easily from my fingers, dropping the elaborate dress.

"It's a journal or diary." Rachel lowered it to my eye level and flipped it open.

We peered into the worn leather book.

"'Sylvia McGavitt.'" I traced the slanting brown ink. "'Port Quincy, Pennsylvania, nineteen-thirty.'" I flipped to where her writings ended. "The last entry is December fourteen, nineteen-thirty-four. There might be a clue about where the paintings are hidden in here!"

Rachel had already lost interest and handed me the journal, and was pawing through the trunk of clothes. She set a small cloche hat on her gleaming waves at a jaunty angle. "Do you think I could pull this off?"

"Definitely." I sunk to the floor, engrossed in the diary. I spent the next hour there, getting lost in

Sylvia's teenage world. My present troubles were long forgotten.

"So, her maid caught her doing the deed with her secret fiancé, the gardener." Rachel flipped through to the end of the diary as I had. "I didn't even think they had sex back then." My sister closed it with an amused look.

"Watch out!" I motioned to the cup of tea perched precariously close to the old diary.

"Oh, please." Rachel gave me the stink eye. "You were reading this in the tub!"

"I was super careful." My cheeks grew hot. It was true. I had taken the diary with me for a long soak, now that we'd scrubbed the old claw foot clean. "And, of course, they had sex! Even out of wedlock. And we already knew Sylvia eloped with him. It isn't surprising they were, um, together beforehand. At least now we know his name."

My sister flipped to the end. "Yeah, Albert Smoot." She giggled. "Wow. Her maid was *pissed*."

My ears heated, too, as I leaned over to re-read the entry. I'd read the beginning of the diary, when Sylvia was fourteen. Her days had been filled with private governess lessons and all of the diversions and privileges of wealthy daughters of robber barons living in Pittsburgh's East End. Then her father had moved the family to Port Quincy, to keep a closer eye on his glass factory. Most of the staff had been new, and Sylvia had had no friends, except for her maid and the gardener.

I'd skimmed while I soaked in the bath, trying to

find any clues about the paintings. Sylvia mentioned yearly trips to Europe, where her mother and father sated their thirst for artwork. Some pieces she mentioned by artist, and others she referenced obliquely. Any three of them could be the paintings in question.

Sylvia had started a relationship with the gardener, Albert Smoot, who'd promised to take her away from Port Quincy and back to Pittsburgh. On the eve of their elopement, Sylvia's maid had found her and Smoot in a compromising position.

"I guess Sylvia and Albert eloped because she was afraid her maid would tell on her, and Sylvia was going to take the paintings to finance her escape, but someone found out and hid them first?"

"Or maybe they burned and we're just wasting our time," Rachel sighed.

"Eek!" I dropped the diary, which tumbled to the floor. Little bits of leather flaked onto the floor. "Someone's at the window."

It was Zach, and Rachel bounded up to let him in the back door. I averted my eyes as he brushed my sister's lips with a swift kiss. *That was fast.* I chastised myself for being bitchy. I wanted my sister to be happy, and Zach seemed to make her light up inside.

"You need to get that front doorbell fixed. I saw your car out front and figured you were home. I have good news." He beamed as Rachel poured him a cup of tea. "A buyer."

"Who?" I perked up.

Zach's face fell marginally. "It's a gas company—"

"Absolutely not. That's not what Sylvia wanted." I recalled Will Prentiss's deposition, his catalog of wrongs and injuries, and shivered.

"I know." Zach nodded in agreement, a blond lock bobbing along.

Rachel reached over and smoothed it back in place for him.

He returned her gesture with a syrupy gaze.

Jeez, get a room!

"But it isn't Lonestar Energy, at least. It's one of the smaller fracking players. Frankly, you're going to have a hard time selling this place to someone who wants to *live* here. The cost to renovate, not to mention that someone was killed here . . ." He slipped me a piece of paper. "That's the offer."

"Yeah, yeah, I know." I bit into a peanut-butter cookie, ignoring the folded paper. "These are amazing," I said through a mouthful of peanut-buttery crumbled goodness.

"Thank you. Don't change the subject." Rachel was well versed in my evasion techniques.

"Just consider it," Zach said. "It's sweet you're trying to honor Sylvia's wishes, but you need to think of yourself. This house could bankrupt you, especially if you're still living here in the wintertime."

I cringed and swallowed the rest of the cookie in one bite. He was right. There was no way I could afford to heat all three floors, even just to keep the pipes from freezing. The mansion had been built in a time of cheap and plentiful coal, and now we were in a time when energy was dear. That was what had led to this whole fracking business in the first place, an insatiable need for new sources of energy. I shivered again, no longer thinking of the horrors that had befallen Will Prentiss. Instead, I was thinking of my dwindling bank account. I opened the piece of paper and nearly choked on the last bit of cookie. "Holy crap!"

Zach gave me a smug smile. "Think about it."

Rachel reached for the paper, but I was too quick. I shoved it into my pocket. She shrugged. Zach would probably tell her later.

"What is this?" Zach gingerly picked up the worn leather diary. Bits of dry burgundy leather crumbled off like burnt bacon.

"It's Sylvia's diary." I could hardly bear watching him flip through the pages, though he was doing so with great care.

"Wow." He let out a low whistle. "I bet Tabby can't wait to see this."

Rachel frowned at Zach's mention of his old flame, by her pet name, no less.

"She doesn't know yet. I caught Keith in here looking for something. Maybe this was it? We had all of the locks changed."

Zach looked up in surprise. "That's not necessary, is it?"

I shrugged. "Keith has a little problem with boundaries. Threatening him won't keep him out. Will Prentiss changed them for us."

Zach knitted his blond brows together. "Will helped Sylvia a lot with the upkeep on this place, but he's kind of creepy."

"He's just shy." I leapt in to defend Will. "And he's been through a lot, what with the gas explosion and his injuries."

"He seems nice," Rachel agreed. "Why d'you think he's creepy?"

"I guess that's the wrong word," Zach back-pedaled. "I'm not sure if he did such thorough work helping out Sylvia. She just kicked him the odd job because she felt sorry for him. Look at this place. He could have done more to keep it up—that is, before his accident."

"Be that as it may, he did a good job changing our locks. And he seems to know a lot about the house." Then again, maybe he wouldn't need to take odd jobs soon. I was sure Lonestar would be settling with Will and, judging from the extent of his injuries, the settlement would be pretty sizeable.

"Where did you find this?" Zach was still leafing through the diary.

"The attic," I said slowly.

"Maybe this will help you find those paintings." He shook the book gently, as if it would reveal its secrets with some prodding.

"I don't think so. It ends the night before the fire, the night before Sylvia and Albert Smoot eloped."

Zach nodded, as if familiar with the old story.

"You sure know a lot about the McGavitts." I reached for the book. I couldn't help it.

Zach handed it back with a smile. "We all do. This whole town wouldn't be here if the McGavitts hadn't started the glass factory. My father worked there before it shut down. And my grandma worked here at Thistle Park and practically raised my father right next to Keith's father. And I used to date the town historian."

Rachel pouted and crossed her arms, letting out a huffy sigh.

"I've got to get back to the office." Zach dropped a kiss on the top of Rachel's head.

Her frown began to disappear in marginal degrees.

"Think about that offer, Mallory."

* * *

The offer was all I could think about on the drive to the Port Quincy Historical Society the next day, after leaving work early again. Dollar signs danced in my head like little green sugar plum fairies with Benjamin Franklin's face. It wasn't a crazy amount, but it would allow me to pay off a sizable chunk of my student loans. And decide to do something else if I didn't make partner after all, especially in light of Alan's talk the other day.

Just like Keith suggested. I recalled the last day of our engagement, when I'd stood with Keith in front of that empty lot, surrounded by hulking McMansions. Keith's words mocked me but rang with a peal of truth. *Do you even like practicing law? You could do something else, something you really want to do, when you figure that out.*

"Whatever," I muttered. "I'll figure out what I want to do, and it'll be my choice, not Keith's or Helene's or my mother's." But could I really go against Sylvia's wishes and sell to a gas company?

"Park and c'mon in." Tabitha rushed down the steps of the Port Quincy Historical Society, her step and her smile buoyant. "But be quiet, the Daughters of the American Revolution biddies are here, and I don't want them to see us. They'll drag it out of you that you're researching those paintings." She looked up through her bright red fringe and blew several strands off her forehead. "And Helene's here. She's DAR president."

I groaned. "Is there any way to get through the back? I'm having problems at work because of her. I can't promise I'll behave."

Tabitha directed me to park in the alley behind the building, then led me to a side porch of the restored old house that served as the historical society. She peeked in and, when the coast seemed clear, pulled me along.

Helene's fake aristocratic voice floated down the hall. "Settle down, ladies. We need all hands on deck for Founder's Day."

We tiptoed the last few feet to Tabitha's office, and she locked the door behind us.

"I'm sick of sneaking around this town. It isn't big enough for Helene Pierce and me."

"Tell me about it." Tabitha typed away. "The DAR takes over the historical society for their weekly tea every Thursday afternoon. When I started working here five years ago, they asked me to join. I explained that my parents are Polish and Welsh and that my family came over here after nineteen hundred, so I wouldn't qualify." Her pretty face hardened. "So Helene pointed out that since I couldn't join, it wouldn't be a bother for me to brew their tea and serve it while they met. No thank you! We only let them have the best room for their meetings because the last historian let them do it."

I laughed bitterly. "That sounds like Helene."

"Forget her." Tabitha tapped away at her keyboard at a startling speed. "She's just a bitter woman who trades on the fact she married into the McGavitt and Pierce families." A printer in the corner whirred to life. "I pulled some strings and got the records from the gallery the McGavitt family used. The Kirsch Gallery records show McGavitt bought a lot of good art. If any of this stuff is hidden in that house, even one single painting, you need to be the one who finds it." She swiveled her printout around so I could read the names of the artists and the works on the sheet. Monet. Degas. Cezanne.

"Oh my God," I blurted out. I wasn't an art expert, but even I knew they'd fetch a lot. Screw leasing Thistle Park's land for shale gas. I could pay off all of my six-figure law school debt, renovate Sylvia's house in Gilded Age style, open the grandest B and B this side of the Alleghenies, and host gorgeous weddings.

"There's a catch. Sylvia's parents sold almost all of them, and we have proof." Tabitha leaned into her computer screen and rattled off works and their dates of sale or appearance in auction catalogs as I checked them off the list.

"So, if anything is hidden in that house, it would be these three." I tapped the listings for the Sargent, the Renoir, and the Pissarro.

Tabitha nodded. "Sylvia's father took the family with him to Europe in nineteen-fifteen, when Sylvia was a baby. He purchased the Renoir and Pissarro on that trip and commissioned the Sargent portrait. That one would be particularly valuable, since Sargent closed his studio years before and there aren't too many portraits after that."

"They're tiny." I read off the dimensions of the Renoir and Pissarro. They were diminutive landscapes.

"The Sargent wasn't. It would have taken up a lot of wall real estate."

"Oh, I almost forgot!" I dug a small pile of photographs out of my purse. "These are from the house. They might show the paintings. Some of them are labeled."

Tabitha and I spread out the pictures. I'd brought

over every picture I could find with a painting in the background. The paintings were not the focus of the pictures, so it would be hard to tell if any of them matched the descriptions. One by one, we squinted at the background of each photo, then flipped it over. They were labeled neatly in faded ink.

"Here's one of Sylvia when she was a baby, with her mother." The same beautiful woman from the oil painting in the back hall held a chubby baby on her lap, her round face peeking out from a lace bonnet.

There were later photos, showing Sylvia as a mother, her hand resting on the shoulder of a boy in a sailor suit, presumably Keith's father. Another photo showed the same boy playing under a tree with another boy. They could have been twins, but for their different clothing. One boy's outfit was clean and fresh and fit him like a glove. The other's was a bit too big for him, like a hand-me-down.

"Robert and Gerald," I read on the back of the photo.

Tabitha rolled her eyes. "Gerald Novak was Zach's father. Zach's grandmother worked at Thistle Park."

"So I've heard."

"Look at this." Tabitha slid a small photograph over.

"That's the dining room!" I was pleased to recognize the room.

"Yup, and I think these are the three paintings."

The Sargent hung above the fireplace. The faded photo wasn't the greatest, but you could tell the painting was fairly large. On the canvas Evelyn once again held baby Sylvia on her lap, and her husband stood behind them.

"And here are the other two paintings." Tabitha

tapped the small landscapes flanking the fireplace, no bigger than sheets of notebook paper.

"The fire probably started from that fireplace. McGavitt had it recreated just the same, which is why you recognize it as the present version of the dining room. Well, except for the paintings. They were the most valuable ones left at the time, so that's probably why Evelyn ran back to get them."

"And why she thought her daughter was planning on taking them to finance her elopement."

I leafed through the other photos in the folder. It was odd to see men and women in old-fashioned clothes posing in the house where I now lived. If I could restore it to its former glory, it would make one hell of a B and B and venue for weddings. I stopped at a photo of two young women and a man, outside in the garden.

"That's Sylvia again, isn't it?" I pointed to the woman at the left side of the photo. "And the gardener, Sylvia's first husband, Albert Smoot, in the middle. Who is the other woman beside him?" Albert Smoot was handsome, with dark hair, a mustache and a very intense expression. Both women gazed at him, but he only had eyes for Sylvia.

"I think she was their maid. She might be Zach's grandmother. Well done about Smoot," Tabitha said. "How did you know?"

"Sylvia described him well in her diary." I pulled the book out of my purse with a flourish.

"This is amazing." Tabitha turned the diary over in her hands, her face still with reverence. "I can't wait to read this!"

I glanced at her door. Every few minutes, Helene's voice penetrated Tabitha's office. I caught a snippet of her conversation. "She'll ruin the integrity of the house, but perhaps we'll oust her before then. . . ." I shuddered to think what she'd do if she knew I was here, with a tool that might help us find those paintings.

"I read the beginning and skipped ahead to the end because it stops the night before the fire. She doesn't specifically mention hiding places in the house. Why would she? Maybe there's some other clue in the diary. Zach reminded me Helene would want to get her mitts on this."

Tabitha narrowed her eyes at the mention of her ex. "Just don't let it out of your sight."

I stood to go.

"I can help you and your sister out with the house if you like. It must be overwhelming."

I smiled at her offer. "I'd like that." I started to unlock her door when Helene's cackle made me pull back as if the doorknob was a live coal. "Will they see me?"

Tabitha glanced at her watch. "They usually go until six, so you'll be fine. I'll walk you out." We shuffled soundlessly down the hall as someone at the DAR meeting gave a report.

We were almost free when I smacked into Yvette Tannenbaum, the singer from Sylvia's funeral and the first lady of Port Quincy.

"I'm so sorry!"

"Hi, Yvette." Tabitha kept her voice low. "I was just walking Mallory out."

Yvette sighed and wilted against the doorframe as she hugged her spindly arms to her stomach. "I wish I could leave with you. My husband makes me come to these. Too bad I have one measly ancestor who fought in the Revolutionary War." Yvette turned to me. "Helene Pierce makes these meetings even more unbearable than they normally would be."

"Is she still here?"

"She's on the front porch." Yvette pantomimed smoking. Perfect. Helene was indulging in one of her Virginia Slims and wouldn't see me exit the side of the building.

"I hear you might have some paintings in that house of yours." Yvette cocked her head.

"Who told you that?" Nothing was a secret here.

"Helene, of course." Yvette laughed. "Good luck finding them." She glanced at her watch then across the street where her father's auto body shop was visible. "The meeting's technically over. I need to get to work."

Yvette slipped back into her mousy persona and headed down the hall.

"That was unexpected," Tabitha said when we were safely outside. "Yvette barely says two words to anyone. She must like you."

"I met her and Bev Mitchell the day after Shane Hartley was murdered. She congratulated me on cancelling my wedding. Why would she attend those meetings for her husband?" I dug around in my cavernous purse for my keys.

"He's the mayor."

"I know, but that doesn't mean she should have to go to events or join clubs she doesn't want to."

Tabitha shrugged. "He wants her to be involved."

"But she's so . . . introverted. Except when she's singing." I recalled her shy smiles and muted hellos when we ran into each other in town. "How does she handle attending events and political things?"

"Not well. She doesn't sound too happy in her marriage if she's complimenting you on not going through with yours with Keith." She glanced over her shoulder, a slow smile warming her face.

"It seems you have an admirer." I turned around to see Garrett Davies, who stared unabashedly from across the street. He raised his hand and waved; then his face cracked into a wide grin, identical to Summer's, except for the braces, of course.

He pointed to his watch apologetically and continued on his way.

"Seems like you feel the same way." Tabitha smirked as she went back into the historical society.

A small smile played at the edges of my mouth as I buckled myself into the Mini Cooper. What was it about Garrett that could distract me from all of the awfulness raining down? I turned the engine over and made a left out of the alley, which placed me at the very top of the big hill that dipped down and then up, creating the grand valley between Port Quincy's downtown before it ascended toward Thistle Park.

Port Quincy's main streets had bricks instead of pavement. The yellow brick road made a soothing thrum under my wheels as I drove. I felt like Dorothy on the way to Oz. I'd come to love driving through town, approaching Thistle Park and the turrets of the grand Victorians on Sycamore Street peeking out over the trees.

But today the ride wasn't smooth or picturesque. I gathered speed like a slalom skier, and I had no brakes. *Wait, I have no brakes?*

I pressed the pedal all the way to the floor of the car but met no resistance.

I looked around frantically for a place to pull over, but both sides of the street held tidy rows of houses. I yanked the parking brake and gritted my teeth for the impending stop. Nothing happened.

A little boy, perhaps counting on me to stop, began to cross the street in a crosswalk. He was about eight, with a striped T-shirt, grubby shorts, and red shoes. He concentrated on his ice cream cone instead of the road or the beagle at the end of the leash in his hand. He hadn't seen me. He didn't know his life was about to irrevocably change.

"Oh God, get out of the way!" I pulled hard to the right to avoid the little boy and his dog and shut my eyes, sending up a more fervent prayer. The car jumped the sidewalk and made impact in a screech of compressed metal and shattering glass. Time slowed down, and I stupidly thought how pretty the windshield looked as it crumbled, before I closed my eyes against the bursting air bag. Next came my screams, which didn't stop until the ambulance and the police rolled up, their sirens wailing, drowning me out.

Chapter Nine

"You're lucky." Chief Truman stood before me, hands on hips. His bulky frame blocked me from leaving the ambulance.

"I don't want to go to the hospital." I tried to slide off the stretcher and make an escape.

"Hold on a second." An EMS worker listened to my heart while another took my blood pressure.

"Any dizziness? Neck pain?"

I shook my head and gasped. Sharp needles danced up the back of my neck and made my head throb in time with my heartbeat.

"Yeah, right. You might have whiplash, or a concussion. We'll take you to the hospital and they'll check you out."

I dared not move again, but my eyes strayed over Truman's head. I had fared better than the little rental, which had obliterated a sturdy picket fence and was now embedded in a giant fuchsia azalea bush. The front end was crushed, and shards from the windshield sparkled all over the sidewalk. The air bags that had burst into action were now deflated.

I stared in disbelief through the space where the windshield had been. The little boy and his dog had safely crossed the street. The little boy must have dropped his ice cream, as his beagle was happily lapping it up when his mother emerged from a nearby house and pulled him and his dog inside.

The owner of the house with the azaleas had run out within seconds of the crash, and I'd crazily thought I was going to get a talking-to. I hadn't realized I was sobbing into my air bag. The woman had been more concerned about me than her yard, and as I'd climbed out of the car on my own, she'd given me a once-over and gingerly embraced me, promising, "Oh, honey, that fence has seen way worse."

"Your brakes were cut," Truman said grimly. "We'll talk later." He reached out and patted my arm, the good one, in a fatherly way. I blinked back tears and tried not to be overwhelmed by the events of the day. Being threatened at work. Finding Sylvia's diary. Seeing Garrett. And I missed my mom and stepdad. I wished for the first time I hadn't convinced them not to come from Florida. I'd tried to hold it all together, but, in light of recent events, I'd failed miserably.

Truman retrieved my purse from the wreckage, and I texted Rachel to meet me in the emergency room, although I wasn't sure how she'd get there now I'd totaled our wheels. I was shocked to see that the town hospital was the McGavitt-Pierce Memorial Hospital. Maybe that was why Keith had always had a sense of entitlement about him, one I'd tried to deny and ignore. He'd grown up with his family's name splashed all over town. No wonder Helene acted like she owned everything.

I was told I had a mild concussion and my left arm was sprained. I was discharged by a hospital volunteer, who wheeled me out to wait for Rachel and Chief Truman.

"That poor woman. Her husband was murdered." The volunteer clucked under her breath and motioned to a heavily pregnant woman making her way slowly over to an old-fashioned car that had pulled up to the curb.

"That's Deanna Hartley?" Shane Hartley's wife. I leaned forward for a better look, ignoring the muscles in my neck when they knotted up in protest. The car was nouveau vintage, a dinged-up, wood-paneled PT Cruiser. A man was driving, a baseball cap pulled low over his forehead. Curiosity got the best of me and I strained to get a better look, but he peeled away.

"Who would want to hurt you?" Chief Truman asked as he drove me home from the hospital.

I rode in the back of his squad car, and Rachel sat shotgun. My sister turned around every three seconds. Her mouth was pressed in a thin, tight line, her face pale and grim. She had morphed from a carefree twenty-two-year-old into our mother in the space of an afternoon.

"Who wouldn't want to hurt me?" I wearily answered Truman's question as I closed my eyes. It hurt to talk, to string together coherent sentences. "Helene Pierce, Keith Pierce, my law firm, Russell Carey? Take your pick." My eyes fluttered open.

Chief Truman raised his eyebrows at me in the rearview mirror.

"Maybe someone connected to Shane Hartley

wants me dead. Maybe they think I killed him. Where are you with that?" My question came out more harshly than I meant.

Chief Truman ran his hand through his thinning salt-and-pepper hair. "Frankly—"

"You don't have jack squat, do you."

Truman narrowed his eyes at me in the rearview mirror but said nothing. Rachel looked back at me nervously.

We finally reached Thistle Park, and Truman drove excruciatingly slowly, probably to soften the ride on the uneven gravel driveway. My neighbor's curtains fluttered again. *Great. Now I'm the town spectacle again.*

I reached into my purse. Rachel had gone through it at the hospital to ferret out my health insurance card. I expected to feel the rough, cracked leather of Sylvia's diary. Instead, I felt my wallet and the cold metal key ring to Thistle Park nestled among other bits of purse detritus.

"Sylvia's diary! It must've fallen out of my purse in the accident." It was gone.

Rachel leaned over the front seat and gently pushed me back in mine. "You need to calm down."

"We need to go back to the accident. Where is the Mini Cooper?"

Chief Truman raised his bushy eyebrows. "The car is impounded, and there was nothing on the ground except remnants of the windshield and front end. If anything was in that car, we'll have it as evidence."

I sat back in the seat and closed my eyes as we came to a stop.

"Has anyone cut this grass since you moved in?" Truman surveyed the lawn.

"We don't have a mower," Rachel began.

"Cut the grass? I've been a bit busy, what with hosing down the blood from the *murder*, attempting to clean up this dump, and trying to save my job! Not to mention canceling my wedding, trying to find a bride to take it over, and kicking out people I've caught trespassing, looking for God knows what. Cutting the grass—I'll get right on that!" I burst into tears.

Truman gently lifted me out of the backseat, hoisted me into his arms, taking care to avoid my left arm in its sling, and carried me up the front walk.

"I'm fine," I snuffled into his shoulder, getting his uniform wet. "You can put me down."

"Just relax." He gingerly patted my back, which made me cry harder.

Rachel opened the door, and he set me down on the fainting couch.

"Get her something to drink and eat," he commanded, and Rachel scurried off.

He handed me an old-fashioned cloth handkerchief. It was embroidered with a small *TD*.

"Thanks." I marveled at his solicitousness and honked into the handkerchief. All a girl had to do was cry to turn this cranky man into a doting teddy bear. "Sorry." I waved the hanky. "I'll wash this." I was embarrassed by my outburst and back to people-pleasing mode. *That didn't take long.*

"Don't worry about it. We have bigger things to worry about now."

"Yup. Someone tried to kill me."

Rachel returned, her face a sickening yellow. "Chief Truman?" Her voice trembled. "Can you come check something for me?"

I sat up, my temples pounding with the rush of blood.

"You stay right there," he said sharply, hot on Rachel's heels.

I didn't listen, of course, and found them both in the dining room.

On the wall, above the fireplace, where the Sargent portrait of the McGavitt family had once hung, was a smeary message, written in blood:

Leave now or end up like Shane Hartley.

"Ketchup." Chief Truman licked the red substance from the tip of his index finger. "It tastes like the cut-rate stuff too, not Heinz." He seemed more put out by the fact the perpetrator used something other than Pittsburgh's finest ketchup to paint a threatening message on our wall than the contents of the message itself. It was half an hour later, and we had all calmed down enough to contemplate the message.

"Not your ketchup, is it?" He tilted his head in the direction of the dining room.

Truman had called Faith for back up and she was now busy dusting for prints.

"Nope."

"They came in through the dining room window, is my guess." He pulled out a kitchen chair. "You ladies leave that window unlocked?"

We'd noticed the curtains fluttering in the breeze over the dining room's bay window, right after we'd gotten over the shock of the death threat on the wall.

"Absolutely not!" Rachel said shrilly. "I made sure

everything on the first floor was locked. We only leave the upstairs windows open, because it'll get too hot for Whiskey and Soda. Since Mallory found Keith in here, we're not taking any chances."

I tossed my sister a grateful look.

"Anyone else have the new keys to the house?"

"No. Keith, and I presume Helene, had the old set, but now that the locks have been changed, it's only us two."

My sister set down a tarnished silver tray with some toast and tea, her hands shaking.

"You need to eat." She buttered a slice. "What if someone tried to kill me, not you? Maybe they thought I was the one driving the Mini Cooper."

"The brakes worked just fine when I drove to the historical society." I forced down a bite. It was probably delicious, since Rachel had made the wheat bread, but it tasted like sand. "They were cut while I was there."

"Which was when?" Chief Truman took out a small notepad.

"I met Tabitha around four. I was only there for an hour. Then I got in the car, turned out of the alley, and straight down the hill." I left out an explanation as to why I'd visited Tabitha.

"Why were you there? You and Tabitha Battles are friends?"

Rachel stiffened at the mention of her presumed rival for Zach's affection, and as she poured tea, the arc of pale gold liquid wavered, sloshing the kitchen table. "Sorry."

"Yes, we are friends." I left it at that.

"Maybe"—Rachel didn't dare to look up as she

buttered her toast with excessive care—"Tabitha cut your breaks."

"Rachel." I dropped my teacup and tea spilled over the edge of the table and scalded my thighs. The delicate china hit the floor, the impact knocking the foot of the teacup off.

Chief Truman mopped up the table and rescued the poor teacup from harm's way.

"She knows about the paintings, and she has as much motive as anyone." Rachel stared at me fiercely. "She salivated over the antiques the first day we met her, and she mentioned that she wished Sylvia had donated the whole house to the historical society. She has an unhealthy interest in Thistle Park."

"You just don't like her because she dated Zach for years!" I no longer felt a rush of sisterly love. No way would Tabitha cut my brakes. She was helping me find the paintings. That didn't mean she wanted them for herself. *Did it?* She'd stepped out of her office for five minutes to make copies down the hall, just long enough to cut my brakes. "She's the town historian. Of course she's interested in this house and whether the rumor about the paintings is true." But I was no longer sure.

"Whoa, what paintings are you talking about?" The chief looked up, his pen poised. "Ladies?"

I sighed and, for five minutes with no pause, I wearily told him the whole tale, beginning with the note we'd found in the dining room pocket door. I tried to do the story justice, and Rachel didn't break in to correct me. I lingered over the incident of Keith's trespass and attempted not to rub it in that Truman hadn't taken it too seriously. I included the

Helene-induced threat I'd received at work this morning and the fact Alan Brinkman had mentioned a business relationship between Helene and Lonestar Energy. I ended with Helene's personally delivered threat to sue me for the house while we were at the veterinarian's office.

"That's quite a story. But I don't see how it connects to Shane Hartley's murder."

"It might not. But he's dead, and someone just tried to kill me, too. And if it wasn't Tabitha"—I ignored my sister's dagger eyes—"then it was obviously Helene. She was at the historical society. She could have slipped out and cut my brakes."

Truman burst out laughing. "You think Helene Pierce got down on her hands and knees, in an alley strewn with litter, crawled under the car, and sliced your brake line?" He chuckled again and finally helped himself to some toast.

It *was* preposterous to try to picture Helene under the car. "You have no idea what she's capable of when she wants something. Don't let her genteel old lady act fool you." I shivered and recalled how she'd pinched my waist the day of the wedding tasting, stinging me like a wicked bee.

"Or maybe it was Keith."

Truman had raised his brows when footsteps startled us.

"Keith might be a jerk, but he doesn't want to kill you." I did a double take as Garrett Davies walked into the breakfast room and stood by Truman. "Faith let me in." He pulled up a chair. "You guys really need to get that doorbell fixed."

"What brings you by?" I tried to muster a smile. I

failed miserably, but at least my tears were now quelled.

"Dad asked me to cut your grass. I'd be happy to." He gave me a smile in return that would melt a glacier. "Are you all right? I heard about the accident. It couldn't have been more than five minutes after I saw you." His eyes were tender as he surveyed my arm in its sling.

"He's your dad?" I swiveled my neck to look at Chief Truman and instantly regretted it as my muscles ached and twanged in protest.

"Of course." The chief wore an amused look. *A familiar face.* Gears clicked into place. *Duh.* Garrett looked a hell of a lot like the police chief. The chief had a big belly and salt-and-pepper hair that was balding at the crown. But both men were tall, and they had the same eyes, electric smile, and initially gruff manner. Garrett would be the spitting image of his father in about twenty years. What was with Port Quincy? There were zero degrees of separation between everyone.

"But," Rachel said, also incredulous, "your last name is Truman, and yours is Davies."

The chief snorted. "Everybody calls me Chief Truman because that's my name. Truman Davies."

"And you live together, with Summer."

"That's right." Truman smirked. "My allergies will never be the same since you conned my son into keeping that kitten. And I already knew about the paintings, because Summer told us about the note that night at dinner." Truman laughed when my jaw dropped open.

"But you're the chief of police, and your son does criminal defense work," I sputtered.

"It makes for some very interesting dinner-table dynamics," Garrett said drily. "Do you have a lawn mower?"

"There might be one in the shed or the carriage house."

Rachel retrieved the key ring from my purse and handed it to Garrett.

"Will opened the door to the shed with the big brass one. Are you really going to cut the grass in that?" Garrett looked yummy in his three-piece gray suit.

"I'll take my jacket off." He removed it, shouldering it around a chair. He took off his tie and undid his top button.

I swallowed and became very interested in the black-and-white checkered floor. When I looked up again, Truman stared at me with greater interest than when he was merely trying to figure out who wanted me dead.

"Be right back." Garrett gently squeezed my shoulder as he left.

I sat up straighter now that Garrett was gone. "This message in ketchup? You can't deny it has something to do with Shane Hartley's murder. The threat references him by name."

"I agree." Truman was deferential for once. "Is there anything else you haven't told me?"

I shook my head slowly, trying not to aggravate my concussion.

Rachel looked down in her lap and tapped her nails together. "Tell him about the photos." Her voice was apologetic.

"What photos?" Truman and I said in unison.

Faith entered the room and echoed the question, while Rachel shot me a look laden with regret.

"It's for your own good. Sorry, Mall."

"Oh, *those* photos." My stomach dropped.

"Spill it," Truman commanded, playing bad cop for the first time today.

"I'll go get them," I said icily. I'd let the pictures speak for themselves. No way would I try to put their contents into words, as the only thing more humiliating than having someone else see them was forcing myself to describe them. I might have been on my way to getting over Keith, but I didn't need to see the cause of our end played out in the lurid stack of photos.

A few minutes later, I'd retrieved the pictures from the bottom of my suitcase. The envelope felt like it contained kryptonite, glowing with evil. It was all I could do not to throw them in the trash. Instead, I dropped them on the table in front of Truman.

"Sheesh." He quickly rifled through them.

I averted my eyes, not wanting to revisit Keith doing the horizontal hokeypokey with Becca Cunningham.

"So this is why you called off your wedding," Faith said, not unkindly.

I studied the table, not meeting their eyes. I said a silent prayer that Garrett would remain safely out back and wouldn't choose this moment to return.

"It's probably too late for fingerprints." Truman took note of the Port Quincy postmark and lack of return address.

He kept us busy for the next hour, asking many of the same questions. Faith joined in, since dusting for prints in the dining room yielded nothing. I could see Garrett cutting the grass from the window, straining against the tall weeds with an ancient push mower, sweat trickling down his back, staining his vest and glistening on his forehead. *Delicious*. I blushed to the roots of my hair.

"Something wrong?" Truman stopped his questions.

"You look all flushed, Mallory." Faith gave Truman a glance. "I think we've had enough for today."

"Do you think it's safe to stay here?" I tried to banish Garrett from my mind.

"We've been over every inch of this house, and as long as you make sure everything is locked, you'll be fine. Keep the lights on outside to deter anyone and call us if anything happens. But you really do need to install an alarm system."

Garrett burst in from the hallway, his shirtsleeves rolled over his elbows. He was sweaty, smiling, and glorious.

"I found you a new car."

The thing was a boat, a vintage Volvo station wagon, circa 1976. It was in pristine condition, the color of burnt butterscotch inside and out. It was like a big, tan hearse. Garrett had found it under a tarp in the carriage house.

"I remember this car." Truman walked into the carriage house with an amused expression, as if it were a time machine that would spit out other 1970s relics. "I remember Sylvia tooling down Main Street in this thing."

Garrett arranged for the car to be serviced, and as

the sun was setting, Mazur's Auto Body Shop towed it away.

"With any luck, it'll work just fine, and you two will have transportation. They'll need to update the license plate and change the title, but it'll probably be ready tomorrow."

"Thanks." I watched the *Brady Bunch* special of a car as it was towed away. "It's really mine?"

"Sylvia deeded you everything on this property. I'm sure she meant the car too."

The next day at noon, a mechanic drove up in the car. It was a good thing, too, as I would need new wheels to get to work. I'd begged off another day to nurse my concussion, but I'd have the Volvo to return on Monday. A woman followed the mechanic in a different car, presumably to take him back to the auto body shop. It was similar to the one that had picked up Deanna Hartley yesterday, but this one was smooth and black, with no dings or marks. Sylvia's car rattled, a big Butterscotch Monster on wheels.

"Here she is." The mechanic handed me the keys. "She's a beaut, in mint condition." He gazed admiringly at the car. "Didn't need much work to get 'er up and running."

"What do I owe you?"

He waved my offer away. "Garrett Davies took care of it. Enjoy the car, miss."

I frowned as he got into the car with the woman, her face shielded with sunglasses. "I'm not sure how I feel about this." I turned to Rachel. "Mom depended on Dad to take care of everything. After he ran off, she had to become self-sufficient overnight."

After my parents' ruinous divorce, my mom often said if she hadn't relied on our father as much, she wouldn't have been taken to the cleaners. My father had definitely gotten the better deal in the divorce, and his attorneys had been ruthless. "Be a lawyer, Mallory. Then no one can push you around," she'd told me over and over. I'd listened to her advice and vowed to always take care of myself. Except it didn't always work out that way. Now I knew you could be self-sufficient, and you still might not see disaster coming.

Rachel rolled her eyes. "Oh, c'mon. You scurry around like the good girl trying to make everyone else happy and someone does something nice for you for a change. Just say thank you and move on."

I raised my eyebrows at my sister. "Well, excuse me."

"Ahem." Someone cleared her throat behind us.

"Oh!" I jumped. The woman leaned out the car window and waited for us to stop bickering. It was Yvette Tannenbaum.

"My dad's shop gets all of the cars that are towed after an accident, and he took in your rental. Truman asked us to be on the lookout for an old leather book, some kind of diary?" She paused.

"Hate to say it, but nothing like that was in the car." Her father, the mechanic, looked contrite.

I let out a breath I didn't realize I'd been holding. "Thanks for checking."

"I'm glad you're okay." Yvette pushed her sunglasses up into her lanky hair. "The police will catch whoever did this to you. Take care, Mallory."

I thanked her as she and her father drove off, then I slumped against the Volvo.

"That sucks," I chastised myself. "I never should've taken the diary out of the house. It was safely tucked away in that trunk for what, eighty years, and the day we find it, I lose it."

"You mean the day you were almost killed, the diary freakishly disappeared. This is beyond your control. You're being too hard on yourself."

I kicked at the gravel and wouldn't look at Rachel.

"Besides," she ventured slowly, "I need your help. This isn't great timing. I entered myself last minute into the baking contest for Founder's Day, and I don't know if I can pull it off. I thought I'd have more time, but with your accident and everything . . ."

I groaned and rubbed my aching neck. Come to think of it, I remembered Helene mentioning something about Founder's Day when I was at the historical society. "What's Founder's Day?"

"Port Quincy has a festival each July to honor the town founder, Ebenezer Quincy. He was the first settler here, and he fought in the Revolutionary War. He was also part of the Whiskey Rebellion. You know, Port Quincy played a small part in the Whiskey Rebellion. In the late seventeen hundreds, all over western Pennsylvania, people protested the tax on homemade whiskey—"

"I've heard of the Whiskey Rebellion, Rach. I was a history major." My head throbbed. "What's it got to do with a baking contest?" I added more gently.

"Zach told me about it." Rachel twirled a strand of hair around her index finger. "I was pretty sure they wouldn't let me enter, but the head of the contest said due to a low amount of entries this year, I could bake something."

I tamped down a smile, the corners of my mouth twitching. Both Rachel and I were inveterate procrastinators. It was one trait we shared, and working as an attorney at a frenetic pace had managed to correct my habits. But left to my own devices, I also put off things until the very last second.

"Of course I'll help you. What are you making?"

"Don't get mad." Rachel let go of her hair and began to trace a pattern in the newly mown grass with her bejeweled purple toenail and dug her fists deep into the pockets of her cut-offs.

"Why would I be mad?" A wave of doubt washed over me.

"I'm-making-schweddin-cake," she said in a rush. "It has to incorporate whiskey, and I know a really sophisticated recipe for orange whiskey cake. It'll be amazing." She dared to peek through the sun-kissed waves of hair hiding her face.

"Schweddin cake? Oh, you mean wedding cake." I imagined a lifetime of people forbidden from mentioning anything related to weddings. *That's the one who was jilted*, people would whisper behind my back. *Don't breathe a word about weddings or she'll flip out.*

I gave my sister a hug, trying not to gasp. A sash of bruises from the seat belt had blossomed overnight.

"You don't need to tiptoe around the rest of your life avoiding the subject of weddings." I steeled myself as Rachel hugged me back. "Let's go make your cake. It'll be fabulous."

I gathered ingredients with my good right arm, including the last of the aged local whiskey the cats hadn't managed to knock over. Rachel dug out Sylvia's ancient cooking bowls and cake pans and amassed everything on the large prep table in the middle of the room.

"I'm not a fan of Tabitha." Rachel tied her long waves in a bun. "Especially since she might be a murderer, but on one point she's right. This place would make a perfect B and B, and we could host weddings here. It would be much better than that gross old country club."

I sank into a chair and let out a laugh. "That's why you're making a wedding cake. To drum up prospective business and convince me to keep this place." Rachel was tireless when she wanted something, and even though I didn't think we could turn this place into a B and B, I was touched she wanted to go into business together.

"It's worth a try." She dared to smile. "Plus, other people will be making things like pies and small batches of cookies. I can get a lot of people to sample the wedding cake. We'll reach more prospective customers that way."

Prospective customers? I began to get nervous.

"This had better be some cake," I muttered. "Are you sure you want to bake a whole wedding cake? You only worked at that bakery in Florida for what, four months?" I instantly regretted it, not wanting to hurt my little sister's feelings.

Rachel's face crumpled. "Just wait and see. I might not be a fancy attorney, but I'm good at what I do when I put my mind to it."

"I know." I tried to backpedal. "I just don't want you to get upset if the B and B idea doesn't work out. I just don't see how I can keep my job at the firm, raise enough money to fix this place up . . ."

"Maybe this is meant to be. It's fate. Just loosen up and give it a try."

"I would love to make Thistle Park into an inn and hold weddings, but I have to live in reality."

Rachel's green eyes flashed and churned. "At least I'm chasing my dreams, Mall. How did I even learn to bake? From watching you. You used to love cooking and helping Mom with her decorating business. And you secretly loved planning your wedding, even though Helene called the shots. This is perfect for you, and you know it. You just won't take the risk."

I met my sister's gaze, which was sad and sincere. Then she whirled around and continued to amass baking ingredients. "We need to go to the store. I need fresher ingredients. We can inaugurate the car."

"When is Founder's Day?"

Rachel averted her eyes, then cleared her throat. "It's tomorrow."

Chapter Ten

Rachel baked with a fury when we got home from the grocery store, and I helped by measuring as best as I could with one arm. It was fun to collaborate on the recipe, and together we tweaked it to add more orange to play off the aged whiskey. I admired her confidence that the cake would turn out perfectly. I retired to bed as she began to ice the cooled layers of cake.

"Whoa," I said when I entered the kitchen the next morning. The cake stood on the scarred wooden table, in all three tiers of glory. It was pale peach, a dreamy creamsicle of a confection, with white swirls of buttercream waltzing around the sides and little orange flowers kissing the edges where the piping met the top of each layer. The top tier had a crown of rosettes and more ribbons of peachy-colored buttercream.

Rachel's face was solemn. "You really like it? Like, *really* really?" She channeled Sally Field at the Oscars.

"It's gorgeous! Where did you learn to do this?" I

marveled at my sister's handiwork. Scones and cookies were one thing, but the cake was stunning.

"The bakery, silly. I was the best at decorating by the time I left, and I was only there for four months. And you got me started with cooking and baking, don't forget that. I just hope it tastes as good as it looks." Rachel beamed. I was sorry I had doubted her. No matter what happened with the house, my sister had found her calling. That was, if the cake tasted even half as good as it looked. I was sure it would.

We carried the cake gingerly out to the Butterscotch Monster, my left arm throbbing. We secured it as best as we could in the back portion of the station wagon. Rachel drove to the Founder's Day fairgrounds at ten miles per hour, earning the ire of several cars stuck behind us as the Volvo coughed and sputtered, pokey and emphysemic. The entrance to the event was under a giant blue banner. It proclaimed PORT QUINCY FOUNDER'S DAY, SPONSORED BY LONESTAR ENERGY. I was curious to see how the townspeople felt about the frackers.

"Mallory!" Olivia called as we set the cake on a table designated for Rachel.

"You made it." I gave my best friend a hug. I'd bribed Olivia to drive from Pittsburgh for the day, since Rachel would be busy manning her station, then slicing and serving the cake after the judges made their decision.

A pale young woman, chubby and tentative, stood before Rachel's cake in awe. "It's beautiful." She reverently stepped back to take in the confection. Her round face lit up as she walked around for a better look.

"What's your name? Are you interested in a cake?" Rachel pounced, switching into businesswoman mode with alarming alacrity.

The girl glanced at the petite ring on her left hand.

"I'm Kayla Lang." She fiddled with the ring. "My fiancé is deployed, but he's coming home next week. We're saving for a wedding." She backed away sheepishly. "But we'll never be able to afford a cake like that, or the kind of wedding that goes with it."

"You'd be surprised." Rachel dug into the pocket of the cute apron she'd donned this morning. It was vintage, peach and cream flowered cotton, with a frilly eyelet edge. It matched the cake's icing perfectly. I wondered if she'd found it somewhere in Thistle Park and if it had inspired the cake. My sister lowered her voice and edged closer. "Our wedding and events packages will be quite affordable. Don't hesitate to call me to set up an appointment." She pressed a small card into the woman's hand.

"Okay." Uncertainty weighed down her voice. "I've got to get to work." She glanced at the card before she cast the cake one more longing look, then disappeared into the throng of people walking by.

"What did you give her?" I lunged for Rachel's apron pocket and grabbed one of the cards sticking out. It read THISTLE PARK BED & BREAKFAST: PORT QUINCY'S PREMIER INN & EVENTS VENUE, WITH WEDDINGS BY THE SHEPARD SISTERS. The reverse side featured a beautiful picture of Sylvia's house, one I recognized from the historical society, taken at least fifty years ago before it had all gone to hell.

"We're not opening a B and B, and we're not hosting weddings!"

Rachel offered me a serene, yet smug smile. "Calm down."

"I'm selling the house. I *want* to sell the house. Your new boyfriend *Zach* wants to sell the house. There won't be a place for you to launch this ridiculous idea." I made another grab at her pocket to filch the rest of the cards.

"Mallory!" Rachel executed a ballerina-like spin that put her on the other side of the table. "I'm just following my dream. *Your* dream too, if you'd admit it. Now shoo. I have potential customers to attend to." I stared at her, open-mouthed.

"C'mon." Olivia steered me away from my sister. "Just hear her out."

I calmed down marginally—that is, after I got a funnel cake with extra powdered sugar. She handed me a napkin to attend to the spray of powdered sugar that fell over my blue sundress.

"It might be good for her. A project."

"A project is crocheting a scarf, Olivia. Rachel can do what she loves—it just can't hinge on that house."

"She looks like she's doing pretty well." Olivia pointed to my sister's booth, which was crowded with people. Rachel beamed and schmoozed her would-be customers. I hated to admit it, but this was right up her alley. I was grudgingly proud of Rachel. I just wished her success didn't depend on my keeping the house.

"She's in her element," I admitted. My heart swelled with pride for my baby sister. "But I don't know a damn thing about running a business, much less operating a B and B or throwing events."

"You planned a wedding for three hundred people, and you were taking orders from Helene. It'll be

similar working with customers," Olivia pointed out.
"You're the most organized person I know, and you
have good ideas."

I reflected for a moment. Planning weddings with
all of their attendant details, and soothing brides and
family members might not be too far off from dealing with troublesome clients, talking partners down
from the ledge and coordinating trials. But something was holding me back, namely money.

"But something usually has to come to fruition to
be considered a success. The wedding never happened."

"Are you sure you can handle this hoopla today?"
Olivia's eyes strayed to my left arm in its sling.

"Positive." I caught myself from nodding at the last
second. My head still hurt, my neck still ached, and
the bruises underneath my loose, gauzy cotton dress
were beginning to turn from purple to a lovely shade
of green.

We passed booth after booth of delectable fair-
ground food: cotton candy, corn dogs, elephant ears,
pierogies, sausage and cabbage, and the feature of
the celebration, little complimentary shots of locally
made whiskey for those who could prove they were
over twenty-one. Little stations were set up to collect
votes for the best food and drink.

We deftly avoided the row with the DAR display,
which was unnecessary, as Helene didn't seem to be
around. But Tabitha was there, standing sheepishly
behind the historical society booth with brochures
and Revolutionary War replica items.

"Don't laugh," she scolded as I introduced her to
Olivia. Tabitha was clad in costume from the days of
the Whiskey Rebellion, when Ebenezer Quincy had

founded the town. She sweated in a homespun brown skirt, a rough white blouse, and no makeup. Her brilliantly dyed hair, Ariel-the-mermaid red, peeked out from under her white cap. It was a vivid shade no Colonial woman ever sported, and her skirt was too short, exposing modern periwinkle flip-flops. She giggled as she caught me looking at her feet. "The historical society encourages us to wear this, and I usually love it, but I accidentally shrunk it in the wash. And it's too hot for the leather shoes."

I burst out laughing. Olivia and I chatted with Tabitha for a bit, then left her and followed the crowd, which seemed to be amassing around a podium and stage set up just beyond a small ball field.

"Can I have your attention," brayed a large man. He was squat and beefy, in his mid-forties, with a blond buzz cut and a florid complexion. He looked like a linebacker gone to seed, and he was clad in a loud checked sport jacket, despite the midday heat. He wore it over a clashing striped brown shirt. He relished his role as emcee and grinned at the crowd.

"Thanks to everyone in Port Quincy who made this year's Founder's Day such a smashing success. Ebenezer Quincy would be proud to see what this town has become." A small cheer went up around him. "As you know, I'm your mayor, Bart Tannenbaum, and I'm going to announce the winners of the food and drink contests."

"That's the mayor?" I murmured in disbelief. "I've met his wife, and they seem very different." I scanned the dais for Yvette and spotted her sitting behind her husband. She wore another faded flowered housedress and looked as bland and diminutive as ever as she picked at her cuticles.

The mayor announced the winner of the best whiskey-themed dish, the best homemade spirits, and finally, the best whiskey-infused baked good. I stiffened as he started his announcement, then relaxed when he called out, "Miss Rachel Shepard, for her whiskey-orange wedding cake!"

My sister squealed as she bounded onto the small stage, eager to claim her certificate. I cheered even though it made my head throb, and Olivia let out a loud whistle.

Rachel paused to have her picture taken by the Port Quincy *Eagle Herald* photographer, holding a slice of her cake. She flashed her most charming smile, elated with her win. It was picture perfect, until I noticed the mayor's hand straying rather low on my sister's back, where her T-shirt and apron separated from her jeans.

"Ew, stop touching my sister, creepster!"

"He is kinda handsy, isn't he?" Olivia frowned beneath her black bangs.

Rachel looked around for me as she clambered off the stage. She gave me a triumphant thumbs-up when she spotted me waving, before she disappeared to distribute the rest of her cake to the crowd, no doubt drumming up even more business.

The mayor resumed his announcements, this time about the baseball field behind him. "It is my great pleasure to dedicate the Lonestar Energy Baseball Complex, in honor of Lonestar Energy's contributions to this community and their very generous donation of new bleachers."

The crowd clapped and hollered enthusiastically,

and a small woman struggled to rise from her seat, three spots down from Yvette Tannenbaum. She was young and slight, with dark brown hair gathered in a bun at the nape of her neck, and big, lustrous kewpie doll eyes. She carried her most arresting feature out in front of her. She was massively pregnant, her big round belly preceding her by a foot as she waddled over to the mayor.

"She's ready to pop." Olivia stared at the woman.

She was very pregnant, but she was glowing, and she was quite pretty.

"I'd like to introduce Mrs. Deanna Hartley, wife of the late Shane Hartley."

The crowd hushed, and I snapped my head up too quickly, causing shooting pains to radiate down my left shoulder. I leaned against Olivia.

She propped me up, her face knotted with concern.

"That's the wife of the man we found on the lawn." I hadn't seen her face as she'd exited the hospital. Seeing her up close made me think of Shane Hartley. It was a shock to see parts of his life, up front and center. He had been a real man, not just a caricature on my front porch, or in the depositions I'd read.

"Deanna made a special trip back from Houston to be here for this Founder's Day dedication. She'll cut the ribbon for the new field, on behalf of Lonestar Energy."

The woman took a pair of comically large ceremonial scissors from Mayor Tannenbaum and slowly made her way over to the edge of the stage. She perched on the end next to a yellow ribbon tied across a span of new, bright blue bleachers, each one emblazoned with the Lonestar Energy insignia.

The strapping mayor must really have a problem keeping his hands to himself. He gently guided heavily pregnant Deanna Hartley by the small of her back. You could read it as chivalry, or you could read it as ick. Maybe that was the source of the severe frown marring Yvette's face. It must not be easy to see your public-figure husband putting his hands all over every lady he came across—my luscious sister and the octogenarian who won a prize for her savory whiskey baked beans included.

Deanna Hartley struggled with the ungainly scissors as the throng of people held its collective breath. She still wore a heavy wedding band, visible from the stage, the diamonds winking and flashing from her finger like little disco balls. It made the bauble Keith had given me look like chump change. Her style was definitely Texas oil-and-gas spouse chic.

The sympathy for this pregnant, widowed woman, far from her home state, seemed to roll off the crowd in palpable waves. Deanna finally managed to cut through the ribbon, then turned to the crowd with a relieved smile. The crowd clapped and cheered, but the revelry was short-lived.

"This is *not* a day of celebration." A clear, but disembodied voice blared from behind the crowd. We all tried to turn en masse to see the source of this pronouncement. It was a young blond woman with a bullhorn. She stood on the other side of the ball field. "Lonestar Energy is poisoning our water and our future, and you have a right to know about it."

"Get the hell out of here," a portly man yelled at her across the field.

"No one asked for your opinion," a young woman said, as the man next to her chucked a bottle of Gatorade toward the protestors. The bottle burst open, sending a splash of neon yellow liquid into the air.

"Don't drink the water! Don't drink the water!" the protestor chanted, along with the twenty or so people with her. I squinted across the field and noticed Bev Mitchell, the jolly seamstress who had welcomed us to town with a zucchini casserole, among the protestors.

Deanna Hartley's face crumpled. She took a step back and nearly fell off the stage. The mayor grabbed her, set her firmly in a chair, then attempted to gain control of the situation.

"Everyone move along back to the fair." His voice was high and panicked. He cleared his throat and tried again, louder this time to be heard over the din of the protestors' chant, puffing up his chest with importance. "Go sample some of those award-winning recipes!"

A few people from the crowd heeded Mayor Tannenbaum's directive and ambled away from the ball field, but more stayed.

"Nothing to see here, people." Chief Truman Davies approached the protestors. Faith followed closely behind. They talked quietly with the group of protestors, who stopped their chanting. The people of Port Quincy listened to Truman, not Mayor Tannenbaum, and began to disperse.

"Who is the woman leading the protest?" I asked the man next to me, who was muttering some choice words.

"Naomi Powell and her band of environmental

whackos. Should be arrested. Don't people know Lonestar is good for this town?" He spoke with real venom, his hands gripping his baseball cap.

I pulled away from him.

"Let's go try some of Rachel's cake." Olivia put her arm around me.

We left the field in search of my sister.

I couldn't get the demonstration out of my mind. While it appeared that plenty of the denizens of Port Quincy appreciated Lonestar and the jobs and revenue it brought to town, there was a sizable group compelled to demonstrate against them. The very group that might be interested in seeing Shane Hartley meet an ugly demise. So, later that afternoon, I went to the Amarillo Steakhouse. The Amarillo seemed fairly new, a cavernous, lodge-like roadhouse, complete with Tex-Mex-themed dishes, a wooden square floor for impromptu line dancing, a mechanical bull and enough animals mounted on the wall to fill a taxidermy museum. It fit in well in rural western Pennsylvania, land of the horseless cowboy. I'd heard this was where the Lonestar executives liked to eat, a little corner of Texas right here in Port Quincy.

I was at the restaurant treating Naomi Powell, the environmental protestor with the bullhorn. It was pretty sedate on a late Saturday afternoon, especially since most of the town was still at Founder's Day. Zach had promised to pick Rachel up from the fair after holding an open house, so I'd returned home, found Naomi's phone number online, and called her on a whim. I'd offered to buy her dinner if she'd talk to me about Shane Hartley and Lonestar Energy. To my surprise, she'd instantly accepted. It wasn't that I didn't trust Truman and Faith to find out who killed Shane or whether his death was related to my accident or the ketchup threat, but it wouldn't hurt to do a little investigating myself. *Right?*

"You think I killed Shane Hartley." Naomi folded her long legs under the booth.

"Of course not!"

"The police already cleared me." She dragged a chip through salsa. "I was on a date."

I sagged in the booth.

"You're a lawyer, right?" She cocked her head to the left and tucked a strand of straight, wheat-colored hair behind her ear. She couldn't have been out of her early twenties. She was passionate and sure of herself and her cause. I liked her frankness.

"How'd you know that?"

"Friends in Low Places" blasted out over the speakers. Two little girls tried to climb onto the mechanical bull. Their mother pulled them away, back to their chicken fingers and chocolate milk.

"I like to do a little reconnaissance before I meet with someone." Naomi smiled. "It's not hard—your bio is right there on the Russell Carey law firm website."

I'd done some of my own Internet reconnaissance before our meeting. Naomi Elizabeth Powell had grown up in Port Quincy, won a scholarship to boarding school at the nearby Dunlap Women's Academy, and studied environmental science at Oberlin, where she graduated two years ago. She'd been working at Environment First's Ohio Valley office for the past year and specialized in anti-fracking grassroots campaigns. *Thank you, Google and LexisNexis.* She was zealous about her cause and had been arrested twice for protesting. It was a long way from arrest for a demonstration to murder, but it was possible.

"This isn't about a lawsuit. I'm not here in my capacity as an attorney. This is personal. This is about the dead man on my lawn."

Naomi's gray eyes grew big. "You inherited Sylvia's house? The newspaper articles just said Hartley was found in her yard, I didn't know you were living there."

I said nothing, hoping she'd continue. I'd learned some better interrogation techniques these last two weeks from Truman and Faith. Maybe if I shut my mouth, she'd fill in the silence.

"I didn't like him." She took a long pull from the Shiner Bock in front of her. "Everyone here is dazzled by the gas industry." She opened her eyes wide in disbelief. "They're not seeing the poisoned farm animals or the water buffaloes people are forced to use just to get clean drinking water." Naomi was on her soapbox, and I encouraged her soliloquy with little nods.

"What are water buffaloes?"

"Per some of the settlements, Lonestar has to provide families with tanks of fresh water since they've poisoned their wells. Sylvia understood what was going on." She giggled. "She called every single person on Sycamore Street and convinced them not to grant gas leases to Lonestar. I think she helped our cause because of the damage her family's glass factory did to Port Quincy. She understood the environmental effects of fracking."

I raised my eyes in surprise.

"Sylvia left our nonprofit a hundred thousand dollars in her will." Naomi bit into a chip, her eyes triumphant. "It was payback. Shane Hartley was relentless, hounding Sylvia nearly every day at the nursing home, then calling her when she had him blacklisted from visiting her. I got him to stop by threatening to write an op-ed for the *Eagle Herald* about everyone's favorite gas executive badgering little old ladies in nursing homes."

"I bet Helene Pierce was thrilled Sylvia left your organization money."

"Hardly. I hear she's contesting Sylvia's will. She'll argue that Environment First convinced Sylvia to change it, to cut her and her son Keith out of the inheritance."

"Get in line," I said joylessly. "Helene has threatened to sue me too."

"So you're trying to figure out who killed that—" She paused and started over. "Who killed that fine citizen, Shane Hartley, and left him dead on your front yard."

I frowned. I had been tempted to trash talk Shane too, after the only encounter I'd had with him while he was alive was so awful. But I recalled his wife, heavily pregnant, now alone in the world, and a wave of sadness washed over me.

"Yes, I want to know who killed Shane, now that I've been threatened that the same thing will happen to me if I don't leave Sylvia's house and Port Quincy."

Naomi set her beer down and un-pretzeled her legs. "Seriously? Someone threatened you?"

"With ketchup." I explained the threat written on the dining room wall and the cut brakes.

"Do you think the same people who killed Shane want you dead too?" Naomi's pupils grew wide.

"Or they don't want me to figure out who did it."

"Let me think. There are a whole bunch of people here in Port Quincy who think Shane Hartley and Lonestar Energy saved them. From the brink of fore-closure, from bankruptcy, from medical bills they couldn't pay and college educations they couldn't afford. People's land is worth more than they ever dreamed if they can get some gas out of it. And Lone-star gives its employees decent health benefits. They're employing half of this town, not counting all the people who've moved here from Oklahoma and Texas. But . . ." She looked around behind us. "In addition to what they're doing to the town's water, they're not the most careful."

"Go on." I leaned in, eager for more details.

"First, there're the Mitchells. They nearly lost their horses and their dogs. They wouldn't dare allow drilling on account of their animals, but the reten-tion pond holding the fracking waste water from their neighbor's drilling site leached through the water table and poisoned their well."

"You mean Bev Mitchell? The seamstress? She was protesting with you today." I thought of the friendly woman and how she'd expressed her distaste for Hartley the day I'd met her.

Naomi cocked her head. "Bev definitely hates Lonestar Energy, but it's her son, Preston, who I could see flipping out and going after Shane. They didn't get the best settlement, which technically they're not allowed to talk about, and now no one wants to buy their land. So they're stuck there, re-liant on Lonestar to truck in their water. Preston is a good kid, and he isn't known for being violent, but it wouldn't surprise me if he snapped. Bev is a widow, and he looks after his mom. Then there's the Prentiss family."

"I know about them." I thought of our gentle handyman.

"How?" Our food arrived, and Naomi paused over her bean burrito.

"Will was Sylvia's handyman, and he helped us with some locks. Um, I also read the pleadings in his suit. Russell Carey defends a lot of Lonestar cases."

"Of course!" Naomi playfully smacked her forehead. Her eyes glittered. "You have access to settlement information?"

I dropped my fish taco back onto my plate. "Yes, but it's confidential." I suddenly felt very protective of my firm.

"Right." Naomi deflated a little.

"Will Prentiss though?" I questioned. "He wouldn't kill. And this is going to sound really cold, but I only spoke to Shane once, the day before he was murdered. From that experience, I can see why someone would want to kill him, and he was only there for five minutes. I actually shoved him, and I'm not a violent person. Now I feel awful about it."

Naomi laughed. "I couldn't see you laying a finger on anyone."

"Try me." Before Keith cheated on me, I hadn't thought I had it in me. Now I wasn't so sure.

"I probably shouldn't be telling you this." Naomi dropped her voice and scanned the restaurant. There were a few die-hard drinkers starting early at the bar and a smattering of families having a late lunch. Everyone else in town was still at Founder's

Day. And the restaurant was huge; no one else was
sitting by us. Not to mention, no one could hear over
the Garth Brooks song echoing through the room. I
leaned in close across the lacquered table.

"Helene bought a whole bunch of stock in Lonestar a few months ago. She was waiting for Sylvia to
die so she and Keith could drill on the land. No one
else in your neighborhood would grant a gas lease,
and they're really hot and bothered to drill there."

"So that's the business deal."

"What business deal?" Naomi took a swig of beer.

"A partner at my law firm threatened me this week.
He mentioned Helene had a business relationship
with Lonestar Energy. Although Lonestar is a client
at the firm, I don't do any energy work, and I didn't
know what he was talking about."

"They had an actual contract," Naomi said miserably.

"What?" I squeaked. "Like a hit on Sylvia?" My
blood turned icy as I pictured Helene arranging it.

"No, a drilling contract. Helene and Keith Pierce
thought they'd pull a fast one on Sylvia. They treated
her like a doddering old lady and were just biding
their time until she died. Then her house would be
willed over to her loving grandson, Keith, and they'd
let Lonestar drill and be even richer than they are
now. But Sylvia figured it out and left you the property."

"How do you know this?"

Naomi grinned wickedly. "We have a mole working at Lonestar, an administrative assistant. She
catches all kinds of little anomalies."

I sat up, eager for her to continue.

"No one else for two square miles would let them

drill, and Lonestar was getting antsy. Sylvia was as healthy as a horse. She could have lived to be a hundred and five. And Helene wanted a return on her investment in Lonestar. They were going to raze Sylvia's mansion, retain some land to drill, and build a housing development. You, or rather Sylvia, foiled their plan."

The wheels began to churn slowly in my head. I was having trouble putting it together. I stared at the elk head mounted on the wall. He gazed back at me with doleful, big black eyes. Prickles began to dance up and down my spine.

"Do you think they killed Sylvia? If they didn't know she'd changed her will and deeded me the property?"

Naomi put down her beer. "Helene? It's not a stretch to imagine her killing Sylvia. And Keith, well, they say the apple doesn't fall far from the tree."

Our check had been cleared long ago, and a different waitress showed up to clear the table.

"Yinz can sit here as long as you like." Her thin blond hair escaped the ponytail at the nape of her neck.

"You're Kayla, right?" She was the woman from the fair this morning, who had been so taken with Rachel's cake.

"That's right," she said, a hint of suspicion in her voice.

"I have a proposition for you."

"Keith did not off his grandma." Rachel snorted as she chopped a tidy pile of walnuts. She was high on her baking contest victory and tore through Thistle

Park's kitchen, testing recipes from old cookbooks. I couldn't wait to tell her I'd cornered Kayla at the Amarillo Steakhouse and offered her my wedding reception, and she'd accepted. I no longer had to advertise the wedding. Rachel had been out on a date with Zach when I'd returned Saturday night, and it must have been a good one, because she wasn't home Sunday morning. She'd texted she'd be spending the day with Zach again, on a trip to a nearby casino for some gambling and shopping. I'd finally caught her Monday when I returned to Port Quincy after work.

"I'm working on our business plan," Rachel gushed. "We can feature turn-of-the-century recipes for the breakfasts and wedding menus."

My heart began to beat faster. It was the same idea I'd had. I was itching to look through the cookbooks, but a wave of doubt crashed over me.

"Rach, there needs to be a business for your business plan. And it won't be here."

My sister didn't even blink. "Maybe not for you, but I have two orders for wedding cakes."

"Make that a third." Mixed feelings made my voice low. "I gave away my wedding reception at the country club." I wanted Rachel to succeed, but I didn't want to be tethered to this house forever if we couldn't turn it into a B and B and wedding venue.

Rachel tossed down her knife and whirled around with a squeal.

"Careful!" I cried as the knife ricocheted off the counter. I picked it up just as Soda the kitten raced into the kitchen to inspect the noise.

"Who'd you give the wedding to?"

"Kayla, the woman who admired your cake so

much. It's super short notice, but the reception is paid for. Nothing else, like a DJ or a photographer—"

Rachel almost knocked me over with the force of her hug.

"That is so sweet." She held me at arm's length. "It's great that you're able to move on. And Kayla's wedding will be a good test run to launch our business venture."

I pulled away from her and tried to change the subject.

"First off, I don't know if I could channel my inner Martha Stewart and hold weddings here, even if we could renovate. It would be a business launched with Sylvia's murder." I raised my eyebrows. "I have strong feelings about this."

"Sylvia died in her sleep. But if she *was* murdered?" She chopped walnuts into smaller and smaller pieces, her knife flashing in a blur. "I could see Helene killing her mother-in-law."

"It would be hard to prove." I sipped some lemonade. Rachel had made it with real mint leaves again and plenty of sugar. "Since she was ninety-nine, no one's going to challenge the conclusion that she died of a heart attack during her afternoon nap."

I closed my eyes and thought of work. This morning, I'd searched the thousands of Lonestar Energy documents on the internal system, specifically for the contract Naomi Powell's mole had seen in Lonestar's office. I wanted proof Helene and Keith were making hinky contracts.

The little hourglass symbol spun as my work PC churned, then spit back a surprising result: *0 documents available.* I squinted at the screen in disbelief. The firm had had thousands of Lonestar documents just the other day. But below the first figure was a different one. The search results revealed over three thousand documents mentioning Lonestar Energy, and now they were all password-protected. I swallowed and quickly exited out of the document system.

Someone had encrypted every single firm document mentioning Shane Hartley's company. Perhaps because the system had alerted them to my prior searches. And now I'd done it again. Some algorithm would inform the powers that be at the firm that I was snooping where I didn't belong.

Chapter Eleven

The next day, I arrived at work before the sun rose and finally pulled back into the driveway at seven, ready to forgo dinner and move straight to my sinking brass bed. But I had a visitor sitting on the front porch who stood to meet me before I could even extricate myself from the station wagon. I shielded my eyes against the low sun with my hand and realized it was Truman. I stifled a groan. "How can I help you, Chief?"

"Cut the Nancy Drew bull crap." Truman's hands were on his hips, his face twisted into a scowl. "You're messing up my investigation." His eyes were cold, his mouth set in a hard line, like the first day I'd met him when he thought I'd bludgeoned Shane Hartley.

"I don't know what you're talking about." I breezed past him and entered the front hall. Sheesh. Where was the solicitous, caring man who carried me into this house just a few days ago? I continued down the hallway, Truman dogging my heels.

Rachel met us in the breakfast room.

"I made spaghetti." She glanced nervously at Truman. "Would you like some, Chief?"

"No thanks. I won't be here long. Just wanted to tell your sister I don't appreciate her asking people questions, trying to solve Shane Hartley's murder."

Rachel glanced mutely at me and headed to the kitchen.

She returned with a small salad, some fresh bread, and two steaming plates of spaghetti. I speared some lettuce with unnecessary roughness, and the fork squeaked across the plate.

"Look, Truman, I'm just trying to stay alive. We don't exactly feel safe here, and there's nowhere else to go. Have *you* made any headway on who killed Shane Hartley?" He must have figured out by now I'd talked to Naomi Powell, and that's what this little talking-to was about.

"We have some leads." Truman jutted out his chin. He was bluffing.

"Good luck with that." If Truman couldn't figure out who had killed Hartley and cut my brakes, I would do it for him.

"We already interviewed everyone you talked to. We know how to do our job. Leave the detective work to us."

I took a bite of bread instead of responding.

"There's something else. I actually stopped by to tell you about the fingerprints we lifted from those photographs of Mr. Pierce and Ms. Cunningham."

I abandoned the bread, no longer hungry. It took all my self-possession to finish chewing and to swallow the lump in my mouth, instead of spitting it out.

"They were Sylvia's prints."

"*Sylvia* sent them?" I dropped my fork with a clatter.

"She probably thought it was important you knew the truth about her grandson."

Sylvia's words the last time I saw her echoed in my head. *It's good to listen to your instincts, Mallory.*

"She tried to warn me, without resorting to the actual evidence." I shook my head. "I admitted I was having some misgivings about the wedding, and she told me maybe it was cold feet. That I should trust myself. But I was going to go through with it." I shivered. "Until she sent those photos."

"How do you have Sylvia's fingerprints?" Rachel set down her water.

Truman chuckled. "We had to book her once. Back in two thousand two. She threw her pocketbook at Helene and broke her nose. It was a heavy thing, and Sylvia had pretty good aim, even though she was in her eighties. Helene pressed charges, and we charged Sylvia with assault."

"Good for her!" I howled with laughter.

"My son represented Sylvia and convinced the DA to drop the charges."

"So that's how Garrett started as Sylvia's attorney?"

Truman nodded. "They became friends, and she had Garrett handle her legal matters, including her will. Made the Pierces furious, because Helene wanted Keith to draw up the will to their liking. In fact, they did just that, until my son straightened things out."

We chatted a bit more, Truman's gruff admonition to stay out of his investigation nearly forgotten. He stood to go. "You don't want those pictures back, do you, Mallory?"

My face heated.

"I don't need them anymore."

"Promise me one thing. No more amateur detective stuff. I'll find out who threatened you and who killed Shane Hartley. But you have to stay out of my investigation."

"I promise." I hid my crossed fingers under the table.

As soon as Rachel and I finished dinner, I changed from my pantsuit into a more expansive pair of PJs. I'd crawled into my sinking bed at half past eight for some much needed sleep, when Rachel knocked on my door.

"You have another visitor." Her eyes lowered with concern. "I can tell him to go away if you want."

"Who is it?" I asked groggily.

"Keith." Her face fell.

I swung my legs out of bed and marched from the room.

"I can tell him to buzz off," Rachel said as I traipsed down the stairs, threw open the front door, and was greeted to the sight of Keith pulling the rest of my belongings out of his trunk. My eyes slid to the backseat of his BMW, and I pictured him there with Becca all over again. *Thank you, Sylvia.*

"See, I'm not breaking and entering this time." He made his way over to the porch. He carried a thick envelope.

"Only because you've figured out I changed the locks." My eyes adjusted to the dimming light. I glanced back at Rachel. The sun was setting behind the house, rimming it in gold against a melon-colored sky, but before me it was darkening to a deep, cobalt blue. Whiskey the cat came out of the house and began to growl.

"Good guard kitty." I bent to scratch her chin. Keith rolled his eyes and set the envelope on the porch. He returned to his car and hoisted the final item from his trunk, attempting to balance it atop a high pile of boxes and bags spilling out all the clothes, books, wedding favors, and knickknacks I'd left behind at his apartment. I was thankful that at least now I'd have some decorations to use for Kayla's wedding. The heavy garment bag kept slithering off the pile and onto the grass.

I realized in horror he was trying to put my would-be wedding gown on top of the boxes.

"I won't be needing that." My voice was thin and high. Keith gave up and let the ball gown slump onto the grass, where it sat like a white chocolate Hershey's kiss, the hanger peeking out of the top like a slip of paper.

"Let's at least be civil, Mallory." He joined me on the porch and took a step toward me, and I took one back. Whiskey paced before me.

"I can't believe you were in an accident. I was so worried when I heard." He took another step, closing the gap.

I began to laugh. "Were you worried about me when you were boinking Becca Cunningham on that backseat and planning to walk down the aisle and pledge your undying fidelity?"

"I'm sorry." Keith addressed his shoes. "I'll do whatever you want."

"Just keep your psycho mother away from me." I paused and really looked at him for the first time.

Something was off. The stress from these past few weeks had deepened the bags under his eyes and made his cheeks sag. His hand flew to his chin, which he stroked self-consciously.

"Becca made me shave it." He wouldn't meet my eyes, his sentence trailing off in a mumble.

I stared at him as if he'd gone mad. Keith had had a beard since the day I met him. I'd never seen his face naked. His chin was small, with a little cleft, and made him appear to have an overbite. No wonder he'd never shaved it.

I also couldn't believe he had been obtuse enough to mention Becca's name in my presence. I peered more closely at his car, half expecting her to pop out of it like an evil blond jack-in-the-box.

"Here's a tip." I tried to keep my voice from becoming a shrewish shriek but failed miserably. "Don't *ever* say her name in front of me. You need to leave, right now."

"I want to apologize properly. Since you haven't let me. I didn't get a chance to explain to you what happened."

"I saw, remember? Some guardian angel showed me what happened, right there on your front seat." I jabbed my finger toward his car.

Shame momentarily clouded Keith's face, but he didn't retreat. It was on the tip of my tongue to tell him his grandma Sylvia had sent the incriminating photos.

"Things changed between us." Keith stumbled on. "The wedding was too big to cancel. I was going to deal with this in a few months. I need someone who will take care of me. Someone willing to work less. I know it was bad timing, and I should have told you earlier. With Becca, it's different—"

I'd had enough of listening to Keith describe our wedding as a too-big-to-fail pageant. I'd turned to retreat into the house when Rachel cleared her throat and announced, "The third gentleman caller of the evening."

I was happy she had listened in on my conversation with Keith. It saved me the trouble of recounting it to her later.

"Ha, ha." I thought she was joking. "Just leave the stuff on the lawn. I'll deal with it when Keith leaves."

"No, I'm serious."

I turned to see Garrett Davies advance around the side of the house, smiling, a skip in his lanky step. He carried an accordion folder under his arm. When he saw Keith and the precarious pile of boxes and bags, his face clouded over.

"Behave, boys," I said under my breath.

"Keith." Garrett climbed the stairs and positioned himself between me and the scoundrel.

"Garrett. Funny, I hear you keep popping up around here."

"Just being neighborly." Garrett took a step toward Keith. Their noses were almost touching. "Making Mallory and Rachel feel welcome in Port Quincy."

Keith snorted and looked Garrett up and down. "I'll bet you are." He tried to pull in his paunchy stomach and square his jaw. I could practically see the air crackling between them.

"Um, Garrett?" I wanted to diffuse the situation

before they broke into fisticuffs. "Do you want to come in? Keith was just leaving."

"You heard the lady." Garrett inched even closer to Keith. "She asked you to leave."

"You're making a giant mistake, Mall." Keith's voice was quavering.

"Excuse me?" Garrett took a step closer still and stared at him with absolute malice. "You cheated on your fiancé." Tiny flecks of spit landed on Keith's now-alarmed face. "Three weeks before your wedding. Let's not talk about mistakes."

"It'd been going on for at least five months." My voice was flat. Both men turned, their stare-down broken. "There was snow on the hood of the car in those pictures."

Keith began to sputter a response, but I wearily held up my left hand, finally free from its sling. "You're not wanted here, by me or by Sylvia." I paused to collect my courage. Might as well tell him if it got him out of here. "Truman Davies just told me. Your grandma sent those pictures. She wanted to make sure I didn't marry you. She helped me avoid what would have been the biggest mistake of my life."

Keith's knees sagged, as if I had delivered a swift kick to his diaphragm. It was like Sylvia had freshly chastised him from beyond the grave. The blood drained from his face, then came rushing back, making his newly shorn red face look like a cherry tomato. He stalked off to his car.

"And I know about the contract you and your mom made with Lonestar."

Keith froze, his hand on the door handle.

"You helped Sylvia along, didn't you?" My voice

cracked. For the millionth time, I regretted not having tea with Sylvia the day she died. Maybe I could have attended to her. Or stopped her from being murdered, since that was what I now suspected.

Keith whirled around. "What are you saying? I killed my own *grandma*? How could you?" His eyes filled with disgust. "Besides, I was with you when she died. We were looking at the plot of land my mother bought us."

"You and Helene would never stoop to killing her yourself. It would be too messy. You probably hired it out. You've been cheating on me for who knows how long, and you were going to marry me. I have no idea what you're capable of." My voice caught on the last word, and Rachel placed her hand on my arm.

Keith just shook his head, got into his BMW, and reversed hard down the drive. A woman's voice yelped. Becca extricated herself from the floor of the backseat. She peeked over the seat as he sped off, like a scared prairie dog emerging from its subterranean hole. Bits of gravel pinged the undercarriage of his car, and he turned out in a cloud of dust. She'd been in the backseat this whole time. I felt extra-humiliated, if that was possible.

I sank to the porch stairs.

"You were right," I said to my sister. "We should have sent him away. He had nothing important to say."

"Helene is trying to get an injunction against you." Garrett pushed a sheaf of papers across the breakfast room table. We'd retreated to the house after we brought in my belongings strewn about the front yard.

I skimmed the papers and burst out laughing.

"An injunction? That's the dumbest legal move I've ever heard of." Injunctions were for emergency, time-sensitive situations, like barring demolition of a building or stopping a protest. Not for anything Helene could claim I was doing. I continued to read the document.

"What? She's claiming not only do I know where three valuable paintings are in this house, but I'm going to destroy them out of spite, and that this is a crime against humanity!"

"It would be comical if it weren't so psychotic." Garrett shook his head with disgust.

"I don't know where the damn paintings are, I swear. They might not even exist. And if they do, and I find them, I certainly won't destroy them!"

"Helene's just trying to intimidate you and get your attention. If she had any real claims, she'd wait and sue you properly. I'm sure she and her attorney have thought of everything possible. Thanks to Sylvia, she doesn't have anything. I can't believe her attorney went for this. It's embarrassing."

"I'll need to find representation for this joke fest."

"The hearing is on Thursday."

"In two days? I never got notice!"

Garrett's eyes strayed to the envelope Keith had brought over and cleared his throat.

"Helene's attorney filed the injunction yesterday and probably had it served at your Pittsburgh address so you wouldn't get it. If you look at the filing, they tried to get a judge to decide without a hearing.

I'm sure you'll find the same notice in the envelope from Keith."

Some attorneys, including ones at my firm, played dirty tricks like this. They accidentally-on-purpose transposed people's addresses, so notices of hearings arrived too late. I would never do anything like that, since litigation could be nasty enough even when you played by the rules.

"So he was doing something nice, kind of, when he brought this over." I winced at this admission. "I've never sought an injunction for a client, but I think I can handle this myself, since it's a farce."

"I'll represent you, if you'd like. I'd love to see the look on Helene's face when it's dismissed."

"Why do you dislike her so much?"

"Her *and* Keith." Garret shook his head bitterly. "There's always been bad blood between us. Keith and I have known each other since kindergarten. He was over here a lot to see his grandma, and my back-yard connects. He was always a jerk, but his father kept him in line. Keith's dad died when he was thirteen, and he went off the rails."

I was familiar with the story. "Keith didn't talk about his dad much, just to say that after his dad passed away, he got a little wild."

"It was more than a little wild. With his dad's good influence gone, Keith became a punk in high school. My dad wasn't the chief then, but he was a police-man, and he brought Keith in for shoplifting and toilet-papering people's trees. Keith always got off. Helene used her influence to make things go away."

"Some things never change." I hadn't heard Keith

talk about his youthful brushes with the law. What else didn't I know about him?

"We went to college together, and Keith rubbed it in my face that he was the McGavitt Glass heir. His father had been some big-shot lawyer and I'm a cop's son. I went to Quincy College on a scholarship and attended classes in Pierce Hall. When we graduated, Keith went off to Penn for law school, and I left for Harvard. I transferred to Pitt after a semester when I found out my girlfriend here was pregnant. Keith said I transferred because I couldn't hack it." He shook his head and laughed. "If he only knew."

"Where's Summer's mom?" I regretted blurting out the question as soon as it had left my lips.

"She's not in the picture." He softened a degree. "She left soon after Summer was born. I haven't heard from her since."

"I'm sorry."

Garrett gave me a level gaze. "It's probably better that way. It wasn't meant to be."

"My dad walked out after Rachel was born. I understand."

I reached out and squeezed his hand as he had done earlier. We sat for a few minutes at the kitchen table, the crickets chirping outside in the darkness.

"Would you like to have dinner with me sometime, Mallory?"

My heart began to beat fast. I hesitated for only a moment, from shock more than anything. But it was enough.

"I'm sorry." He stood. His face was marred by hurt feelings. "That was too forward."

"No, it wasn't! I just—"

"I shouldn't have," Garrett interrupted. "Summer adores you. I could never get involved and then have it not work out."

"Garrett—"

"If you have kids someday, you'll understand." He gave me a sad smile, let himself out the back door, and started his long walk home through the dark backyard.

Chapter Twelve

The next day, I was distracted and distraught, haunted by the thought I'd blown it with Garrett. It didn't help matters when I pulled into the driveway after work to find Zach and Rachel canoodling on the front lawn. I was happy my sister was happy, but I didn't need to see her relationship up close and personal.

Get a room. Or just disappear to one of the many in this house. Anywhere but here.

I exited the station wagon as loudly as possible, slamming the heavy tan door. Rachel faced the house and Zach wrapped his arms around her. He kissed her ear, sending her into a fit of giggles.

"Hi, you two." I was all saccharine sweetness. I stifled an inner gag, then chastened myself. *Just because you blew it with Garrett doesn't mean you shouldn't be happy for Rachel.*

"Zach was pointing out where the house was rebuilt after the fire." The lovebirds broke their embrace, and I joined them, my heels sinking into the grass.

"Right there." Zach pointed to the left side of the house. "Do you see it?"

It was barely perceptible, but the exterior wall encasing the dining room was slightly different. It extended out a bit longer, with a deeper bay window, which marred the smooth symmetry of the house.

"I think so."

"This house was built by Otto Fassbinder, a world-famous architect." Zach was practically drooling.

It was evident what he and Tabitha had in common now. Tabitha was obsessed with this house, and Zach was obsessed with houses in general.

"There's no way he would have designed the house like that. The side of the house was definitely rebuilt."

"Maybe the paintings are still in there after all." Rachel leaned back to peer at Zach.

"Or maybe they burned down with that part of the house," said a voice behind us. The three of us turned. Tabitha was approaching, a big box in her arms. "I came to get the glass for the exhibit." She motioned to her car parked on the street and offered a terse smile that didn't quite reach her eyes. I knew Tabitha thought the paintings did exist, but she was being contrary to disagree with Zach.

"I have to go, Rach, but I'll see you tomorrow at the office." Zach and Rachel kissed. To his credit, Zach tried to make it a quick one, but Rachel grabbed his lapels and pulled him in for a long, slow smooch. Her tactic worked, as Tabitha let out a loud sigh.

"See you later." Zach tipped an imaginary hat at us as he always did. He headed for his car, which looked different. The black Lexus sedan he had been driving had been replaced with a small green convertible. It couldn't be comfortable for chauffeuring prospective home buyers.

"What's tomorrow?" I asked Rachel as soon as he drove away.

"I'm meeting with the manager at his office about becoming a real estate agent."

My eyes went wide. "But I thought you wanted to turn this place into a B and B and run it with me. And do you have time to do that with Kayla's wedding?"

Rachel gave me a look that said I was nuts. "First, everything will get done in time for Kayla's wedding. And second, you've turned me down a bazillion times. I can't keep waiting for you to make up your mind. You'll never quit the law firm. They'd have to fire you first. I need to move in a new career direction."

It stung hearing Rachel fling my own arguments back at me.

"But do you really think it's a good idea, training with someone you just started seeing?" I pressed.

"Zach is very demanding to work with, not that you're asking for my advice." Tabitha smirked.

"Exactly. I didn't ask for advice. From *either* of you." Rachel tossed a hurt look in my direction and stormed off to the house.

Tabitha shifted the box to her other hip. "Sorry, that was uncalled for. It isn't any of my business."

"Is he really that bad?" Zach's slick good-boy looks and heavily laid-on charm rubbed me the wrong way, but Rachel seemed utterly taken with him. And he had been forthright about Sylvia's opinions on fracking on the property, even if he didn't agree with it.

"Just trying to save your sister from the inevitable realization that Zach is very ambitious. And intense. A little too into certain extracurricular hobbies." Tabitha peered into the empty box.

"What kind of extracurriculars? Nothing illegal, right?" My protective older sister antennae were triggered and alert.

"No, just that he likes to live fast, faster than this town. He likes to go to Vegas and to spend a lot of money. Then again, maybe that's right up your sister's alley."

I sighed. "Rachel is already planning a trip to Vegas with Zach. They're going together in September."

Tabitha's eyebrows shot up, and she blinked hard. "Oh. I probably shouldn't be mentioning this, but . . ." She stared off into the street, following Zach's zippy convertible as it crested the hill of downtown Port Quincy. "I think I saw Zach's car get repossessed yesterday. Although," she continued hastily, "maybe he was just getting it towed."

I frowned. "Are you sure? What makes you think he wasn't having car trouble?"

Tabitha bit her lip. "I'm not sure. I have a tendency to jump to conclusions when it comes to Zach. Forget I said anything."

Should I bring up Tabitha's hunch with Rachel? No, she was a big girl, and she'd never forgive me for gossiping about Zach with his ex.

We went into the house, and Tabitha selected small pieces of glass. She wrapped each one carefully in tissue paper and bubble wrap before placing it in the box and documenting it in a notebook.

"You're a little glum." She stopped her work and peered at me.

"I'm all right. I just screwed things up with Garrett. He asked me to dinner, and I hesitated. Then he pulled the offer off the table."

Tabitha snorted. "Figures. He's only dated a handful of women over the years. He's probably just rusty. Maybe you should ask him out instead."

"He didn't want to start anything because of Summer." I was still stung by what he'd said. "He's afraid to get involved and then have it not work out."

Tabitha sucked in her breath and set down a glass lighthouse. "He can't use that excuse forever. And Adrienne didn't break his heart that badly, although what she did was unforgivable. Besides, it was thirteen years ago."

"Adrienne? That's Summer's mom?"

"I wouldn't exactly call her Summer's mother, no," Tabitha said carefully. "She got pregnant right before Garrett went off to Boston for law school. She told him about the baby at Thanksgiving, and he transferred back here in January so he could marry her. Summer was born, Adrienne decided she didn't want to be a mom, and she ran off. To California, to be an actress."

"Poor Summer and Garrett. He hasn't dated anyone since?"

"Oh, he's dated. He's one of the more eligible bachelors in Port Quincy. But he's picky. He likes you, Mallory. I'm sure he'll reconsider if you ask him."

"I was supposed to get married this Saturday. Maybe now's not the time to be chasing after Garrett Davies."

Tabitha's gimlet eyes shone with mischief. "Revenge

might not be the best motive, but I'm sure it would really piss off Keith."

"Garrett mentioned Keith always got away with murder and how they were rivals, just like you said the other day."

"You have no idea." Tabitha considered a glass angel, then placed it back on the credenza. "Always trying to best each other. Garrett graduated valedictorian of Quincy College, and Keith salutatorian—"

"Wait, Keith always told me he was valedictorian." It would be just like him to slightly aggrandize his achievements, I now realized.

"No, it was Garrett. I remember. You have no idea how much Keith gloated when Garrett transferred to law school back home. He told anyone who'd listen that Garrett must've failed out. When, really, Garrett was stepping up for a baby he was having with a woman he didn't love. He would have married her, too, if she hadn't run off."

We fell into silence. I thought about almost marrying someone I didn't love.

"Talk to him, Mallory. Give him a chance. He's just out of practice."

"We'll see."

After Tabitha left, I returned to obsessing over Kayla's wedding extravaganza. I only had three days to pull it off. We'd spoken on the phone every day since I'd offered my reception to her. Over a series of brief conversations, I'd tried to coax out of her what she wanted for her big day.

"You know, country-casual." She was infuriatingly dreamy and non-specific.

"Super!" I replied each time, then pitched idea after idea, from hay bales to checkered tablecloths, to lanterns and pinecones and picnic fare.

"I trust you. Do whatever. I'm just so happy Travis and I are finally getting married, and at the country club!"

It was going to be damn near impossible to pull off "country-casual," whatever that meant, at the country club, with its old dark woodwork and tarnished brass. Not to mention pulling it all together with only three more days to spare. And that was including the day of the wedding. I leafed through the bridal magazines Keith had left on the lawn, scoured wedding websites, and rifled through the favors and decorations I'd amassed for my wedding. Unfortunately, my would-be reception hadn't been anything close to country-casual. The ostrich feathers, miniature crystal votive holders, and silver vases wouldn't transfer over to Kayla's wedding.

"Kayla doesn't really have the money to buy decorations, and neither do we," Rachel lamented.

"I know. But we have something better than money."

"What's that?" Rachel wrinkled her nose in distaste, as if I were speaking crazy-talk.

"We can go shopping right here, in this house." I gestured around me. "Think of all the stuff we've run across looking for the paintings."

So, for the next hour, Rachel and I and tore through the house, looking for props for Kayla's wedding. We came up with navy gingham tablecloths hidden in picnic baskets in a linen closet and intricate cotton lace doilies faded to a caramel brown.

Multiple laundry loads later, and they both were ready to be pressed into service again. The greenhouse yielded white trellises that needed a fresh coat of paint and copper lanterns, rusted to a soft mint green patina. The best find was a set of small glass candleholders, shaped like daisies, that threw off a soft yellow light.

"You can do this in your sleep," Rachel assured me when we returned to the kitchen hours later.

I contemplated my wedding dress in its garment bag. I'd left it hanging on the back of the kitchen door, mocking me in all its grand pouffiness.

"I know your wedding didn't go off, but what you planned was amazing. And you weren't even implementing your own vision, just Helene's. But it would've been something."

"I had a year to plan my wedding. I'm glad most of Kayla's family lives in Port Quincy and can come on such short notice. Now all I have to do is use this stuff to convert Helene's version of the perfect wedding into Kayla's, and do it in record time."

I went over the to-do list for Saturday. It was shorter than the one I'd had for my botched wedding, but there were still many tasks, now that I'd committed to my vision for Kayla's wedding. Rachel, Summer, and I were going to make flower arrangements from the abundant blooms in Sylvia's garden, with mason jars from the basement serving as vases. We would tie them with grosgrain ribbon scavenged from the sewing notions in the attic, in line with the bride's country-casual theme. Kayla's sister and mother were feverishly making cookie-cutter wedding favors and shopping for matching dresses for her three bridesmaids. Her aunts were baking up a storm to supply Kayla's cookie table with hundreds of confections, in keeping with Western Pennsylvania tradition. I was meeting with the chef at the country club tomorrow morning before the injunction hearing and work to beg him to tweak Helene's menu choices on extremely short notice. He remembered the compromises I'd brokered between Helene's wishes and what was technically possible, and was willing to help me out. Kayla still hadn't found a DJ, nor could she pay for one. And as of yesterday, she was still looking for a wedding dress that didn't need to be altered.

I squinted at the straining garment bag. "What do you think Kayla will wear?" An idea percolated in the back of my mind. Kayla was a little taller than me, and a few sizes up, but with flats and an added panel in the back, my gown just might work.

"No way. I see where you're going with this. Your dress would need major alterations, and you'll never find someone to do them by Saturday." Rachel held her nose as she poured out another mason jar of ancient preserves down the drain, preparing it to stand in as a vase.

I plucked a business card from the front of the refrigerator.

"It's worth a shot."

Ten minutes later, I drove to seamstress Bev Mitchell's house. She'd agreed to alter my dress as much as possible by Saturday morning, as well as give the trellises a fresh coat of paint, and Kayla had sounded tickled pink over the phone. Kayla agreed to meet me at Bev's house, and I hoped the dress would be to her liking, or at least fit. And with a flutter of guilt, I also hoped I could find out some info about Bev's son, Preston. Based on my conversation with Naomi Powell, I wanted to know whether he was capable of murdering Shane Hartley.

I parked the boat of a station wagon behind a rusty Cavalier and hefted the heavy garment bag from the backseat. In front of me was a neat ranch house with marigolds and begonias marching up the walkway in gold and red precision. A pale blue statue of the Virgin Mary stood in front of the house, her arms outstretched. Bird feeders, rife with robins and cardinals, hung from the maple trees edging the yard, and little solar lights shaped like butterflies lined the driveway. Three horses grazed in the distance, and odd, pill-shaped white structures dotted the landscape.

Bev flung the purple door open before I had a chance to knock. Kayla peered over her shoulder. Bev was as accessorized as her lawn, with jingly purple bead earrings, butterfly clips in her blond beehive, turquoise rhinestone-encrusted glasses, and a busy batik dress. She grabbed the heavy garment bag and bustled me inside.

"What a lovely gesture." She deposited me on an overstuffed plaid couch. She was enveloped in her signature cinnamon smell. "You just sit tight while I see what we can do with this dress." She set a small plate of snickerdoodles and a glass of milk on the coffee table, disappearing around the corner with Kayla, whose eyes were glued to the garment bag in anticipation.

The front door opened, and a teenager entered

and removed his baseball cap. He was much taller than his mother, as skinny as she was stout. But he was as cheerful as Bev, his eyes dark and winking.

"You must be Mallory. I'm Preston." He smiled broadly as he sat in the recliner across from me. "Real nice thing you're doing for Kayla."

I smiled politely as Preston leaned over and took a cookie, then inserted it in his mouth and ate it with one bite. I admired his teenage metabolism.

"The Port Quincy Country Club wouldn't refund my reception, and I didn't want my wedding to go to waste. Kayla's fiancé's deployment ended, and they want a wedding. I happened to have one to give her." My smile faltered, as I wondered how my next statement would sound. "You were at the protest, on Founder's Day." I tried to keep my prying light and conversational.

Preston chuckled. "My mom loves a good protest. She says it reminds her of the sixties."

"So I take it there's no love lost between you and Lonestar Energy."

"That would be correct." Preston gave me a wary look, suddenly more on edge. He ran his hands through his blond hair. "You're not thinking of letting them drill on your property, are you?"

"The very day I found out Sylvia Pierce left me her house and I moved in, Shane Hartley came to talk to me. I wasn't too endeared."

"I try to forget what he did to my mom and me." Preston sat up so fast the springs in his La-Z-Boy whined. He reached lightning-quick and grabbed a snickerdoodle. He popped it into his mouth whole. He then retreated to his chair, chewing with ferocity, his cheeks red.

"Preston, calm down." Bev fluttered as she rounded the corner, her earrings jingling. "That man is a sore spot in this house."

"Damn right," her son said through a mouthful of cookie. "Said his fracking was safe, and we wouldn't even notice our neighbors had a well on their land. It worked out okay for them. They got to retire. But their retention pond full of toxic goo leaked and ruined *our* land, nearly poisoned *our* dogs and horses, and trapped Mom here forever. He's made this land worthless. Thank God my dad isn't here to see all of this." Preston gestured out the large picture window to acres dotted with those strange white cylinders.

"What are those white things?" I squinted at the lozenges on the horizon. I didn't point out that Shane hadn't personally destroyed the Mitchell family's land and water. He was just Lonestar's representative. It was automatic lawyer-think, regarding the opposition as a company representative, not a private actor.

"They're water buffaloes." Bev hovered next to her son. "We had well water, but it's ruined now." She reached out and lightly touched her son's shoulder. But her eyes were filled with anger as well, and she was breathing in shallow little spurts.

So that's why she assured me the first time I met her that the zucchini from her casserole wasn't grown on this land.

"Who provides the water buffaloes?" I carefully studied the plate of cookies.

"Lonestar." Bev shook her head ruefully. "As a condition of the settlement."

"Which you never should have signed, Mom." Preston's voice was thick with regret. "Sorry, but you should've refused it and gotten out of here. You could've taken them to court, and then everyone would know what they did to us. Hartley promised he'd provide us with fresh water and dig a new well from a deeper aquifer. Every month they try to worm out of filling the water tanks, interpreting the settlement this way and that, always to their benefit. Mom has to call and call to get them to follow through with *their* settlement agreement."

"Where were you the evening of July eighth?" I tried to sound casual.

Preston laughed, his deep voice breaking to a higher register. "If I could have killed that jerk, I would have. I had a baseball game, and near a hundred people saw us. The team, Mom, and I went out for pie afterward at the Greasy Spoon, like we always do, then straight to bed. I'll take it as a compliment you think I killed Hartley." Preston actually smiled at the thought.

"Preston!" Bev chastised her son, anguish marring her usually cheerful face. Though I did recall she hadn't seemed too upset the day after Shane died. Quite the contrary.

"I guess I'll be going." I rose from the couch. I was completely mortified. Instead of helping Kayla, I'd obliquely accused Bev's son of murder. Then again, judging from his hostility toward Hartley and Lonestar Energy, and the fact he could have snuck out of this house while Bev slept, I wasn't so sure Preston Mitchell was innocent. He definitely had motive to kill Hartley. Even though he was technically not an adult yet.

"You will do no such thing, Mallory. Stay right here." Bev shot her son a nasty look.

"Sorry, Mom, and sorry, Miss Shepard. I need some air." Preston disappeared to the back of the house, and a door slammed shut.

"I shouldn't have questioned him." I recalled my promise to Truman Davies not to meddle.

"His bark is worse than his bite," Bev assured me. "He'd never hurt anyone, but he does detest Lonestar Energy, Shane Hartley in particular."

"I'm ready," a small voice said behind Bev.

We turned as Kayla tentatively entered the living room, and all thoughts of solving Shane's murder drifted away.

She looked resplendent.

For my wedding, I had insisted on a rather plain dress, a sheath of cream-colored silk. It was perfectly understated, well-matched for the courthouse wedding and small reception Keith and I originally planned. Helene had freaked out, reasoning that I needed a dress of stature to go with the reception that had ballooned to hundreds of guests. So I'd switched to a ball gown. But I'd balked at beads and sequins. The bodice of this dress was plain cream satin, with a full ivory tulle skirt, frothy and as stiff as meringue. It was gorgeous, although I'd felt like I was playing princess dress-up in it, not like it was my real wedding gown.

The dress had been waiting for Kayla all along. She looked beautiful and demure and regal but comfortable. She floated over to the full-length mirror in the corner of Bev's living room and burst into tears.

"If you don't like it, you don't have to wear it." I rushed over.

"Of course I want to wear it." Kayla began to bawl. "I'm just so happy!"

"There, there." Bev handed Kayla a box of tissues. "This is a good reaction to have. This dress was meant for you, honey. It just had to find you."

I grew misty-eyed. When I'd planned my wedding, I'd been mystified by the reality shows where women searched for the perfect gown, tearing up when they found a dress, proclaiming it "the one." I'd thought it was hyperbole, but Kayla was genuinely moved, and I was too.

"What about this?" Kayla felt behind her, where the zipper gaped open down her back.

Bev frowned, her glasses slipping down her narrow nose. "We'll have to convert it to a corset with a panel."

"That sounds complicated. Do you have enough time?" Kayla's luminance dimmed a degree.

Bev shoved her glasses back up. "It'll be tight, but this is worth it. I can skim a bit off the underskirt to make the panel. Oh, sweetheart, you'll be a beautiful bride."

I recalled Helene's similar words for me back at the wedding tasting, a few weeks and several lifetimes ago. But Bev meant it. And it was true. Kayla was radiant.

We fussed over her and discussed the flat shoes she'd wear to keep the hem low and debated whether the veil her mother had worn in her wedding a quarter century ago would match the dress. I'd gathered my things to slip out and grabbed a cookie for the road when Kayla spoke up.

"Mallory, you were talking about Shane Hartley earlier, when, um, Preston got so annoyed."

"I regret it." I glanced at Bev. "I didn't know it was

such a sore subject." My cheeks heated. I'd known it was a touchy subject and hoped to get some information out of Bev and her son. I should've kept my bumbling efforts at investigating separate from planning Kayla's big day. Truman would be furious if he knew I'd poked around.

"The Hartleys' marriage wasn't the strongest." Kayla was barely audible.

"Why do you say that?" I sat back down.

"Deanna was unhappy. She and Shane were trying to have a baby, but it wasn't working out."

Bev made a dismissive sound, then removed the pins she'd been holding between her lips. "It looks like it worked out. That woman is about to pop any day now."

"Who told you this?" I dropped a cookie to the floor. A basset hound appeared out of nowhere and wolfed it down in one bite, much like its master, Preston.

"I'm a waitress at the Amarillo Steakhouse on weekends, but during the week, I'm the receptionist at the fertility clinic." Kayla concentrated on picking apart the frayed edge of a purple pillow. She looked up warily. "You can't tell anyone this came from me. Do you pinky swear?"

Bev, looking amused, crooked her little finger around one of Kayla's, as I did the other.

"The Hartleys were patients. Mr. Hartley was shooting blanks."

"Then whose baby is she carrying?"

Kayla shrugged, seemingly nervous to have all of our eyes boring into her. "Mrs. Hartley had been having tests done with us, and it all came back clear.

She couldn't convince Shane to come in and get tested. Some men can't face the music that it might not be their wife's issues keeping them from having children. But he finally came in and gave a sample. That very afternoon, Deanna called back to say they didn't need our services anymore because she was pregnant. We tried to call Mr. Hartley to tell him his results. He never called back."

"Wow." Bev's eyes lit up at this tasty morsel of gossip. "No one would've guessed that."

Kayla frowned at Bev, her face already dulled with regret. "That's confidential, Mrs. Mitchell. The doctor treating them knows, and I do too because I had to open his chart to get his phone number. But no one else. I probably shouldn't have read the chart, or said anything." Kayla looked miserable, no longer glowing and ethereal.

"Of course, sweetie." Bev patted Kayla's arm but looked hungrily at her cell phone on the coffee table. I wondered how long it would be before Bev spread the gossip of Deanna Harley's baby's questionable paternity.

Preston came in just then with a second basset hound.

"I apologize for mentioning Sh—um, you know who." I said this to Preston, who looked as hangdog as his pet.

"And I apologize for going off. I need to settle down. He's dead. It's time to move on." Bev's son offered me a shy smile as I left Bev and Kayla in a cloud of tulle and satin.

* * *

After I pulled away from the Mitchells' house, I found myself drawn to the Davies residence. At least I thought it was their house, if our backyards were connected. I idled outside for a minute and tried to muster enough courage to ask Garrett to dinner. Then I pictured Summer, Truman, and Garrett's mother listening in and lost my nerve.

I wasn't ready to join Rachel at home, so I drove around the outskirts of Port Quincy, wondering for the billionth time who'd killed Shane. Preston Mitchell definitely had a temper. But could he really have killed the gas executive? Maybe, if provoked. And only if he'd known Shane was going to be at Thistle Park. I could check his baseball team's schedule and the Greasy Spoon diner, as long as Truman didn't find out I was snooping around again.

Like a magnet, I was drawn to the housing development where Keith had wanted us to live. I parked in front of the plot of land Helene bought for our wedding gift. She must have sold it, since builders had already broken ground. A giant foundation rose out of the sparse grass lot. I was looking for a sense of closure but felt none. I turned around in a nearby cul-de-sac. One of the houses had a pile of teddy bears, deflated Mylar balloons, and poster-board signs on its porch.

RIP Shane, read one of them.

Deanna Hartley. I pulled into the driveway and blinked back the thought of Chief Truman ordering me to mind my own beeswax. The large house looked impassive and cold. A FOR SALE sign hung in the front, emblazoned with Zach's name. The yard was a bit unkempt, but other than that and the makeshift porch memorial, you wouldn't know tragedy had befallen the woman who lived inside. I cursed my nosiness and rang the bell. The same doggedness that made me a good attorney would earn me no favors with Chief Truman if he found out I'd been here.

"Can I help you?" Deanna answered the door in jeans and a striped red and white T-shirt, which seemed to make her bump appear even bigger. She had a towel around her head, and wet strands of dark hair escaped to curl around her face. Her doll-like eyes blinked at me against the late afternoon sun. She didn't seem to recognize me.

"I'm Mallory Shepard."

Deanna gave her head a brisk rub with the towel. With one deft movement, she gathered her heavy hair, twisted it into her trademark bun and pinned it at the base of her head. She looked at me expectantly.

"I live on Sycamore Street. I inherited Sylvia Pierce's house."

"You were there when Shane was killed." She motioned me in.

I followed her into what was probably the living room. It was hard to tell since every surface, the couch included, was piled with boxes.

"It must be hard to move so close to your due date, especially when it's so hot."

She moved to clear some space for me to sit.

"Hey, I'll get that." I eased a heavy-looking box out of her arms and settled it on the floor.

She'd looked so young at Founder's Day. Up close, she was about my age, with the start of crow's-feet etched along her eyes.

"Thanks." She sat with an oomph. "Actually, this heat isn't bad. Y'all are softies. Port Quincy's got nothing on a Houston summer. I'd offer you something, but most of the glasses are packed away."

"How soon until you move?"

She looked at her swollen belly. "As soon as he's ready to come out." She placed her hand protectively over her stomach. Her giant wedding band was gone. "My due date is tomorrow"—she gave a content smile—"but everyone says first-time moms are late. I'll head back to Texas a few weeks after he's born." Her smile waned. *Cut the chitchat, lady*, her glance seemed to say. *What do you want, other than to be a ghoul and relive the moment my husband was killed outside your window?*

"I have some questions."

"About Shane?"

"About who killed him."

Deanna's mouth twisted into an approximation of a grim smile. "I should be asking you that since you were there when it happened."

"But I didn't hear anything, honest."

She looked at me for a second, then nodded. "I believe you." She tried to make herself comfortable on the small patch of couch not holding any boxes, but gave up. "A lot of people in this town have welcomed Lonestar Energy. We've brought good jobs. But some folks—"

"Like Naomi Powell."

"Yes, like Ms. Powell, made unnecessary trouble for my late husband. And others took matters into their own hands, people who weren't happy with their settlements. Shane got plenty of threats, and they egged this house. But like I told the police, I don't really have a clue who murdered him." She stated this wearily, as if resigned to the fact her husband's killer would never be found.

I swallowed to prepare for the next question.

"Who's the father of your baby?"

I'd never seen a pregnant woman move so fast. She jumped up and jammed a manicured finger in my face, her whole body shaking. "Show yourself out."

"So it's not Shane's." I held my ground, although I was quivering inside. "Okay. Maybe the real father killed your late husband?"

"Don't you dare—" Deanna began, then seemed to think better of it. She narrowed her eyes and changed tactics. "What do you want from me?" She was one cool cucumber; I'd give her that.

"I'm not blackmailing you. I just want to know who bashed in your husband's skull and left him to die on my front lawn and, better yet, why."

Deanna's shoulders gave a barely perceptible shudder at my description of what had happened to her husband. She switched topics back to what was really bothering her. "Who told you about my baby?"

I paused for a minute, not wanting to expose Kayla. This woman made me nervous.

Deanna guessed anyway. "The fertility clinic. I was worried about that. Thank God Shane was a chauvinistic pig, and as soon as we found out I was pregnant, he wanted nothing to do with them. He would never consider that something might be wrong with his plumbing, not mine." Deanna spat out this last bit, unknowingly echoing Kayla. Her eyes narrowed and she looked off in the distance.

Whoa.

My next observation drew a long pause from

Deanna. "You don't sound too unhappy about your husband being dead." In fact, she sounded like she had as many grudges against him as everyone else.

"I didn't kill him, if that's where you're going. We had our problems, but I'd never murder my husband." She sniffed delicately, restored to her prim persona.

I'd gotten more information from her with blunt statements. "You wouldn't kill him, but you would cheat on him."

Deanna walked to the French doors overlooking the backyard and rested her hands on the small of her back. The low angle of the sun illuminated her profile. Her shoulders were tense, and a cord twanged in her neck. She turned back to me with tears quivering at the ends of her thick Kewpie lashes. "We tried for seven years. It took all that time for Shane to even consider testing. Do you know how much stress that can put on a marriage, all the charts and waking up to take your temperature? Especially when you have to carry it yourself, because your husband refuses to get any diagnostic tests? Not to mention I hate it here in Port Quincy. Shane was just a wildcatter when I met him. He wasn't very good at the gas business. I was a geologist, and I taught him everything. I never really agreed to leave Texas, where I had family and a job I loved. So I got a little comfort somewhere else. You can judge me all you like, but I'm not the only person in this town with skeletons in her closet."

Her little speech resonated too well. I wasn't here by choice, either. And if I'd stayed with Keith, we'd be settling in two streets over. I tamped down that thought and focused on the task at hand.

"Who is the father?"

"Does it matter?" Her tears ceased. She flicked the last ones away and rubbed at her mascara.

"You know it does."

She sighed. "He's in a loveless marriage, same as I was. We were going to divorce our spouses and be together." She said the last part with a bit of wistfulness.

"He *was* going to divorce? Is your boyfriend abandoning your plan and staying in his marriage?"

Bull's-eye.

"I don't think it's any of your business." She bristled, her expression huffy and panicked at the same time.

I smirked. "That's rich. You conducted an affair. I don't think your boyfriend's wife would see it that way."

I regretted it as soon as I'd said it. I flinched at the cattiness in my voice. This truly wasn't my business, and I was probably taking out my own anger toward Keith on this woman. She might not have had a good marriage, but she'd still lost her husband in a violent murder.

"I'm no home-wrecker. His marriage has been over for years. Decades, even."

Interesting. That would make her lothario quite a bit older, if his marriage had truly been over for decades as she claimed. Something zipped across my brain. A wood-paneled PT Cruiser, the one that picked her up at the hospital.

"He's just waiting for the right time to break it to her. She'll be devastated, and he wants to soften the blow." Deanna sounded like she was trying to convince herself.

"There's never a right time." I thought of the glossy stack of lurid photographs Sylvia had sent me anonymously, then switched subjects. "Tell me about the night Shane was shot."

Deanna sighed. "Shane left after dinner to go back to the office, to look over the new offer letter the attorneys had drawn up for you. My boyfriend came over, but only for a little while, because we knew Shane would be back soon. He'd only been here once before. We couldn't go to the place where we usually met, because . . . well, anyway. He left here around ten."

Rachel and I had been asleep by then. "Couldn't your boyfriend have left here, then killed your husband?"

"No! He had no reason to. He knew I was leaving Shane."

Yeah, right. Just like this mystery man promised to leave his wife.

"Why couldn't you go to the place where you usually met? Why didn't your boyfriend just pick you up later, after Shane came back and went to sleep?" Another thought skittered through my head. Two rosy marks appeared on Deanna's doll face, as red as if she'd drawn them on with paint. She looked at me, an odd mix of defiance and shame making her lips twitch.

"Oh my God, you used my attic."

Deanna turned mutely to look out the French doors again and answered in the affirmative with her silence.

"It was perfect." She finally turned around to face me. "There was a key in the third-floor door, and we took it with us. No one ever noticed us there.

We met at night when Shane was back in Houston for business."

"You didn't remove anything from the house, did you?"

Deanna gave me an indignant glare, and all of the contrition vanished from her face. "Of course not." She snapped ramrod straight, holding her belly beneath her. She seemed more insulted than when I'd accused her of adultery. "We're not thieves!"

"Did you happen to see any paintings?"

"Paintings? Of what?" She looked at me as if I were crazy.

"Never mind. I'll be going now. Sorry to bother you."

Deanna snorted.

"There *was* something odd." She rubbed the small of her back. "The last time we were there? There was a light on. In the carriage house."

"When was this?"

"About a week before Shane died." She wrinkled her pretty face in thought.

I stood to go, so I could get back to Thistle Park and begin exploring the carriage house, a shovel or knife in hand.

"Let's just call the cops," Rachel suggested when I proposed a trip to the carriage house. We hadn't been there since the day Garrett unearthed the station wagon.

"We'll just take a teensy little peek," I wheedled. "It's still light out, just barely. Besides, I'm sure there's not even a place to hide."

"But Deanna Hartley definitely saw something?

How do we know she's telling the truth? Wouldn't Garrett have noticed something when he was looking for a lawn mower?"

"Not necessarily. If we find evidence of someone having been there, we'll tell Truman."

We trekked deep into the backyard. Rachel held a dull serrated knife at her side, and I sported a rusty cast-iron skillet. When we reached the door to the carriage house, we stood solemnly before it. We were close to the creek, and dragonflies dive-bombed around us, gobbling mosquitoes and gnats, their iridescent wings translucent in the waning sunlight.

"You first." Rachel gestured grandly toward the door.

"Why me?" I took a step back, my pan at the ready. Although I wasn't sure how much good it would do as a weapon. That sucker was heavy. It would be hard to lift and strike someone.

Rachel sighed with impatience. "The heroine in the movie who goes looking for trouble is always the one who gets it in the end. I think we should call Chief Truman. But if you're dumb enough to make us go in there, you should go first."

I set the skillet on the newly mown grass. My sister had a point. "I promised him I'd stop snooping around, so I can't very well tell him I dropped in on Deanna Hartley and interrogated her at her house, now can I?" Truman would kill me.

"Then what are you waiting for? She probably just imagined the light anyway." Rachel shielded her eyes from the low angle of the sun.

"You're stronger." I retreated from the door.

"Don't play that card with me." Rachel reached for the handle, the key poised. The door swung open before she made contact, and we both screamed and ran back toward the house.

"Wait." A man raced after us, dragging his right leg behind him, his gait uneven but fast.

"Will?" I wheeled around and searched for the skillet I'd abandoned in the grass.

"I didn't mean to scare you." Will Prentiss finally reached us.

"Too late!" Rachel shrieked, her voice shrill and frantic.

I was breathing heavily and tried to put some space between us. "What were you doing in the carriage house?"

"Sylvia knew," he said defiantly. "She let me stay. Even offered to let me live in there." He motioned to the house with a jerk of his arm. "But I'm doing just fine in the carriage house. Made myself a little space in the loft." So that was why Garrett hadn't noticed him.

"Too bad Sylvia's not around for us to confirm." Rachel's hand clenched around the knife, ready to spring.

"How long have you been in there?" I tried to calm down, or at least keep from hyperventilating.

All of the air deflated out of him. He seemed to think we weren't going to flip out.

"Off 'n' on. I lost my house after my accident. My mom went to live with my sister. She sleeps on the couch. But it's too crowded there. My sister has her husband and four kids. I got tired of sleeping on the floor, and I lived in my truck all of June, till it got repossessed. I just moved in here the week before Sylvia passed."

No wonder he'd gotten here so quickly the day I'd

called about changing the locks. He hadn't driven over, just walked up the street with a toolbox. He must have left the carriage house, cut through the woods, and emerged out on the street.

"I asked Sylvia and everything, I swear. Like I said, she offered to let me stay in the house, but I just made do out here."

For some reason, I believed him. *Almost.*

"Were you here the night Shane Hartley died?"

"No, ma'am."

Argh! What was with the ma'ams again?!

"That night I was out drinking, sorry to say, and I passed out on my friend's couch."

"Likely story." Rachel snorted.

Will lowered his eyes. "I'll be clearing out now. Sorry I scared you, but I didn't hurt Shane Hartley, even if you think I had a reason to." He didn't bother to collect his things, just shuffled off around the house toward downtown Port Quincy.

"*Now* can we call the cops?" Rachel flung her knife down in the grass in disgust.

"Sure." I sunk into the grass as well. "I have them on speed dial."

Chapter Thirteen

The police picked up Will Prentiss for questioning as he was on his way into town, minutes after I called. Soon after, Truman and Faith got to work inspecting the carriage house.

"Do you think he did it?" I wore a path in the grass, pacing back and forth between the broken angel statues and the back porch. I didn't want to believe Will had killed Hartley, but it wasn't looking good. "Ouch! These mosquitoes are eating me alive." I slapped my leg, rubbing the welt that prickled up.

Faith looked grim. "I can't say whether Will killed Shane or not. It doesn't look good that he's been hiding back here. We're holding him downtown as long as we can."

"He had access to the house." Rachel's eyes narrowed into flinty lines. I hoped she never became a judge; the defendants wouldn't have a chance.

"Let's not be hasty." I squinted in the failing light. Technicians were busy inside the carriage house with Maglites, inspecting every rusty tool, looking for signs that one of them had been used to kill Shane Hartley.

"Sylvia trusted him, after all. Although . . ."

"Although what?" Truman zeroed in on me, one eyebrow cocked. "Spit it out, Mallory."

"Um, I know he's suing Lonestar. The suit, especially the depositions, seems extra contentious." Lonestar's counsel had made Will's mother cry during her deposition, with a particularly callous line of questions. The Lonestar attorney was one of Russell Carey's fiercest, designed to break the will of those testifying.

"And why would you be privy to that information?" Truman's nostrils flared.

Busted. "I happened to see the depositions at work."

"You happened to. What kind of law do you practice again?" His voice was so low I had to strain to hear it. I'd rather hear him shout than this.

I twisted my small citrine pendant and addressed my feet. "Commercial litigation. Mostly mortgage class actions. A little bit of pharmaceutical defense, some insurance work."

"So why would you be looking at documents that involve energy cases? I thought we had a talk about not playing girl detective. Don't you dare jeopardize my investigation by snooping around where you shouldn't be." By now, the sun had officially set, and Truman flicked on his flashlight. His face shined in its glow, and his expression suddenly softened. "I'd be careful if I were you. Your firm must consider Lonestar to be an important client. They weren't really on your side when they called me to ascertain whether you were a suspect. They're not looking out for you, Mallory." Truman strode off to his squad car after this sobering reminder, not even bothering to say good-bye. I let out a shaky breath I hadn't known I was holding.

"We got this. Trust me." Faith gave me a beseeching look I could barely read in the dim light from the back porch. "It isn't worth prying at work. Let us do our job. And don't do anything to jeopardize yours."

I gulped and looked at my feet. I hadn't told Truman or Faith why Rachel and I had decided to inspect the carriage house. They didn't know about my impromptu questioning of Deanna Hartley, or her admission she and her beau were the ones using the third floor as a love nest. It was information they should definitely know, but I selfishly held it back to avoid falling out of Truman's good graces.

"We'd feel better if it seemed like you had any leads," Rachel mumbled.

Faith made a dismissive noise and stalked off after Truman. Rachel and I went inside to iron linens and wash out more mason jars for Kayla's reception, before we settled into an uncomfortable sleep. The next day dawned far too soon.

I parked the station wagon in front of Garrett's office building and climbed the stairs as I had almost three weeks ago. So much had changed since then, it seemed like a lifetime. At least I had worn matching heels today, so navigating the three flights was relatively easy.

"He's waiting for you, honey." Garrett's secretary grinned, her aubergine locks gleaming under the fluorescents. "Good luck."

I smiled weakly. I was dressed conservatively, in a gray skirt suit, the kind I wore to represent a client in court. I'd tried to tame my hair, but renegade strands kept unraveling from my bun and slowly reverting to curls. I tucked one behind my ear and gave Garrett's door a soft knock.

"Come in." His smile was pleasant, but his tone was all business. "Ready?"

"I think so." After Truman and Faith had left last night, there had been a missed call from him, which I'd returned with my heart in my throat. But it hadn't been a personal call. He'd wanted to go over what would happen at the hearing. Dinner hadn't come up, and he'd gotten off the phone amiably but professionally, closing the door on personal chitchat. Garrett had warned me that the hearing would be more involved than the preliminary opening salvos in court I'd handled for clients, because the judge would be handing down a ruling that day.

"I want to talk about what happened in my kitchen the other night." I picked at a piece of thread hanging from the button of my suit. "About dinner. I made a mistake."

Garrett stared at me like a trapped deer and cleared his throat. "No, you didn't. It isn't a good time for us to start anything. I have a daughter who could get hurt, and you just broke off your engagement."

My shoulders slumped, and he must have seen me trying to choke down my pride, because his face softened. "I just don't want to complicate things."

He doesn't want to go out with you. Just quit it already.

I glanced at the clock over his desk. "We'd better go."

The walk over to the Port Quincy Courthouse was tense. Tense because I'd basically asked Garrett out, and he'd said no, and tense because I'd never been one of the parties in a lawsuit. I had represented clients in court many times, and I'd felt nervous for them, anxious to secure a favorable decision, but I'd never had a personal outcome staked on a case.

As we crossed the street, a Lexus slowed and Zach leaned out the window to wave. Tabitha must have been wrong. His car hadn't been repossessed. She'd probably just seen it being towed. I was glad I hadn't brought it up to Rachel and given her more ammunition against Tabitha.

Garrett and I shuffled through a metal detector and up the stairs of the ornate courthouse. It was cloaked in Pepto-pink marble. A central atrium displayed four floors beneath a vaulted stained-glass ceiling. "This place looks like the Bellagio, if the Pink Panther had designed it." I craned my neck to take it all in.

Garrett laughed. "Port Quincy was important once, back when the glass factory was running twenty-four hours a day."

We reached the courtroom, and he surprised me by grabbing my hand and giving it a squeeze. His warm touch sent electric pulses up my arm. "Are you ready?"

"As ready as I'll ever be." My quavering voice betrayed my nervousness. I'd finally reached a point in my legal career when court didn't make my heart beat fast, but that had all gone out the window today.

The heavy double doors grated as we entered. Keith and Helene turned in unison to scan the room. Helene eyed me as I made my way down the middle aisle in front of Garrett, contempt visible on her sour face. She stared me down as if I were an orange jumpsuit-clad perp, handcuffed and ashamed. I stared back at her and made her stiffen when I dared to offer her a triumphant smile. I wasn't entirely confident, but she didn't need to know that.

Keith gave me a curt little nod, the beginnings of a new beard scruffing his chin. I stared back at him, my smile dissipating, wanting to give him nothing. I didn't miss the look Keith gave Garrett. It was one of deep, abiding hatred that had been marinating for some thirty years. Garrett gave Keith a smirk. A shiver raced down my back, my fake poise evaporating in a puff of anxiety.

Ever the gentleman, Garrett pulled out my chair for me and began taking out papers and files.

"All rise," called the court crier as he announced the Honorable Judge Ursula Frank.

Judge Frank swished into the room, and I was treated to a view of her worn Birkenstocks just below the hem of her robe. She hit her gavel and said crisply, "Be seated." She wore gray braids laced around her head like a crown, no makeup and an imperious expression.

Helene and Keith's attorney went first. He was a wizened man, with genteel movements, a suit that was a little too big, and a high, nasal voice. "Your Honor, we have evidence that Mallory Shepard is in possession of three priceless works of art and is making no effort to safeguard these national treasures." He paused for a beat and turned to me, as if he were about to address me directly.

"So?" Judge Frank's voice was bored. "Why should I care? It is her property, isn't it? She can light those paintings on fire and charge people to see it, if she wants. Make it performance art."

I bit my lip to hold back a smile. Helene sniffed, loudly enough for it to echo through the high-ceilinged courtroom.

"Your Honor, Sylvia Pierce was nearly one hundred when she made the hasty and misguided decision to deed her ancestral home to Miss Shepard—"

"This isn't a hearing to determine the mental state of Sylvia Pierce. Try to focus on the topic at hand, which, if I may remind you, is an emergency injunction to avoid irreparable destruction to three 'priceless' paintings. That is, if they actually exist." The judge made air-quotation marks as she said the word priceless and was now studying her green plastic watch.

The attorney cleared his throat and pressed on. "Sylvia Pierce was showing signs of a failing mind, Your Honor. She was not aware of how valuable many of the items in the house were, items that might be hidden. She changed her will seven days before she passed and created a transfer of deed to someone who isn't a member of the family."

My heart stung at his words. I was more of a family to Sylvia than those two ingrates.

"Like I said, so what?" The judge seemed uninterested. She plucked some lint from her robe. "You'll have to do better than that to convince me Sylvia Pierce was losing it. She was as sharp as a tack, and she could deed her house to Mickey Mouse if she wanted to."

Helene stiffened and clutched at her purse, before sending me a dour look.

"And, may I remind you, we are here about an

injunction. If you don't return to the matter at hand, I'll throw you out of this courtroom." She sat up, uninterested no more, and glared at the attorney.

"Yes, Your Honor." The wind let out of his sails. "But my client feels there are bigger issues at stake. Issues of national and historical importance. The paintings, you see, are a John Singer Sargent, a Pierre-Auguste Renoir, and a Camille Pissarro." He leaned back on his heels, flushed and peevish. All was quiet in the courtroom.

Well, at least I know what the paintings supposedly are.

His admission confirmed the tentative list Tabitha and I had pieced together.

If they didn't go up in smoke eighty years ago.

"Fascinating." The judge peered down from her perch. Her tipstaff twitched and readied for something. "What's fascinating is that you dare to come into my courtroom on a fishing expedition. I do *not* have time for this!"

Garrett pinched my arm under the table. "Ow," I cried out, drawing all eyes to me. My exclamation seemed to snap Judge Frank out of her rage.

"You are trying to get this woman"—Judge Frank jabbed her finger at me—"to admit whether or not she's found the paintings. Number one, that's none of your business. Number two, there's as much of a chance of those paintings existing as there is that I'm the tooth fairy. It's just a ridiculous legend."

Oh, my God. This wasn't about stopping me from harming priceless paintings; it was about getting me on the record to admit whether I'd found them or not.

"Your Honor." Helene's attorney cleared his throat and loosened his tie. "If I may respond—"

"You may not. Your clients are furious Sylvia Pierce outfoxed them. This is a joke." She picked up the papers that must have been the injunction, then tossed them in front of her.

"Objection!" It wasn't the attorney who said this, but Helene. She jammed her skinny hand onto the table and turned around to face me.

"Control your client, counselor, or I'll throw her out."

The little old man patted Helene's arm ineffectually, and it was Keith who pushed his mother's shoulder, sinking her into her seat.

"I've heard enough. Your petition for an injunction is denied, with prejudice. All bills assigned to the petitioner." She stood up, banged her gavel, and whooshed out of the courtroom, her clerks jogging to catch up with her. Before she left, I swear she gave Garrett a barely noticeable nod, her eyes alight with laughter.

Helene stormed out of the courtroom, her kitten heels tapping the tiles with such force I expected to see little sparks with each footstep. At the last second, she wheeled around and stared at me, then began to advance. I threw up my arm, the one newly out of its sling, and let out a squawk.

"Mother." Keith shook his head in warning. Helene turned and exited the courtroom. Keith gathered Helene's purse and shuffled after her. Their dejected attorney packed up his briefcase and followed him out.

Garrett and I were alone.

"We did it, and we didn't even say anything!" I marveled at how it had all gone down.

Garrett turned with an irrepressible grin.

"Do you know the judge?" I recalled her slight nod of acknowledgment.

"I'm in her courtroom all the time. And I booked her trial advocacy class back in law school at Pitt." He took a deep breath. "About dinner . . . I made a mistake. I'd like to ask you out again."

I smiled; this time, I was ready. "The pleasure would be mine."

"I wish I'd been there to see the look on Helene's face." Olivia speared the fries adorning her salad. We Pittsburghers never passed up an opportunity to top off our food with a healthy handful of fries, be it salad or sandwich. We were in my office, reliving yesterday's denial of the injunction.

"It was priceless." I leaned back in my chair and stretched like a cat in the sunshine, happy to have something finally go my way.

"Garrett didn't even need to say anything. Judge Frank read Helene and Keith's motives from a mile away. If I had testified, I would've admitted we haven't found anything, and that's all they wanted to know."

Garrett and I had gone our separate ways outside the courthouse. I'd floated to my car, floated home, and floated to work today through the tunnel and over the bridge.

A knock interrupted us, and a young woman opened the door, a timid look on her face. "Miss Shepard? Can you come with me?" She might have been a summer associate.

I stared at my half-finished lunch. "Sure. May I ask what this is about?"

"We're eating lunch." Olivia dismissed her a bit rudely. "I'm sure it can wait."

"The managing partner wants to see you." It clicked in my brain. The woman was from human resources.

I exchanged a frightened look with Olivia and stood to follow the woman on shaky knees.

She led me to the bank of elevators. My heart was pounding in my ears. At Russell Carey, it might be better to get a summons from the grim reaper than someone from HR. The elevator doors pinged open with a peal of finality, and I followed the woman in. I was nearly crushed by the weight of her silence.

I stepped out into a gleaming black marble reception area.

"This way." She walked quickly through the halls. I had to move fast to keep up.

My calves balled up with tension. We reached a closed door.

"Here we are. Just make yourself comfortable."

Fat chance.

She deposited me in the doorway and scurried away down the corridor, not meeting my eyes as she left.

I swallowed the bile at the back of my throat. I was in a small conference room, with a bank of floor-to-ceiling windows overlooking the Allegheny River. The walls were covered with framed lithographs and charcoal drawings, depicting gruesome scenes of swirling water sweeping away screaming people. There were rivers of fire, with wood and bodies poking out amidst fire and destruction.

I was in the Johnstown Flood room. I'd heard all the Russell Carey lore: this was the room where people's careers ended. I stared at the macabre artwork, transfixed. My heart was beating so fast and hard I could see my chest rise and fall. I settled myself into a leather chair and tried to calm down.

"Mallory Shepard." Gordon Nagel strode into the room.

I jumped in my chair, the muscles in my neck nearly twanging. He sat across from me and folded his hands, his countenance thoughtful and practiced.

Gordon was the managing partner of Russell Carey. A friendly-looking, portly man in a gray suit, with gray at his temples and in his complexion. He carried himself like a benevolent administrator, but it was a bad sign to have an unannounced meeting with him. I was certain that before today, he couldn't even have picked me out of a lineup of hundreds of associates.

"I hate doing this. It's never pleasant."

Tears had already begun to prickle in my eyes.

"The time has come to let you go, for reasons that are known to you." He began to enumerate, in a calm voice, the fact that my work had been slipping, even before the personal problems of my broken engagement. "What it comes down to is this. Your work was found to be lacking."

"That's not true!" I nearly rose out of my seat. "Ask the partners I work for about my work! I've always gotten fantastic reviews, and I've billed nearly two hundred hours this month, despite my 'personal problems.'" My jaw dropped open when I realized why this was happening. "Helene Pierce is behind this, isn't she? What a client wants, a client gets, and she wants me out." I was hyperventilating, but I caught Gordon's quick swallow, a brief lapse from his litigator's poker face.

He motioned me to stop. "You'll get three months' severance. Your name will remain on our website, to help you as you look for another position." He studied the lithograph above my head, not deigning to look at me. "You have an hour to collect your things. If you're not off the premises by noon, security will escort you out."

I gripped the table in disbelief.

"I'll distribute my client matters," I whispered.

"Oh, don't worry," Gordon said patronizingly. "We'll take care of that."

He personally accompanied me to my office, where they were indeed collecting my work, the files and folders stacked high on a cart. A documents team glanced at me sheepishly as they wheeled the cart out of my office, KGB style.

I tried to log on to my computer. I'd been frozen out.

"Oh, my God." I moved toward the door, as if to run out, then thought better of it.

The document team had left a large box for me, and I slowly filled it with my things: my framed degrees, books and plants and a picture of me, my mother, Doug, and Rachel from the day I graduated law school, beaming and assured of my fabulous legal career to be. I even found a picture of Keith hidden in a drawer. I threw this last item into the trash. It made a hollow *clunk* as it became garbage, much like my job prospects. My secretary bawled and Olivia swore as they both helped scrub any vestige of myself from the office.

It was just before noon when I got in the elevator and turned in my security badge at the front desk. I marched out of the building, and I didn't spare a backward glance at the place that had monopolized almost every waking hour of my days for the past six years. I dumped the contents of my professional life in the backseat of the Volvo and drove like a zombie until I reached the tunnels. I tossed a glance over my left shoulder just in time to see the city skyline, a jumble of variegated glass, chrome, and cement stalagmites rising up out of a seam in three rivers. I disappeared through the tunnel and out the other side of the mountain, effectively closing one chapter of my life.

Chapter Fourteen

Call me anal retentive, but I like nothing more than trying to solve life's problems with a good spreadsheet. The problem was, no matter how much I fiddled with the figures from my bank account, the house-related expenses, my student loans, and the cost of health insurance after my severance ran out, I couldn't make the math work. The spreadsheets of doom revealed a Hokusai wave of debt cresting ever closer, and no Excel manipulation could change the outcome. I'd be able to hang on through the three months of severance. After I raided my meager retirement, I'd be officially screwed. So, I pretended this wasn't my life and took a nap instead.

"Mallory!" Rachel ran over and fumbled for my wrist to take my pulse. It was still dark out.

"I'm fine." I'd woken up with a start in the middle of the night and come downstairs to tinker with my finances. I'd fallen asleep on my laptop keyboard at the dining room table. The spreadsheet was filled with row after row of keys I'd pressed in with my face. "Just trying to figure out how to avoid bankruptcy."

Today was D-Day. The day I was supposed to marry Keith. The day Kayla would be marrying Travis. I snapped the laptop shut and pushed my personal problems to the back of my mind. The sun hadn't even risen yet, but I had so much to do. I'd made it this far through this crazy month. I could handle one more day and make it a good one for Kayla.

An insane thought skittered through my brain. What if this was fate? What if I was destined to turn Thistle Park into a B and B and host weddings and events? The main thing holding me back had been my job. And I had an opportunity to pull off a lovely wedding for Kayla and Travis and show the town I could do it. There was just the small matter of money.

Forget it. I pushed the fantasy out of my mind. I didn't have the money to renovate, so I'd look for another job. I shook the thought out of my head and launched into the day.

Rachel followed me around the house for the next few hours before the sun rose as we tied up loose ends for Kayla's wedding. Maybe my sister was worried I'd fall apart since I'd been fired, but I was strangely numb. I barely registered this was to have been a day of celebration, a date for anniversaries and remembrances. I was now focused on giving Kayla the most spectacular wedding she could have dreamed up.

"Maybe this isn't the time for this." Rachel sat next to me when we took a break. We'd carried flower arrangements, favors, and programs back and forth from the porch to the station wagon. "You didn't like your job. You worked really hard at it, but your heart wasn't in it. To be honest, I thought after you and Keith got married, you'd quit."

"I think I became a lawyer to make Mom happy." I shrugged. "And I worked at Russell Carey to pay off my loans and to make partner. It doesn't matter now. I need to get a new job, and fast. This place is hemorrhaging money already, and we haven't even really done anything to fix it, just clean."

It was true. Yesterday I'd barely made it home, to be greeted by the sight of a plumber's truck in the driveway. Rachel and the plumber had been in the second-floor bathroom, where he had been fixing a busted pipe. The ceiling below had been dripping and stained with rust-colored water, bowing the creamy tin roof of the butler's pantry. I'd waited until he'd left to tell Rachel about getting fired. The plumber had asked, "You okay, lady?" as I wrote him out a check with hands so shaky it was hard for him to read the amount.

I turned back to my sister. "I hate to even think of it, but if Zach can't find a buyer who actually wants to live in this house, I might sell to a developer. Or a gas company."

Rachel sighed. "I know you want to carry out Sylvia's intentions, but it's not like you can ask her permission. You have to take care of yourself. Do what's best for you."

I was about to agree when the kernel of a crazy idea germinated in my tired brain.

"What if I did ask Sylvia?"

Rachel giggled. "Like hold a séance?"

"Sort of. Maybe I'll visit her grave. We ran out of the funeral, and I haven't been there yet."

Rachel shrugged. "It's worth a try. D'you want me to go with you?"

"I feel like I should do this alone. I'll go tomorrow. Let's set up at the country club."

Rachel gave my arm a squeeze. "If you hurry, we'll still have plenty of time to set up. Just make sure no one sees you talking to yourself at the cemetery. This whole town already thinks we're wacky enough."

I offered my sister a weak smile, gathered my keys, and went out the back door.

I wandered around the grounds of Thistle Park for a good ten minutes, gathering flowers for Sylvia's grave. We'd performed the same task yesterday after I was fired, to make the centerpieces for Kayla's reception. The flowers bloomed in wild bursts around the edges of the backyard. There were flowers native to this part of Pennsylvania and cultivated ones, long abandoned to fan out over the many years. I arranged all of the bounty in a loose bouquet: crown vetch, honeysuckle, tiger lilies, black-eyed Susans, waxy rhododendron leaves, and some thistles for good measure. My legs were scratched from wandering through the thickets of weeds, yet I didn't feel a thing.

This was to be my wedding day, and instead I was marching through Port Quincy with a gorgeous bouquet of flowers. For some reason, this made me laugh instead of cry. I cradled the bouquet, the big bunch of flowers resting in my achy left arm. This bouquet was closer to the one I'd wanted for my wedding—vibrant, fragrant, and wild.

"Roses look best," Helene had commanded imperiously. The florist had looked at me expectantly, prepared for a fight. I had shrugged and allowed

Helene to steam-roll me. I hadn't thought it was worth a spat, and by that time, pink and white roses would fit in better with the traditional, staid wedding I was executing for Helene. It was fitting that I now got my wish but was no longer marrying her son.

As I reached the church, I swear I heard *Lohengrin*'s march in my head. I shook the illusion out. Instead of turning into the building, I bypassed the entrance and unlatched the iron cemetery gate. The hinges creaked in protest and flaked brown rust. The air was damp and cloying, like a wet shirt, with heavy clouds above threatening to spill their contents.

I was glad Shane Hartley wasn't interred here and had been buried back in Texas. It was easy to find Sylvia's resting place in the empty cemetery, crowded with old-fashioned headstones and whole rows of families with the same name. Sylvia's grave stood out as the only one with a modern headstone.

The earth had settled a bit, yet still appeared newly turned. A few blades of tender grass poked up, but otherwise, Sylvia's grave was untouched. I sat before it and looked around to confirm I was alone.

"Hi, Sylvia," I awkwardly addressed her. "Um, thanks for leaving me Thistle Park. And for telling me the truth. About Keith." I placed the big bouquet from her beloved garden by her headstone and traced the letters of her name, freshly chiseled in a sleek black granite slab.

"I'm trying to do what you would have wanted me to do. Things are kind of in flux right now, and it'll be hard, but I'll make the right decision. Thanks for trusting me." I leaned back on my heels and closed my eyes. Bits and pieces of our last conversation floated back unbidden.

"You know, I married a damn fool," I recalled her saying, bright blue eyes twinkling. "But at least I followed my true heart. The first time. The second time, I married for propriety, and for money, and to save my father's company. And Helene married my son for his money, and you see how that turned out!" She'd burst out laughing, drawing in a labored breath from her oxygen mask. "But you'll be okay, sweetie. You can take care of yourself."

I'd looked at her like she was crazy for telling me this.

She'd pressed on. "It's never too late to listen to your intuition. To change one's mind and set off on a different path."

"I'll make you proud, Sylvia." I finally stood.

It began to rain, the drops cool and fat. The hot asphalt beyond the cemetery hissed as each bead of water hit and a Jurassic mist rose from the pavement. I laughed and peered at the sky above me. I'd take it as a good sign. Rain was good luck for a wedding day, and I wanted Kayla to have all the luck she could get.

The graves surrounding Sylvia's were older, more worn. I touched the one to her left, the limestone letters illegible from years of exposure and acid rain. To Sylvia's right was a taller marble headstone adorned with frilly scrolls and carvings, whimsical birds, and angels. This one read EVELYN ROSAMUND McGAVITT. Sylvia's mother. Evelyn's date of death was the same day Sylvia had run off.

I touched Sylvia's headstone one more time and shut the cemetery gate behind me with a clang. I started off down the hill, my heart lighter than it had been for weeks. I was sweaty and my legs were nicked from picking flowers in the backyard, but I felt purposeful and clear.

Things might be a complete mess, but I promised myself I'd do things my way.

I'm not alone. A little smile tugged at the corner of my lips. *I have my sister right here, and Mom and Doug are a plane ride away. And I have something I haven't had in a while, a place that feels like home. I'm right where I belong.* I turned onto Main Street and gained speed in my haste to get home, to set up the country club for Kayla, to give her a beautiful day.

Chapter Fifteen

It was a blessing in disguise that the Port Quincy Country Club hadn't let me out of my contract. I could have used the refund, what with my financial life imploding just like my personal life, but it was destiny for Kayla to get her wedding. Rachel and I arrived with a reprisal of her winning whiskey orange wedding cake and our mason jar centerpieces bursting with flowers gleaned from Thistle Park's gardens, miniature versions of the bouquet I'd brought to Sylvia's grave.

"We're cutting this awfully close." I set out Kayla's wedding favors of heart cookie cutters at each place setting, atop the navy gingham tablecloths we'd ironed earlier this week. Rachel was rearranging the flowers in the jars, carefully balancing the proportion of black-eyed Susans, daisies, lilacs, and day lilies with infuriating slowness. She reminded me of our mother, the decorator, as she stepped back to adjust one of the beribboned jars with a critical eye and pulled out a single daisy.

"That looks amazing." I gave her a quick hug. "Only *seven more* tables." I gave my watch an exaggerated glance. Thank goodness Kayla was having a more manageable hundred guests instead of my originally planned three hundred. The two of us bustled around, placing candles and pinecones, while waiters and waitresses set down bread plates and goblets. Rachel climbed a stepladder and hung white twinkle lights from each of the eaves, glancing at her watch and biting her lip in concentration. Kayla and Travis would be married on the deck, and her guests would move into this room for the reception. I had paid for the whole country club, and for Kayla I chose the smaller banquet room, more intimate than the main ballroom. The floor in this room was wooden rather than the ballroom's fusty floral carpet, and with the lights dimmed, we just might pull off Kayla's country-casual themed reception.

"It's beautiful!" Summer bounded into the room, her father in tow.

"Well done." Garrett turned around in a slow circle.

Both Summer and Garrett had dressed up, Summer in a purple dress, and her father in one of his suits, to help us out with Kayla's wedding.

"It's a little spare, but I think Kayla will be pleased. I'm so glad someone will get a happy day out of this." But something was missing. There were supposed to be bales of hay and the white trellises Bev had offered to repaint to hold more twinkling lights.

"Where's Bev?" Rachel must have realized at the same time that key props had yet to arrive. We had three hours until the wedding began.

"I don't know." My phone vibrated in my pocket. Bev's name showed up on the screen. "Hello? Oh no." Bev was panicking about her car. "We'll be right there."

Kayla called me on the way over to Bev's house.

"Do you happen to know where my dress is?" Kayla was trying to be polite, but I recognized the panic that set her voice on edge, making her mellow tones brittle and frenzied. She sounded close to tears.

"Bev is having some car trouble, sweetie. We'll be back very soon. We have plenty of time." I revved the station wagon harder as Rachel and I tried to make it to Bev's without speeding too much.

Rachel gasped as we pulled in front of Bev's ranch. Her gray Toyota had gotten a thorough beating. All four tires were slashed, and her front window was bashed in, the glass spiraling out in a messy spider-web pattern around a jagged hole. A note lay atop the broken glass on the front dash, the large font clearly visible: *Don't be nebby—stay out of the Hartleys' affairs.* Nebby means nosy in western Pennsylvania parlance, and the message was driven home by the damage done to the car.

"I'm so glad you're here." Bev gave us swift hugs. She was in a tizzy. She walked back and forth in front of the car and took short puffs of air while fussing with her jewelry. "Preston is fishing or I could use the truck to bring over the dress and the bales and trellis."

"Did you call the police?"

"Or your son?" I reached out and held Bev at arm's length to search her face and to calm her down.

"Not yet." Bev blushed scarlet, her tall, blond tower of hair shaking. "I'm embarrassed."

"Embarrassed about what? Some psychopath working over your car?"

"No, about the note. I told a few people about Shane Hartley's . . . condition."

I felt sick and dropped my arms. Bev's gossip about the paternity of Deanna's baby had made her a target. Why would paternity be such a big deal now? Shane was dead. Who would care so much? Unless it was linked to his death.

"I'm calling the police," I said firmly. "Then we'll load this stuff into the station wagon and get it over to the wedding."

"Where's the dress?" Rachel and I carried heavy bales of hay and the trellises to the back of the station wagon. My bum left arm screamed in protest, but I ignored it when I glanced at my watch and saw we didn't have a minute to spare.

"It's in the house," Bev said, giving us the first good news of the day. "Thank goodness it wasn't in the car." She wore a wobbly smile and looked up at the sky in silent thanks.

I gulped as I took in the slashed tires, her dented car and decimated windshield. I couldn't agree more.

Twenty minutes and three run traffic lights later, the hay bales were artfully placed around the banquet hall. The trellises were set up and adorned with more twinkling white lights. Kayla's aunts tended to the cookie table, piled high with delectable treats made by all of the women in her family, in keeping with western Pennsylvania tradition. Flaky lady locks stuffed with cream held court next to golden peanut butter blossoms and delicate, lacy pizzelle. The once-gloating country club manager was nowhere in sight, which suited me just fine.

Garrett placed his arm around me as I whispered to him what had happened. His gesture was not lost on Summer. She blinked once, then grabbed my hand.

"C'mon, Mallory. I want to show you my DJ setup." She pulled me over to a small table with an open laptop connected to speakers.

"Summer thought it would be a good idea to collaborate with my mom on some playlists. For the old people and slow dances, she said." Garrett followed us.

I laughed and relaxed and saw the room fully for the first time.

Tea lights flickered inside burnished copper lanterns salvaged from Thistle Park's greenhouse, throwing light and shadows on our flower arrangements. The country club's white linens had been replaced with crochet doilies pilfered from the many small tables in Sylvia's house, set atop navy gingham tablecloths salvaged from Thistle Park's musty linen closets, washed and ironed into service. The daisy votives twinkled a soft yellow around the base of Kayla's cake. A fresh post-rain breeze wafted in from the open doors overlooking the river. We'd arranged the trellis and lights right after we handed Kayla her dress, finishing our final adjustments as the first guests trailed in and made their way to the deck.

"Phew. This was way closer than I wanted it to be." I slumped against the wall as more guests entered the room, marveling at our handiwork. It was gorgeous and suited Kayla better than the typical wedding held at the country club.

"But you pulled it off." Rachel beamed. "This went from country club to country, and you did it in less than two weeks."

"*We* pulled it off," I corrected my sister.

Rachel's green eyes turned misty as she fished for some Kleenex in her bra.

Kayla made her grand entrance on the arm of her father and, with the dress completely altered, it didn't even look like mine. I let out a breath I hadn't known I was holding. The gown looked like it was designed for her. The corset Bev had painstakingly added nipped in Kayla's waist, and her mother's veil floated atop her hair. Curled blond strands softly spiraled out of her updo. Travis looked handsome in his dress blues, and he cried when his bride met him at the altar on the deck. A few guests brushed tears out of their eyes, including yours truly.

"Thirteen-year-olds make perfect wedding DJs, don't you think?" Rachel asked me after the ceremony. Summer played DJ with aplomb.

I had begged and pleaded with the cook, who'd remembered my epic battles with Helene and taken pity on me. He'd used the same main ingredients but tweaked the menu for Kayla. Guests dined on fried chicken and a carved peppercorn roast instead of the chicken piccata and prime rib that had been on my menu. And it looked like they were having a hell of a lot more fun than we would be having at my wedding. I sighed with relief, thinking of how close I'd gotten. Kayla's wedding was closer in spirit to what I had wanted, even though our styles were different.

What was to be a bloated pageant, predicated on Helene's whims, was now charming and sincere.

"You okay?" Rachel touched me lightly on the shoulder.

I grinned in response. "Never been better." It was true. The party was going in full swing, people were happy, and we'd finished in the nick of time.

After her first dance, Kayla ran over and enveloped me in a bone-crushing hug.

"Thank you," she whispered.

"That was amazing!" I was flushed and happy at the close of my would-be wedding day, something I hadn't imagined would be possible.

Rachel and I practically skipped into the hallway of Thistle Park. It was well past midnight, but I was more energized than I'd been in weeks.

I flopped down on the couch with a contented sigh.

"Now will you reconsider? Let's renovate this place as a B and B and hold weddings." Rachel looked hopeful as she plopped down next to me.

I thought carefully before I answered her. Could I trade cases and clients for color swatches and canapés? Dealing with bridezillas might be easier than dealing with petulant clients, partners, and in-house counsel. Maybe I could pull this off at Thistle Park. But just because I'd whipped together a wedding for Kayla didn't mean I knew what I was doing. I wasn't a businesswoman.

Still, I could picture small luncheons in the dining room. Brides posing on the grand front staircase, their trains cascading over the restored antique rugs. Warm-weather wedding ceremonies performed in the gazebo out back, sweetened by the smell of flowers in the manicured garden. Evenings topped off with dancing in the greenhouse. Candles winking and reflecting off new glass walls. Happy guests staying in Thistle Park, restored to its former glory, fed and sated with my sister's delectable baking and my cooking. Rachel gave me an encouraging smile, and I was sure she could see the wheels turning in my head.

Besides, I've already planned two weddings. Mine, or rather Helene's, and now Kayla's. And one of them went off without a hitch.

"I'd like to."

Rachel cut me off with a whoop of glee.

"It'll be a steep learning curve. We don't know how to run a business. And I'll need to get a loan to fix this place up. Let's see if it's even possible. If it is, I'm game."

"Anything's possible, Mallory." Her eyes were shining. "This is going to be an amazing business venture. I promise."

"Let's toast to it. I'll get us some lemonade." The wild energy I'd felt after the wedding was ebbing, and all I wanted now was a good night's sleep.

I padded down the hall to the kitchen and shucked my heels along the way. I hummed a bar of something Summer had played. The wood floors felt deliciously cool and smooth under my swollen feet, and the rain had broken the veil of humidity that had hung over Port Quincy. A glass of lemonade would be perfect.

I saw Whiskey first. The calico was sitting erect and still, standing vigil over something.

"What's up, mama cat?" I bent to scratch under her chin. I flicked on the light and began to whimper, then scream. There lay Will Prentiss, in a pool of blood, staring at the kitchen ceiling, all the light gone from his eyes.

Chapter Sixteen

"I had hoped I wouldn't be called back here." Truman held a hint of accusation in his gruff voice. "Especially in the middle of the night." He wasn't in uniform, and the casualness of his outfit of khakis, sneakers, and a T-shirt did nothing to diminish his authority. Garrett had rushed over as well, dressed similarly. They really were quite similar, except for the thirty-year difference in age and the big belly time had put on Truman.

"Dad, chill out." Garrett shot his father a peeved look.

There was no murder weapon, but Truman and Faith thought Will had been struck with a heavy object in the back of the head, just like Shane Hartley.

"He died no more than a few hours ago." Truman was subdued. He tented his hands together, then exhaled and began to crack his knuckles, one by one.

I wasn't comforted by how rattled he appeared.

Rachel shook beside me. "I don't know if we can stay here. If we had come back from the wedding early, that could have been us." She flicked her eyes in the direction of the kitchen, where the techs were finishing their pictures and getting ready to take Will's body to the morgue.

"There's no sign of forced entry."

"Will probably kept a key," I choked out, embarrassed by my stupidity. "When he changed all the locks for us, he could've kept a copy for himself." *Why didn't I think of that when we found him in the carriage house?*

"We didn't find a key on him." Faith looked weary and sleepy, her glowing milkmaid countenance gone, replaced by something more grim and gray.

"The killer probably took it." Rachel shivered even harder, though it was a balmy seventy degrees and quite stuffy inside.

"And the killer could be anyone," I added. "Lots of people knew we'd be away at Kayla's wedding."

"I'll arrange to have the locks changed again in the morning," Truman promised.

But what about until then? I pushed the thought out of my mind and tried to focus on the immediate present.

"What was on top of Will's body?" As the police had pulled me from the kitchen, I'd noticed something white resting on Will's chest.

"Another note." Faith looked uneasy.

"And?"

She scrolled through one of the tech's digital cameras until she found a shot of the paper.

"'Find the paintings now or you'll go the way Sylvia did,'" Rachel read aloud as she leaned over.

"I knew it." I balled up my fists. "Sylvia did *not* die in her sleep."

We were all quiet for a moment.

"Right?" I demanded of Truman.

"We weren't called in." He shook his head and his jowls bounced in his tired face. "She was nearly a hundred. It wasn't negligent to presume she died in her sleep. We'll have to reinvestigate and hopefully not exhume her body."

I pictured Sylvia's neat grave and the young shoots of grass poking through. No, I didn't want that.

"Just because she was ninety-nine doesn't mean she wasn't murdered. I know she was. I can *feel* it, Truman. Are you any closer to finding Shane Hartley's killer?" My fingernails dug into my palms, and I fought to keep my voice even, with no hint of accusation.

"Or the person who wrote the note in fake blood in the dining room?" Rachel folded her arms. We had tried to scrub the ketchup off the wallpaper, but it had indelibly stained the old roses and vines pattern, leaving a ghostly pink trace of the message behind.

"Or whoever worked over Bev's car?" I sagged down in a breakfast room chair, eyeing the spot where Will's body had been through the doorway to the kitchen.

"We can't tell you—" Faith began her familiar spiel.

"Yeah. Yeah. You can't tell us about the investigation. But there has to be a reason for all of this, and you're the experts. Shane Hartley was murdered here, and we were threatened with an order to find paintings that may not exist. Bev's tires were slashed and she was left a note." My voice was strident, my attempt at equanimity lost.

"Beverly Mitchell is the biggest gossip in all of Port Quincy. I'm not condoning whoever did that to her, of course, but I'm not surprised." Garrett sat next to me.

I began to sweat as I realized I'd withheld a key bit of information. I didn't want to incense Truman and Faith, not at this hour. Then again, Will was dead. I couldn't see how it was connected. I studied my fingernails and begged my hot face to cool off.

Truman's eyes bore into mine. The jig was up.

"Do you have something to add, Mallory?"

"The rumor Bev was spreading? About the paternity of Deanna's baby? It's true."

Truman leapt up from the bay window and sat across from me, in interrogation mode again.

"And how do you know that?" He went quiet until I was forced to meet his gaze.

"I went to see Deanna Hartley."

Truman, Faith, and Garrett all inhaled sharply. Rachel, who already knew, sent me a miserable look from across the room. She still shivered, hugging her arms to her body.

"It wasn't planned! I was just driving around and I saw her porch, with the memorials for Shane. She admitted Shane isn't the father of her baby and that she and the father used Sylvia's attic to meet." I slumped down in my chair with this admission.

"Damn it, Mallory!" Truman hollered. "When did you talk to Deanna?"

"Wednesday. After Kayla told us about Shane, how Deanna's baby couldn't be his. Deanna told me the last time she and her boyfriend met here on the third floor there was a light on in the carriage house. That's why we knew to look in there and why we found Will." *Who might still be alive, if I hadn't interfered.* My stomach soured.

"It would've been nice to know this three days ago," Faith scolded me, while Truman rested his face in his hands. He wouldn't look at me.

"I can't handle any more of your meddling." He finally raised his weary face from his palms.

I felt horrible, worse than the time I'd spilled my mother's nicest bottle of perfume after she'd warned me not to touch it.

"I should've told you immediately. All of this might be related, and I'm not the one who will figure it out. That's your job."

Truman snorted, probably too tired to scold me anymore.

"You know what I can't handle?" my sister piped up. "This." She gestured to the kitchen, where Will had recently lain.

"She's right. This is the second dead body we've found. This house is cursed."

"Couldn't agree with you more," Truman said resignedly. "We averaged about one murder per year here in Port Quincy. Before you two moved in, that is."

"I don't want you staying here tonight." Garrett glanced out the window, toward his father's adjoining property.

"It'll be okay." I resigned myself to sleeping in this house of horrors. Any last thought of turning it into a bed-and-breakfast and a joyous venue for weddings had been quelled by the grisly scene in the kitchen.

"I might not have thrown the dead bolt." Rachel shook her head with regret.

"Whoever did this would've gotten in anyway, if they really wanted to." I patted my sister's knee.

"Exactly." Garrett frowned. "They still can. You're not safe here."

I thought of my dwindling bank account and swallowed hard. A few nights in a hotel would have been fine before I was fired, but now? I didn't have a dollar to spare.

"I'll stay." Garrett squared his shoulders. "On the couch, Dad." He rolled his eyes at Truman. "I'll be back before Summer wakes up."

Garrett was gone by the time I padded down to the kitchen the next morning. There were fresh bagels and juice on the table, and the kitchen was spic and span, every trace of blood washed away. I'd slept surprisingly well, despite finding Will, probably because Garrett had been here.

"He's a good guy." Rachel bit into a bagel.

"I could do much worse." I studiously avoided the middle of the kitchen, Will's last resting place. "I could be embarking on my honeymoon with Keith right now."

I opened my laptop and began to type.

"What's that?" Rachel pulled up a chair and leaned on her elbows.

"A list of suspects and victims. We're going to figure out how it all fits together."

"No way." Rachel shook her head. "Truman and Faith were furious. You can't snoop around anymore."

Guilt pushed my mouth into a frown. "This isn't snooping. We aren't going to act on anything. But this just might keep us alive."

Rachel was silent, undoubtedly thinking of the note on Will's body, about finding the paintings or else.

"Okay. As long as we don't do anything with the list."

"Our victims are Shane Hartley and Will Prentiss." I typed them in.

"And maybe Sylvia."

"We've been threatened, and also Bev."

"But Bev was threatened for gossiping about Shane Hartley's infertility, and we've been threatened about the paintings."

"But we've also been warned we'll end up like Shane and Sylvia." I shivered and took a sip of chamomile tea to chase away the chills. Too bad they weren't temperature related.

"And our suspects. First, Will Prentiss," Rachel said with an edge to her voice.

"He's dead, Rachel," I said indignantly.

"But what was he doing in here?"

"I don't know, but he's a victim."

"I'm not denying that." Rachel's voice grew strident. "But I don't recall inviting him here while we were at Kayla's wedding. He had a motive to kill Shane Hartley."

"Fine. He's a victim *and* a suspect. I'd still put Helene and Keith at the top of the suspect list. There's something hinky going on with Helene and her relationship to Lonestar Energy. Someone at the firm knew I was searching for Lonestar documents and changed them all to password protected. And Naomi Powell said Keith, Helene, and Lonestar made preemptory contracts to drill here, because they assumed Sylvia would die soon and they'd inherit the house."

"If they're on the list, you need to put Shane as a suspect for killing Sylvia," Rachel reasoned.

"But he was banned from visiting her in the nursing home." I reminded her of what Naomi had told me. The list was a mess, with almost every victim a possible suspect as well. I bit my fingernail, then flexed my fingers.

"What are you doing?" Rachel gave me a wary look. I'd abandoned my list and launched my Web browser.

"I'm going to take a peek at Keith's files."

"Mallory! Were you not just sitting at this table when Truman forbade you from investigating?"

I scowled at my sister. For years, she had been a wild child, getting into scrapes and trouble, and I'd alternately got her out of it and hid it from our mother and Doug, or tattled on her when it was too serious. I couldn't believe things had changed so much.

"I don't even know if I can get in. And if it makes you so uncomfortable, you don't have to watch."

"No, I'll watch. I just want it on the record when you get caught that I objected."

"Duly noted."

I navigated to the website for Drake Lerner, Keith's law firm. I clicked on the link for the internal login and closed my eyes in thought. "What would his password be?"

"Try your name, or your birthday." All of Rachel's prior concerns seemed to have evaporated.

I sniffed. "You mean *Becca's* name or birthday." I typed in her name and hit enter.

"Access denied." Next I tried Snowshoe, Keith's favorite ski resort, plus the year he was born.

"Access denied. Damn it, that's his go-to password."

"C'mon, try your name, or your birthday. People don't change their passwords." She was right, but there was no way he'd get involved with Becca and keep me as his password.

"We should just stop. If we get it wrong, Keith will be frozen out, and he'll know someone was monkeying with his login."

"You should've thought of that before you started this." Rachel pulled the laptop away and tapped in some numbers with rapid speed then clicked enter.

"What the hell are you doing?"

The screen turned white then gray, as the Citrix server resolved itself. It now read, *Welcome, Keith.*

"You're welcome." Rachel was smug. "His password is your birthday."

I stared at the screen in shock.

"What are you waiting for? Find what you need before you really get caught."

There wasn't much in the files I could access with Keith's password. Which made sense, since Lonestar was a client of my former law firm, not Keith's. But I found enough. And I also stayed on the system long enough to get disbarred if anyone found out I'd been poking around in another firm's confidential files. *Desperate times call for desperate measures.*

First, there was a memo written by a summer associate at Keith's firm. It detailed how to contest a building's designation as a historical property. Keith and Helene had obviously worried about Sylvia's inquiry about making Thistle Park an historical building. The summer associate concluded the house would be near impossible to tear down if it achieved historical status.

Keith also had the contract that Naomi had mentioned attached to one of his e-mails, granting Lonestar a gas lease to drill on Thistle Park's property. The mansion would be razed to make room for a new housing development of twenty-five homes. None of the new owners would be able to contest the drilling, as it would have begun before the houses were built.

And there was one e-mail that hinted there would be a big payoff for Will Prentiss if he could find "them." The e-mail was from Helene to Shane Hartley, and Keith was copied. The e-mail had been sent to Shane the day he died, the day I moved into Thistle Park. Shane had written back promptly and alluded to the fact he would hold off on a settlement offer for Will Prentiss until Will recovered the paintings.

There was one more summer associate memo that described lengthy trips to the Frick Fine Arts Library to research the paintings the McGavitt family bought and sold over the years. I smirked, as it replicated the same research Tabitha and I had done. Keith had invented some elaborate story as to why the summer intern needed to research the matter.

"I bet *Helene* sent Will in here to find those paintings," I seethed. "Sylvia trusted him, and he double-crossed her! And it's disgusting that Hartley withheld the gas accident settlement from Will until he found the paintings for Helene. Will's settlement was in limbo. He was flat broke. Helene and Shane counted on him to be extra motivated to find the paintings and get his reward. They figured once he found them, he'd turn them over to Helene, and she'd tell Shane. But that never happened. Will couldn't find them. After Shane died, Will's settlement probably seemed even more in limbo, and he was desperate to find those paintings for Helene. He would have needed the money even more."

"What are you doing?" Rachel hovered nervously over my shoulder.

"I'm saving digital screenshots of the e-mails on my laptop. They won't leave a trail on Keith's end, and unless he figures out I used his password, we're safe." I signed out of Keith's remote digital office.

"Your theory doesn't automatically make Helene a killer. She probably thought we wouldn't notice and Will would fix the house in his role as handyman and find the paintings."

"And Helene waited all these years to find them before Sylvia died, because no one thought they survived the fire. But then I inherited Thistle Park, and we found that note. We need to find the paintings *now*."

"If they exist."

"Rach, if we don't find them, *we* might not exist."

Chapter Seventeen

I spent the rest of Sunday with my spreadsheets, trying to figure out how many months I could afford to stay at Thistle Park. It didn't look like many more unless I could secure a hefty loan, which was doubtful now I'd been fired. All of the visions of turning this place into a bed-and-breakfast and wedding venue evaporated in a cloud of debt.

So, on Monday morning, I summoned Zach. We brainstormed cheap fixes to inch the house closer to going on the market. Rachel followed her boyfriend around listlessly with a clipboard and wrote down his suggestions to make the house saleable. She was annoyed I wasn't going to make a go of it, and she wouldn't listen to my protestations that I needed to sell it. Her dreams of becoming a real estate agent like Zach were long forgotten; she had her heart set on the B and B idea.

"You'll have to polish the floors. And remove the peeling wallpaper. It would be better to replace it with something historically accurate. If not, you can just paint it."

I blew a curl off my forehead in exasperation and Zach stiffened. *Historically accurate wallpaper? Give me a break!* I'd need that money for ramen noodles and health insurance.

"And it would be good to move some of this furniture out, if you can't reupholster it or afford a professional stager. . . ." He must have felt the heat of my glare. "Right, I guess not. Maybe we can move some of it into the carriage house."

I hated walking around the house, thinking of ways to make it sell faster, but I doubted a bank would be willing to let me borrow any dough now that my six-figure job was gone and my law school loans were still due. It was almost the end of July, and I'd try to get it market-ready by mid-August.

"If you were willing to grant a gas lease to Lonestar, or one of the smaller fracking outfits, you'd have enough money to keep the house and fix it up." Zach cautiously sidled up to Rachel as if he knew I was going to have a conniption fit, Mount Vesuvius style.

"I know." I probably surprised him with my calmness. "And if anyone but Sylvia had left me this place, I might. I'm a little desperate for money right now, but I know how she felt, and I'm going to honor her wishes." I didn't mention I was so disgusted with Lonestar after reading the nexus of deceit among Keith, Helene, and Shane that I'd never let them drill.

Zach brightened. "If you guys can actually get this ready, I think it'll sell. And I can try to sniff out what the next owner will do with the land, but if they lease to a gas company, I can't stop them."

Zach left, and Rachel and I spent the rest of the

day sponging and stripping off layer upon layer of wallpaper from the rooms that were already peeling.

My phone rang. I moved to the parlor, relieved to take a break. I sank into the fainting couch. It was Tabitha.

"I heard about what happened with Will. I'm so sorry."

"I might be next."

"What are you talking about?"

I filled her in on the note confirming Sylvia was murdered.

"That's ridiculous! You can't be threatened to find artwork that might not be there. It *could* be in the house, or it could have burned or could have been sold by Sylvia's parents eighty years ago. The paintings might be languishing in some private collection."

"True. But if Sylvia was murdered by someone trying to make her reveal where the paintings were, they won't think twice about killing us. It won't matter I have no idea where they are. Rachel and I have been over every inch of this place." I truly felt like I knew every nook and cranny of Thistle Park, since I'd spent weeks checking each seam, trunk, and cabinet.

"Then maybe it's time to put that idea to bed and for you to leave. I hate to say it, but it isn't safe."

Desperation percolated up a thought from the recesses of my brain. "There is one place we haven't looked. Well, something that could *show* us where we haven't looked."

"What are you talking about?" Tabitha must have thought I was losing it.

"Zach mentioned the architect who built this place—Fastwinder?"

"Otto Fassbinder. He was pretty badass."

"Good, so maybe someone has the architectural plans for the house. They might give us a clue to a good hiding place."

"You're a genius, Mallory."

The night passed uneventfully. There were no dead people on the lawn, or in the kitchen, when Rachel and I awoke Tuesday morning. I no longer had a job, but now I had a mission: to find the architectural plans for Thistle Park and hope they revealed some secret cubbyhole. I loved a good research assignment and was happy to do it, especially if it kept us alive. I popped my head into the kitchen before I left. The table was lined with tins, each sporting a pastel foil shell.

"Muffins?" I sniffed the fragrant, sweet, fruity air.

"Nope, cupcakes. Someone wanted strawberry. For a baby shower. Maybe this baking thing will work out, even if you don't stay here and make it a B and B and wedding venue."

"I hope so." I smiled at my sister. "I'm off to get the plans for the house with Summer."

I drove the station wagon to Garrett's house and Summer bounded out, a small purse swinging from her shoulder. She was uber excited. I hoped this mission wouldn't be too boring for her.

"Mallory!" She flung open the passenger door and settled in before I could even unlatch my seat belt.

I laughed, tickled by her enthusiasm for a trip into Pittsburgh, something I'd taken for granted. "You're all ready to go."

Garrett emerged from his parents' neat brick ranch. He looked tired, but relieved.

"Have fun," he said to his daughter, then turned to me. "Can I talk to you for a second?"

"Sure." I left the car and walked to the front landing, out of earshot.

"Dad just called, and it looks like they've caught Shane Hartley's murderer."

A wave of relief washed over me. *Finally.* An invisible weight lifted from my shoulders, and I almost cried with relief.

"Who?"

"I'm not supposed to say, since they've just gotten a warrant for their arrest. It's—"

He paused and glanced at the Butterscotch Monster, where Summer was staring at the two of us unabashedly. She realized she was caught and gave a sheepish wave.

"Dad, let her go. We're running late!" She glanced dramatically at her small purple wristwatch.

"Just a second, sweetie." I leaned in closer to Garrett.

"It's Bart Tannenbaum."

"The m—" I started to say, much too loudly, when Garrett gently covered my mouth with his hand.

I turned my back to Summer. "The *mayor*?" I whispered this time.

"Yup." Garrett nodded. "He was having an affair with Deanna Hartley."

I gasped. "So he's the father." It fit. He was an older man, in a loveless marriage. I could picture Yvette on Founder's Day studiously ignoring her husband as he led Deanna down the stage to cut the ribbon for the new baseball field.

"Shane wouldn't let Deanna out of their marriage, so Bart Tannenbaum got him out of it."

"I'll never doubt your dad and Faith again."

Bart must have left Deanna's house, headed over to Thistle Park and killed Shane before returning home.

"He had his car repainted!" I thought of the black PT Cruiser Yvette Tannenbaum had driven when her father the mechanic dropped off the Butterscotch Monster, and the wood-paneled one that had picked up Deanna at the hospital. But it didn't explain the other things that had happened.

"What about Will Prentiss? Did Bart kill Will too?

"My dad and I talked about that. Will was probably in the carriage house the night Bart murdered Shane, so Bart covered his tracks. And he probably learned you and Rachel were there the night he killed Shane outside your window, so he left the note to scare you out of the house. You're lucky he just tried to threaten you and Rachel into leaving and didn't take it any further." Garrett swallowed.

I thought this over until little prickles danced up my neck. I whirled around. Summer was staring plaintively out the passenger-side window.

"I'd better go."

Garrett smiled. "We're still on for our date?"

I smiled back. "Wouldn't miss it for the world." And I could actually enjoy it now Bart Tannenbaum was behind bars.

Summer and I headed for the Frick Fine Arts Library in the Oakland neighborhood of Pittsburgh.

July was coming to a close, and a few students were already streaming about.

"Are you ready to go back to school?" We climbed the stairs to the building, which looked like an Italian villa. A man and woman were holding a baby near the fountain in front, and the little one splashed his hands in the water and cooed.

"I guess so." Summer ran her hand self-consciously through her newly shorn hair. "My friend Jocelyn gets back from camp tomorrow, and Grandma is taking me shopping for school clothes. But I don't want vacation to end."

We entered the beautiful little library, and Summer stopped in her tracks to look around. "This is awesome." She turned in a circle. Light poured in through the floor-to-ceiling windows. Books lined both floors, which were open and arranged around a central atrium, where warm wood gleamed. The space was relatively quiet. Only one student sat at a table, a carafe of coffee next to her.

I approached the front desk. "Um, pardon me?" I tried to keep my voice down, which was silly because there were barely any people to disturb.

The young woman standing behind the desk arched her pierced brow. Her hair swayed back and forth in a dramatic genie ponytail atop her head.

"Yes?" She had a pleasant smile.

"I called earlier, about some plans from the architect Otto Fassbinder."

The woman's demeanor changed so fast you'd have thought I'd threatened her outright. Her already fair skin turned a shade paler.

"Are you okay?" I was concerned she'd faint.

"Yes!" she snapped. She closed her eyes for a

moment then fluttered them open and leaned across in a conspiratorial manner. "You aren't looking for the records of the McGavitt house, by any chance, in Port Quincy, Pennsylvania?"

"Yup. The very ones. Thistle Park."

She rubbed her eyes, smearing a trail of green eye shadow.

"We don't have them." Her voice was barely audible.

"But I found them in the online catalog."

The woman looked up as if she expected to be caught. "A man took them out last weekend and didn't bring them back."

"Someone checked them out? I just called you guys to confirm you had them. They've been missing for a week?"

The woman gave the slightest of nods.

"I bet he wasn't *allowed* to check them out." Summer cottoned on faster than I did.

The librarian bobbed her head miserably.

"So he stole them?"

"I only work weekends. No one else knows they're gone. He wanted to see them, so I got them from storage. You can't check them out. He asked to make copies, but they're too big to use with the copy machine. And too fragile. But"—she dropped her voice low—"I let him anyway. Then he wasn't there anymore. And the plans were missing."

"What did he look like?" I held my breath.

All of a sudden, the librarian found her bearings. She stiffened and stood up to her full height, besting me in that department by a few inches.

"I can't divulge any information about patrons."

She looked put out. "Even ones who may have taken things."

"Oh, for Pete's sake, I'm not asking you to tell me his name. Just what he looks like. Young? Old? Heavy? Slim? And he's not even a patron. Technically, he's a thief!"

She seemed to consider for a moment. "I guess I can tell you. He wasn't that old, or that young." She considered me. "Kinda like you." I just managed to keep a polite smile.

"Not big. He was kind of average. And he was wearing a hat—a baseball hat and jeans." She leaned back, uncertain.

"That's it?" Summer shook her head.

I was glad she was outraged on my behalf.

"What color was his hair? What did he sound like? Did he limp?"

"I—I don't really remember." The librarian crumpled again. "I think he had light hair. He was wearing a hat. And I don't *think* he was limping, but I'm not sure."

Keith. Or Bart Tannenbaum.

"It's all right." I didn't really sound sympathetic, but I remembered from my evidence class in law school that almost no one remembered what a suspect looked like after the fact.

"I'm going to have to tell my boss I let him take the plans to the copier." She sat dejectedly. "I was hoping he'd bring them back."

We left her pondering her fate.

"This isn't good," Summer said as we pushed our weight against the heavy wooden doors.

We stepped into the sunshine and drifted back to the station wagon.

"Nope. But if what your dad told me is true, we probably already know who has the architectural plans." I clapped a palm over my mouth, not wanting to reveal too much.

Summer laughed. "My dad and my grandparents try to keep everything from me, but I find out. I know they arrested the mayor this morning."

"Summer, you really aren't supposed to know that."

She shrugged. "The walls are really thin at my grandparents' house. Do you think Mr. Tannenbaum took the plans for the house?"

"Maybe." I hoped it was okay to talk to her about it since she already knew. "The man the librarian described could be him, although his dress usually isn't that nondescript."

Her vague recollection could be anyone. Bart, Keith, or even Will Prentiss. Will had been alive last week, and it seemed like Keith and Helene had liked to hire him on a freelance basis to do their dirty work.

We reached the car, but Summer looked longingly down the street to the Carnegie Museum. "Do you mind if we go? Since we're here?" Her face was so hopeful.

"Sure thing." I'd thought we'd be here poring over architectural plans for hours and had paid for enough parking time for a quick trip to the museum. "I promised Rachel the car, but we can look around for a bit."

Once inside, Summer made a beeline for the Hall of Architecture, shunning the modern art and the natural history portions of the museum.

"This is my favorite part!" Summer raced up the marble steps.

"Mine too." I hurried to catch up.

We made a slow revolution around the room and examined plaster replicas of famous temples and statues.

"Mythology was my favorite unit in school last year." Summer paused in front of a bust of Athena. Her warrior's helmet and her breastplate were embossed with Medusa's head.

"She's so fierce." Summer seemed in awe. "Do you know the crazy way she was born?"

I wracked my brain for a moment. "I think her father was Zeus and she erupted all grown up, from Zeus's head."

Summer nodded. "Zeus swallowed Athena's mother when he found out she was pregnant." She paused. "Do you think his wife, Hera, was mad?" Summer tilted her head. "About all of his affairs?"

"She was. And Zeus might have swallowed Athena's mother to protect the baby from Hera." Something skittered across my brain. I couldn't grab it fast enough. And I wasn't sure how happy Garrett would be that his thirteen-year-old daughter and I were discussing the topic of marital infidelity, whether it was based in classical mythology or not.

Summer snorted. "Why didn't Hera just punish her husband, instead of going after his mistresses?"

"Good question. If I remember right, she also went after the children he had with them." My toes curled in my sandals as I recalled my anger directed at Becca Cunningham, when maybe I should have focused on Keith. I was finally ready to let it go.

"Yeah, I know about Hercules. She sent snakes

after him when he was a baby, in his crib." Summer shivered.

A sick feeling gripped my stomach.

"What's wrong?" Summer grabbed my arm as I took a step back and almost sunk to the cold marble floor.

"Honey, were you telling the truth about the night Shane Hartley died? That first day I met you, you told me you were at the house the day before, tending to the cats when it was still light out. But now that I think of it, Rachel and I didn't see you there."

Summer got very quiet. After a lengthy pause, she finally spoke up. "I saw you and Rachel move in. I didn't know who you were and what you'd do with Whiskey and her kittens. I was watching from behind the carriage house, and I saw you move Whiskey and Soda inside, but not Jeeves. So I went to find him that night."

"Did you see anything?" I tried to make my voice sound light, but it was strained.

"I did." Summer's voice was very soft, and she was twisting the strap of her purse around and around her arm, like a tourniquet, turning her arm red.

"What did you see, sweetie?" I reached out to still her hand and unwind the purse.

"The night Mr. Hartley was killed?" Her small voice got progressively higher and thinner.

"Summer?" Please, please, *please* let her not have seen something totally awful.

"I *was* there." Summer trained her eyes on her flip-flops.

Crap. I tucked my finger under her chin and slowly

raised her face until it was level with mine. "What did you see?"

"It's not like I saw him get killed or anything," she said nervously.

Phew. "It's okay, but I need to know."

"I waited until my dad and grandparents were asleep, and I climbed out my window, 'cause it's just on the first floor. I put cat food and a bottle of water in my backpack. I used my cell phone as a flashlight, and I walked through the backyard."

"You must have been so scared." I wouldn't want to walk through our backyards in the dark, even before Shane Hartley's murder and all of the break-ins.

"I *was* scared, but I couldn't let Jeeves stay out all night by himself. So I got to the back porch and looked around, but I couldn't find him. He must've been hiding under the porch. It was too dark to see. I'd just put out the food and water when a truck pulled in."

Shane Hartley.

"I crouched next to the back porch. I didn't want them to see me in their headlights. Then the truck was turned off and someone got out."

"Who was it?"

"There was a full moon, but there wasn't enough light to tell. And then another person pulled in." She stopped and peered at me.

"What did the other person look like?" I tried to keep my voice even, not to sound anxious or upset. But the thought of Summer so close to the killer made me sick, even in the calm, cool safety of the museum, one month removed from the incident.

"I couldn't see. But they were driving one of those cars, the old-fashioned ones."

"An old-fashioned car?"

"Like in a gangster movie. The ones with the wooden sides."

The same type of car had picked up Deanna Hartley at the hospital.

Summer wrinkled her nose. "I couldn't tell who got out, but he seemed kinda tall. I crawled until I got to the part of the garden with the statues, and then I ran back home. I didn't hear anything, I swear."

My heart leapt into my throat. I came to a sickening conclusion and prayed I was wrong. Too bad the Zeuses of the world couldn't always swallow their mistresses, to protect them.

"Summer, sweetie, let's get out of here."

"Where are you going?" Summer blinked as we stopped in front of her grandparents' house. I'd resisted the urge to call Truman while Summer was in the car.

"I'm going to see your grandpa at the police station." I wanted to be straight with her.

"You're not going to tell him I was out that night, are you?" Summer crumpled in her seat and pouted. "It doesn't matter now. You heard they caught the guy who did it. It's the mayor, and it fits. He drives one of those old-fashioned cars." She turned her hazel eyes to me, pleading.

"Maybe so." I offered her a sad smile. "It'll be okay, Summer."

"My dad will be mad." She glanced at the front door. "And Grandpa will say I held up his investigation."

This made me burst out laughing. "They'll just be happy you're safe and sound. And no matter what, it was very brave of you to go back to check on Jeeves that night, even if it wasn't exactly allowed. Now do I get to see him before I go?"

Summer unbuckled herself and nodded.

On the way home, I'd complimented her on her unwavering care of Whiskey, Soda, and Jeeves, trying to focus on the positive aspects of a thirteen-year-old girl sneaking out of her house nearly a month ago and almost witnessing a murder. Summer had perked up a bit and chatted about Jeeves. She'd begged me to come in to see how big he'd grown and the new trick he could do, a backflip.

"I don't know where he is." She peered under the couch in a comfortable-looking living room.

Pictures of Summer from the time she was a baby to the present adorned one wall, and pictures of Garrett depicting the same covered another.

"He usually comes out when I get home. Jeeves!"

Should I step outside to call Truman?

Summer disappeared around the corner and gasped. "Grandma!"

I raced in to see a gray-haired woman tied to a chair with rope and a kitchen towel stuffed in her mouth. Her frightened eyes, swollen and red, trailed away from Summer to the woman who now had a gun trained at Summer's head. Unfortunately, my hunch from the museum had been correct.

Chapter Eighteen

"I expected the girl to show up, but I didn't think you'd be with her. Or that Lorraine would be home." Yvette Tannenbaum stated this calmly, as if we were two girlfriends chatting over a pedicure. Her mousy hair was frizzy with perspiration, and her floral dress bore deep stains under her arms. This wasn't meek Yvette, but strong Yvette, the one I'd glimpsed at Sylvia's funeral, when she'd sung so incredibly. Now the power was frightening, not sublime.

"What are you doing?" I shuffled over to Summer, who was shaking.

A small whimper escaped from her mouth. Summer's grandmother writhed against the ropes binding her, her chair inching closer to Yvette.

"Stop it." Yvette moved the gun away from Summer's temple and pointed it at her grandmother.

"We can work something out." I attempted to put into play the negotiating skills I'd used as an attorney. They sounded pretty lousy right now.

Yvette snorted. "I don't think so. I've already tried to kill you once. I won't fail this time."

A small bell went off in my stress-addled brain. "You cut my brake line! You were there the day I was at the historical society. I ran into you in the hallway."

"Being the mechanic's daughter comes in handy sometimes." Yvette's smile snaked across her face. "I came back in through the bathroom window, cutting it close when I ran into you in the hallway. I also had my car repainted that evening, in case this brat tried to trace it back to me." I'd never seen her truly smile. Before, she'd just looked meek and dour. Now she appeared powerful, evil, and insane. I had to get her away from Summer, who was now crying freely, taking in ragged breaths.

"Don't whine." Yvette trained her gun on Summer. "You saw me kill Shane Hartley."

"I didn't. I swear!"

"You're lying. I saw you by the light of your cell phone. Little girls should be in bed at midnight, not tiptoeing around strangers' houses."

"I was helping the cats." Summer stood straight, but her knees knocked together. "Where's my kitten?" She frantically looked around.

"Locked in the basement. Damn cat was hissing at me."

I tried to stall for time. "Why did you kill Shane?" I thought I already knew. I hoped I was wrong. "You told me I dodged a bullet by not marrying Keith. Because he cheated on me. You killed Shane because you thought he was Bart, didn't you?" The alternative theory was just too disgusting.

Yvette's chapped lips twisted into a creepy smile. "Bart couldn't control himself." Little flecks of spit shot out of her mouth like sparks. "He was behaving like a lovesick teenager. You'd think I'd be used to it, after dealing with his infidelities for twenty years. But this time was different."

Her eyes got a faraway look, and I tried to control my raspy breath. If I stalled her, maybe someone would figure out this madwoman was holding us hostage.

"He got her pregnant. After he'd said he didn't want to have children, he went and got her pregnant."

"Deanna." Yvette's head snapped to attention. *Oops.*

She pivoted to point the gun at me. "Yes, her," she spat. "I found a letter Bart was working on. He's careless about everything. He was leaving me for her."

"So you went to the place where they always met."

Yvette nodded but didn't move the gun. By now, Summer had slumped to the floor, and I wanted to join her, but I couldn't let Yvette point her weapon at Summer again.

"You don't get it." The gun bobbed with her every movement. "I had an offer to sing opera in New York, but Bart made me stay. He wanted to be a senator."

Summer's grandmother made a wheezing noise. It sounded dismissive even with all of the cotton blocking her mouth.

"I know. I married a joke of a man who spent twenty years on the city council so he could finally become mayor. I didn't know it then. I stayed here, and we gave up on children. Then he found this pretty little Texan, half his age. . . ." Her body shook.

"You thought you killed your husband, not Shane." I could see it. Bart and Shane were both relatively short men. It would be easy to confuse them in the dark. The Hartleys' truck had been in my driveway, and Yvette probably assumed Deanna had driven there with Bart. It wasn't the wretched hypothesis that had bubbled up in my brain back at the museum, but it would do.

But I should have known better. One of the things you learned as an attorney was to never ask a question you didn't know the answer to.

"No." Yvette's smile became even more chilling. "I thought he was Deanna."

A bucket of ice water doused my nerves. It would be possible to mistake Shane, with his short stature and his potbelly for his wife, Deanna, with her pregnant belly and her hair in its trademark bun.

"My life was spiraling out of control." Yvette's voice was barely above a whisper. "Don't you know what that feels like?"

I nodded, knowing all too well.

"I gave up everything. All of my dreams and aspirations. Why shouldn't he?"

"Keith cheated on me, but I didn't kill his mistress. Or Keith, although I may have wanted to when I first found out."

"But you got out in time. You didn't stay in Port Quincy for decades, waiting for him to carry out his dreams at the expense of yours. You didn't find out he was slowly draining your joint bank account to finance his escape to Texas. If I'd found those paintings, it wouldn't have mattered. But that diary was worthless."

"*You* have Sylvia's diary?"

Yvette nodded. "I removed it from the car after your accident. And then I misplaced it a few days later. It didn't have any useful information." Her arm wavered as she assessed me. "You're very determined. Too bad you didn't just decide to sell and move back to Pittsburgh. Then none of this would have had to happen."

"I didn't hear anything that night." So Yvette had placed the threatening messages in the house. "You slashed Bev's tires because she was spreading it around town that Shane wasn't the father of Deanna's baby."

Yvette scowled at the mention of Deanna's name. "Bev didn't know it was my Bart," she said possessively. "But she knew it wasn't Shane. I couldn't take the chance she'd figure it out. I'll take care of her after I'm done here." She took aim at me, then seemed to change her mind and pointed at Summer.

Summer's grandmother's swollen eyes went wide, and I resisted the urge to look left. I could smell my sister's perfume. I gave a little nod and said a quick prayer.

A chair crashed down on Yvette's head, and she shot the pistol. I knocked Summer out of the way as someone screamed and all was chaos.

Chapter Nineteen

Rachel brought the chair down.

I jumped off Summer and kicked the gun away as my sister sat on the chair, trapping Yvette. She flailed and tried to bite Rachel's hands.

"Are you all right, Summer?"

She was slumped on the floor.

"I'm okay."

We were all fine, but the refrigerator hadn't been so lucky. Yvette had shot clean through the door.

"Get my purse," Rachel commanded. She rifled through and removed a pair of small silver handcuffs, adorned with pink marabou feathers.

"Where did you get those?" I was stunned into inaction.

"Never mind. Just help me with this!"

We worked together to roll Yvette over and cuff her hands behind her back. Then we untied Grandma Lorraine and used the rope to bind Yvette's legs.

Lorraine coughed and sputtered after I yanked the kitchen towel out of her mouth. Summer flew into her grandmother's arms once she was free. I opened the basement door and Jeeves appeared, swishing his tiny black tail in annoyance.

"You must be Mallory." Lorraine gave me a shaky smile over Summer's head. "I've heard so much about you. It's terrible that we're meeting under these circumstances." She eyed Yvette, who thrashed against the ropes that now bound her to a kitchen chair, the towel stuffed in her mouth.

Truman burst into the kitchen, Garrett behind him. Garrett swooped down to envelop his daughter and his mother, and Truman replaced Rachel's handcuffs with real ones as he read Yvette her rights.

Garrett turned and embraced me. "You're all fine, right?"

"Thanks to Mallory talking to that nut and buying us time." Lorraine gave me an embrace as well. "And to you, too, for knocking Yvette over." She reached out and patted Rachel's shoulder.

"I'm Rachel, Mallory's sister. She was supposed to be back half an hour ago to give me the car, so I took a walk over here since I knew she was with Summer."

Faith carted Yvette away, wrangling her as she kicked and tried to spit out her gag.

"Bart Tannenbaum made a very large withdrawal from his joint account with Yvette this morning," Truman explained, "and we discovered he'd bought a plane ticket for himself and Deanna Hartley for Houston, for one week from now, since she's given birth to Bart, Jr. He was going to leave his wife."

"Yvette found a letter saying as much."

"We figured Bart had the motive and the opportunity to kill Shane, but Deanna vouched for him, said she was with him that night. It was Bart who clued us in that it was Yvette. She was the one who'd directed her father to repaint their car."

Summer looked at me sheepishly, and I gave her a final hug. "I'll tell your grandpa about what you saw that night. Don't worry about it."

Rachel drove us home. We sat slumped over chamomile tea, spent from our adrenaline crash.

"All's well that ends well." She clinked her cup with mine. I wasn't too sure.

The next day dawned cloudy and gray. Rachel and I were somewhat recovered. My mom was not. She was freaking out in Florida, her anxiety so palpable it oozed out of the phone.

"I'm not sure about Port Quincy. You girls will be safer in Pittsburgh."

"We're all right, Mom." I was warmed by her concern. "Besides, you'll be seeing a lot more of Port Quincy, so you can judge for yourself. I'm going to keep Sylvia's house and turn it into a B and B. It'll be the most beautiful wedding venue in Western Pennsylvania."

"That's wonderful! What changed your mind? I thought you were going to sell it."

"I guess our near-death experience. It will be really hard, and expensive, but I think I can cash in my retirement money and get a loan to fix up the bottom two floors."

"My daughter, a B and B purveyor. And if you fail, you can go back to practicing law."

"Um, thanks, Mom."

I got off the phone and sat with Rachel in the parlor while we waited for a FedEx delivery. The van finally rolled down our driveway around noon, and we ran out to greet it.

The driver chuckled and handed me a tube of cardboard. "Mighty anxious, aren't you."

"You have no idea." We raced back into the house.

Tabitha had performed a miracle and found a second copy of the architectural plans. I'd paid triple to have them copied and overnighted to us.

"Let's see, let's see!" Rachel skipped as I brought the plans into the dining room and unfurled them on the table.

We peered closely at the intricate map of the house and scanned for places where someone could hide paintings. Now that Yvette was behind bars, we didn't need to worry about people breaking in to find them. And if they did exist, they'd more than pay for Thistle Park's renovations.

"I want to start looking before I get ready for tonight." I glanced at the grandfather clock.

"You're still going on your date with Garrett?"

"Just to dinner." I wasn't up for much more but was looking forward to seeing him.

"Zach will be by in a few hours too."

We tried to match what we were seeing on the architectural plans with what was actually in the house.

"The dining room is slightly different." Rachel trailed her finger over the drawing.

"The chimney's changed. It could be where the fire started in the dining room."

"And the original kitchen was in the basement. The current kitchen was originally a conservatory. They must have changed it after the fire."

"Whoa, check this out." I pointed to a wall in the dining room, then at the architectural plans. Inside the wall, where we couldn't see, was a dumbwaiter. The wall appeared smooth, covered in the same damask rose wallpaper as the rest of the room.

"I'll go get a hammer."

The newly repaired doorbell chimed, clear and crisp.

"Are you expecting anyone?"

"Maybe it's Truman." The chief and I had spent a long time on the phone yesterday discussing what Summer had seen the night of Shane's murder. He had been nearly apoplectic, knowing his grand-daughter had been so close to a murder, and I wasn't looking forward to hearing how upset Garrett would be, either. Hopefully they'd cut her some slack, since Yvette had tried to kill us.

"Nope, it's Zach." I peered out the keyhole before I swung the front door open. He jumped back in surprise, a key in his hand.

"You gave him a key?" I stared at Rachel. I hadn't formally put Sylvia's house on the market, and Rachel had been here to let Zach in the few times prospective buyers stopped by. I hadn't thought to give him a key.

"Our relationship is progressing." She beamed as Zach leaned in to brush her cheek with a kiss. "You're early, sweet pea."

"I have good news." He held up a bottle. "Champagne."

I accepted the bottle, chilled and dewy. It was the very same vintage as the glass I'd had at the wedding tasting with Keith and Helene. It had only been a few weeks ago, but so much had changed.

"What are we celebrating?"

"I've found you a family." He was triumphant.

"Pardon?"

"A family for the house. They have four children, and they won't allow any fracking on the property. They've made a great offer. I'm certain you'll accept." He pulled a folded piece of paper out of his back pocket and handed it to me.

"Whoa." The number was substantial. "This is more than fair."

"They know it'll need a lot of work, but they really want to live here. Even with all that's happened."

Rachel glanced at me with trepidation. "Tell him."

"Tell me what?" Zach's face fell a fraction.

"I appreciate all of your hard work, and, of course, I'll compensate you for your time, but I've decided not to sell. We're going to open a B and B and hold weddings here."

A brief flash of anger clouded Zach's face, then dissipated. If I'd been looking elsewhere, I would have missed it. "Are you sure you want to do this? It's hard to run your own business."

His doubt was beginning to annoy me, but I looked fondly at my sister.

"We're a team. I think after this month, we can do anything."

"That's great. I know the two of you will be successful, and I wish you the best of luck."

I smiled at his gracious goodwill for us.

"We still have something to celebrate." He gestured to the champagne. "To your new business venture."

"I know just the glasses to use." Rachel opened a cabinet and pulled out three very dusty, but beautifully cut glass goblets. Large letter Ms were etched into the sides, and vines and daisies curved around the monogram. Rachel blew off the dust and held them up to the light. "The McGavitt Glass Company's best."

"What's this?" Zach was transfixed by the architectural plans spread out on the dining room table. I resisted the urge to shoo him away.

"It's our last-ditch effort to find the paintings, if they're in this house. The money would pay for the renovations."

Zach shrugged and plucked the stemware from us and set them on a silver tray on the sideboard.

"I'll get our toast ready." He disappeared into the kitchen.

Rachel let out a sigh of relief. "He seemed to take it well."

I gave my sister an incredulous look. "You were worried my decision to keep the house would hurt your relationship?"

"Not exactly." Rachel fiddled with the edge of the architectural plans. "I'm just glad he's not too upset."

Zach returned with three goblets of pale gold liquid, bubbles racing up the sides of the etched glass.

"To the Thistle Park Bed and Breakfast." He raised his glass aloft. It sparkled in the light from the chandelier and seemed to wink at us.

"To the bed and breakfast." We clinked and drank.

"Yummy." Rachel drained hers.

"Drink up." Zach nudged my glass.

"Why not." I downed the fizzy champagne. My eyes strayed to the architectural plans on the table. "This is really thoughtful. I hate to cut this celebration short, but I want to get a head start on looking for the paintings. I don't mean to hustle you two along on your date but . . . ."

Zach smiled, but his eyes were strange and hollow. "I'm not going anywhere, Mallory."

"What do you mean?" I stepped back.

Rachel giggled and sat down. "This stuff is *strong*." She stopped laughing and steadied herself at the table. "Honey? What's with this drink?"

He ignored my sister and looked around the room.

"Where are your cell phones?"

"The parlor." My voice grew slurry. I was so tired, I just wanted to sleep. Little alarm bells were ringing, far away.

"Did you drug us?" I could barely understand my own words.

Zach nodded. "I had to. I need the paintings. It has to look like an accident."

"Oh, my God." I was shutting down, growing so tired, but thoughts from the past few weeks flickered through my mind. I fought sleepiness and tried to brush it aside, like a heavy velvet curtain layered on top of my consciousness.

"It was you."

"Don't strain yourself." Zach leaned over me with a concerned frown.

I had sunk into a chair and leaned my head against the table.

Zach disappeared for a moment. The front door opened and closed.

"Roooossssies . . ." Rachel slurred.

What? Ah, roofies.

"He's going to kill us." My sister stared at me mutely, a tear running down her face.

"Yes, I am going to kill you," Zach affirmed. "But

it'll look like an accident. Your car will be found in the Monongahela, and by the time they get to you two, you'll have drowned."

"But why?"

"I've got to find the paintings. I have some hefty gambling debts, and certain private collectors are eager to take the paintings off my hands for an amazing price. Too bad you ladies couldn't move out, or just let me sell the damn house. Now, let's see." He glanced at the architectural plans on the dining room table and smiled. "It's convenient that you have a second set here. I had to leave my copy at home."

"You took them from the Frick."

"I did. And it's a shame I had to kill Will Prentiss. I realize now he was leading me to the correct location."

He jostled the breakfront away from the wall opposite the fireplace.

"I've been so fortunate," he mused, winded from moving the heavy piece of furniture. "Crazy-ass Yvette Tannenbaum snapped and killed Shane Hartley. She took the focus from me."

"What are you doing?" Could he understand my slurred speech?

"She hid the paintings in the dumbwaiter." He validated our hunch.

Who was *she*? Evelyn, Sylvia's mother?

He left us for a minute and returned with a large duffel bag, the kind hockey players carried. He removed a small pickax and began hacking through the wallpaper, each thwack punctuated with a grunt. The metal tore jagged spaces in the jungle of faded wallpaper, raining down plaster and eventually brick.

The chandelier above our heads rattled, the crystals tinkling.

"This is probably chock full of asbestos. They made these dumbwaiters fireproof, thank goodness for the paintings. But you won't live long enough to worry about that."

The last layer of plaster and brick gave way, and underneath was a wooden door, now scarred by the pickax. Zach opened it, revealing a worn rope.

I saw this all sideways, as my head was too tired to lift from the table.

"You killed Sylvia." I would be sick, if I could ever sit up again.

Zach shrugged. "She wouldn't tell me where the paintings were. She could've let me sell the house, and then I would've found them on my own. I do know this house like the back of my hand. I used to tag along while my grandmother cleaned."

"How did you kill her?" I hoped I could stay awake long enough to stall him. It had worked with Yvette, but would I get lucky again?

"I smothered her with her pillow. She'd just gotten off the phone with you, nattering on about rescheduling a tea date. She told me she'd just deeded you the house, which she shouldn't have done."

I moaned into the table.

"Although I should be thanking you. I didn't come looking for the paintings all these years Sylvia was in the nursing home, because I thought they'd burned in the fire. It wasn't until you found the note that I realized they might be hidden, safe and sound. No one believed my grandmother, but she was right."

"Your grandmother?"

"The Pierce's maid, Ida Smoot."

I struggled to sit up; my head weighed a thousand pounds.

Rachel snored softly on the floor.

"Your grandma can't be a Smoot. Smoot was Sylvia's first husband's name." Then I thought of the day Tabitha and I had looked at the photographs from this house. I thought of the picture of the two boys who could have been twins, one nattily dressed, the other in hand-me-downs. It clicked. Gerald and Robert. *Not twins, but half brothers.*

Zach turned from his work in the wall and faced me with a sneer. "My grandmother slowly went insane. She raved on and on about how she'd married the gardener, and they were going to run off together. But he left her, pregnant with my father, to be with Sylvia. He couldn't marry Sylvia, because he was already married to my grandmother. And he didn't die young—he dumped Sylvia when he realized her parents had cut her off for running away with him. Sylvia's son and my father were raised side by side, half brothers. Sylvia got to bear the name, even though she had no right to it. Sylvia cheated my family out of their life. It's time to make amends."

"Your father and Keith's father were half brothers." Whiskey twined around my almost-numb legs. She left me to sit beside the giant vase sitting next to the fireplace. I was so tired. *Isn't there something in the vase?*

"Very good, Mallory. My father grew up right here, in the attic. He got Sylvia's son's cast-off clothes and his half-eaten sweets. And Sylvia got to wear a last name she had no right to and con her new husband into thinking Keith's father was his child."

"But you said Sylvia was good to you and your family." It took all my concentration to sound intelligible.

"You're good to a dog when you throw it some scraps. Not a person. Sylvia knew all of this, but she wouldn't tell me where her mother hid the paintings. So she had to go."

I moaned, unable to open my eyes. So Evelyn had hidden them, to keep her daughter from absconding with the gardener.

"If you'd held on to that diary, you could have figured it out. Sylvia was devastated when she found out her fiancé was involved with the maid. She was going to take the paintings to finance her elopement. My grandmother found out and told her mother, Evelyn."

"How did you get the diary?" I slurred.

"When my car was repossessed, I bailed it out from Mazur's Towing and saw the diary on Yvette Tannenbaum's desk. It was too good to pass up." So Tabitha had been right about Zach's car.

"Wake up, Rach." I couldn't even understand my own words.

My sister snored next to me on the floor. I nudged her with my foot. Zach knelt and shook her awake. She flinched and tried to spit on Zach, but a thread of drool ran down her cheek.

Zach tenderly wiped it away. "I did like you. It's too bad it has to end under these circumstances." Rachel whimpered under his touch.

It must have taken Zach longer than anticipated to pull up the dumbwaiter rope.

I slipped in and out of consciousness. I came to

when I toppled off my chair and landed on the hearth. *The pistol.* Mustering every last ounce of strength, I picked up the fireplace poker and rammed the vase. It shattered, and I belatedly wondered if it was worth anything. I grasped the pistol and pointed it at Zach.

"Are you kidding me?" He blanched, then relaxed. "That's a toy. It won't fire." He dismissed me with a chuckle and returned to the dumbwaiter.

"Mallory, where are you?" Garrett entered the room, flowers in his hand.

"What have you done?" Garrett rushed over to my sister and felt for a pulse, then raised my head from the hearth.

"Don't get any closer." Zach pulled his head out of the dumbwaiter. He retrieved the pickax and took a swing at Garrett. He missed, cleaving off a chunk of dining room table.

I took aim under the dining room table and fired.

Zach screamed and dropped his ax to grasp his mangled ankle. "Damn it, Mallory!" Garrett scanned the room and removed a dusty tassel from the brocade curtains. He deftly flipped a groaning Zach over on his stomach and hogtied his hands behind his back. Then he crossed the room in one step and picked me up and laid me on the dining room table.

"I should have gotten here sooner." He wiped a tear from my eye. "Someone at the nursing home remembered Zach came to see Sylvia before she was found dead. He was such a frequent visitor, he didn't sign in. And Faith interviewed the mortician at the funeral home. He thought one of Sylvia's fingers had been broken but brushed it off because she'd supposedly died in her sleep. Dad's on his way. He's been trying to find Zach to bring him in for questioning." Garrett turned to look at Zach writhing on the floor. "He's not going anywhere."

Something caught my eye. "Could you get that bag?" My eyes moved to the dumbwaiter.

Garrett opened an old burlap sack and removed two paintings still in their frames. It was all for naught. They were warped and stained. I turned away, my vision blurred. Zach, now moaning on the floor, had tried to murder us over two moldy, worthless landscapes. Garrett stroked my forehead, then carefully unfurled the third item, rolled up into a scroll, and held it up for me to see. Only this painting was unscathed from its long entombment in the wall.

There was Evelyn McGavitt, recumbent and sly, a smirk playing at the edges of her full lips. Her dress wrapped delicately around her bare shoulders, her décolletage framing her face. Her husband stood behind her, sternly looking out, his hand on her shoulder. Baby Sylvia sat on her mother's lap, her gaze steady. She seemed to peer into the future. The McGavitt family. The world went black.

Chapter Twenty

It was three whole days until I got to see Rachel. They held us until they figured out what sedative Zach had given us. After we were released from the hospital, Rachel and I spent a week with my mom and stepdad in a hotel. They had rushed from Florida to take care of us, and we needed the time away from the house. Rachel took Zach's arrest especially hard.

"He used me to get to the paintings. Tabitha tried to warn me."

"She knew he was deep in debt because of his gambling problem, but she didn't know he'd go this far." I shivered at how close we'd come to ending up like Sylvia.

"It didn't matter," Rachel said with a bitter down-turn of her mouth. "I was so in love, that wouldn't have been a deal-breaker. Now we know being with someone who tries to murder you is way worse than being with a cheating scoundrel."

We weren't eager at first to return to Sylvia's house. But at the end of August, Rachel and I moved back to Thistle Park. The evenings were cooler, and we were taking things slowly.

My stepdad, Doug, stationed himself at an old grill we'd found in the greenhouse and had scrubbed of rust. Rachel showed Summer how to make daisy chains, and my mother regaled Garrett's parents with stories from her anniversary cruise.

I sidled up to Doug and handed him a beer.

"You did good, kid." He motioned to the house.

Scaffolding crisscrossed the front of the mansion, readied for the construction to commence tomorrow. The two ruined landscapes, the Renoir and the Pissarro, were still valuable. Not as valuable as they would have been if they didn't need major restorations, but their sale would finance the renovations at Thistle Park and knock out most of my law school loans.

The Sargent portrait of the McGavitt family was on loan to the Carnegie Museum. I didn't want anything that valuable in the house ever again, now I knew what curses it would bring. Besides, it was time the portrait saw the light of day, after being cooped up in the dumbwaiter for all those years. The museum made a print of it for us, which now hung in its rightful place over the dining room fireplace. And the dumbwaiter was being restored. It had held secrets for too long.

I'd met with my first bride that very morning to go over the details for the first wedding that would take place in December.

I turned back to Doug. "I know nothing about running a business, but I'll figure it out."

He laughed. "I can picture you planning weddings and Rachel baking, but I can't see either of you changing sheets and scrubbing bathrooms or catering to your guests' whims."

"We'll manage. That actually sounds better than the law firm. It's just great to be alive."

We walked out of the shade, to join the rest of my family in a patch of sunlight.

Please turn the page for some
delicious recipes from
Mallory and Rachel's kitchen!

Whiskey Orange Cake

2½ cups flour
2 teaspoons baking powder
½ teaspoon baking soda
¼ teaspoon salt
1½ cups sugar
¾ cup butter, softened
¾ cup orange juice
¼ cup whiskey
4 eggs
1 teaspoon vanilla extract
1 teaspoon orange extract

Preheat oven to 350 degrees. Grease and flour two 9-inch cake pans. Combine flour, baking powder, baking soda and salt in a bowl. In a separate bowl, cream sugar and butter at medium speed. Add orange juice, whiskey and eggs one at a time and beat until smooth. Beat in vanilla and orange extracts. Slowly add in dry ingredients and beat until smooth. Pour batter into pans and bake until a knife or toothpick inserted in the middle comes out clean, approximately 30 to 35 minutes. Cool before frosting.

Orange Cream Frosting

½ cup butter, softened
4 cups confectioners' sugar
⅓ cup cream

1½ tablespoons vanilla extract
½ tablespoon orange extract

Cream butter in a bowl. Slowly beat in sugar and cream. Beat in vanilla and orange extracts.

Apple Bacon Scones

2½ cups flour
1 tablespoon baking powder
½ teaspoon salt
1 tablespoon cardamom
½ cup cold butter, cut into small pieces
¾ cup shredded cheddar cheese
½ cup buttermilk
½ cup cream
1 egg
2 apples, peeled and cut into 1 inch pieces
5 strips of bacon, cooked, crumbled and
    cooled

Preheat oven to 425 degrees. Line a baking sheet with parchment paper. Combine flour, baking powder, salt and cardamom in a bowl. Use your fingers to rub cold butter and flour together until butter is completely blended into the flour. Add shredded cheese and mix well with your hands. Beat buttermilk, cream and egg in a separate bowl. Fold egg mixture into dry ingredients. Mix in apple and bacon pieces. Knead fifteen times on a lightly floured surface. Shape dough into a 9-inch circle and cut into eight wedges. Bake for 14 to 16 minutes, until golden brown.

Rosemary Cheese Straws

2 cups flour
2 teaspoons dried rosemary
¾ cup cold butter, cut into small pieces
2½ cups shredded mozzarella cheese

Preheat oven to 425 degrees. Grease a baking sheet. Combine flour and rosemary in a bowl. Use your fingers to rub cold butter, cheese and flour together until butter and cheese are completely blended into the flour. (Or you could use a food processor.) Knead dough a few times on a lightly floured surface and roll dough out into a rectangle approximately ¼ inch thick. Cut into 1-inch wide strips or cut out shapes with a cookie cutter. Bake for 7 to 8 minutes, until golden brown.

Please turn the page for an exciting sneak peek of
Stephanie Blackmoore's
next Wedding Planner Mystery

MURDER WEARS WHITE

coming in February 2017!

Chapter One

"So you'll do it?" Whitney Scanlon stared at me with beseeching brown eyes and blinked back a fresh batch of tears. "He only has a couple months left."

Could I do it? Could I move her wedding up eight months and finish renovating my mess of a mansion in time to host her wedding? I looked away from her penetrating gaze and glanced around the room. The furniture in the parlor, including the couch we sat on, was covered with grimy drop cloths. Cans of paint and piles of lumber littered the room. The hum of a buzz saw filled the air and enough sawdust coated the floor to transform it into a sandy beach.

My lead contractor, Jesse Flowers, promised he'd finish the job by the end of October, and I had taken his word for it. I drew in a deep breath, coughed on some dust, and plunged in.

"Of course!"

Whitney enveloped me in a swift and fierce hug. "I knew it, I just knew it! My dad will be so happy to walk me down the aisle." Her tears came freely, and I smiled as I returned her embrace.

Jesse ducked under the arched doorway and stuck his head in the room. He gave me an incredulous stare and mouthed, "you're killing me."

I stuck out my tongue over Whitney's shoulder.

"We'll make sure your dad sees you get married." But my assurance faltered when I saw the disorder. It was one thing to promise the B and B would be ready in four weeks. Quite another thing to deliver. At least the weather would cooperate for Whitney. It was a picture-perfect October in Port Quincy, Pennsylvania. Leaves from gingko trees fluttered to the ground like golden fortune cookies and each day the sun hung like a medallion in a brilliant cornflower blue sky. Mellow smoke from wood-burning fireplaces perfumed the air and geese practiced their long flights south. Evenings were crisp and cool and clear and if I could pull this wedding off, the grounds would be a gorgeous backdrop for a cozy and elegant party. *If* I could pull it off.

And I would pull it off. Whitney's father was dying. His last wish was to walk his daughter down the aisle, and he wouldn't be around for her original wedding date in June. Hers would be the first wedding held at my work-in-progress B and B, the official launch of my wedding planning business.

What would have been the first wedding in December was for an exacting bridezilla who was already running me ragged. Just like when I was an attorney, I couldn't cherry-pick my clients. I was delighted to kick off my new career working with a bride like Whitney. No matter that I'd broken out in a cold sweat when she called this morning. I had nowhere acceptable to meet her. In the end, I'd shaken some dust off the couch in the parlor and decided Whitney should know what she was getting into.

I felt dumpy in the makeshift outfit I'd thrown on for my impromptu meeting. I'd shed my dingy overalls and slipped into a wrinkled turquoise sheath dress mere minutes before Whitney's arrival. I'd gained back all of the weight I'd lost, and then some, for my own cancelled wedding, and the dress didn't quite fit.

"I've never seen you in a dress," Jesse had mused as I descended the stairs to meet Whitney. His lined face twisted into an amused smile, as if he'd caught me playing dress up. The other workers stared at me like I was an alien as I twirled my ponytail of sandy curls up in a messy bun and jammed my feet into kitten heels. I'd worked alongside them since late summer, and they'd never seen me in anything but cargo pants or filthy denim, with my hair protected under a bandana or baseball cap. I smoothed out some wrinkles in the cotton fabric and vowed to look more presentable for clients.

"Thanks for coming through for me." Whitney beamed, seemingly impervious to the chaos. She dabbed at her mascara with a tissue she'd extracted from her tiny plum purse. Everything about her was diminutive. She was my height, five foot nothing, but much tinier and bird-like. She had delicate features and loose strawberry blond curls. She radiated strength, despite her apparent fragility.

"Excuse me, Mallory?" Jesse loomed over me and shattered my reverie. "There's a problem with the bathroom in the green bedroom. I thought you'd like to know. *Right now.*" He must want to grill me for promising this place would be wedding-ready in four weeks.

I shrugged in apology to Whitney.

"It's okay. I'd better get going. I'm so thrilled you can move up the wedding. It means the world to me that my father will be there. You're a lifesaver, Mallory." She rose to her feet and carefully navigated her way around the flotsam and jetsam of hardware in her path to the front hall.

"Let's meet later this week. We'll have a lot to do to plan your wedding in such a short amount of time." I crossed my fingers behind my back and made a wish to magically fix up a professional space amid the mess to meet with her next time.

Whitney turned back to look at me. Her eyes sparkled, immune to the reality of renovation hell. She turned to leave as the massive front door swung open ahead of her. It was Garrett Davies, the delectable man I'd been seeing. His face brightened when he saw me over Whitney's shoulder and his warm hazel eyes crinkled at the corners. He held a large brown bag bursting with lunch for me and the contractors. The gentle autumn sun backlit his tall frame, creating a pleasing silhouette. I was about to introduce him to Whitney, but she froze. Then she took a panicked step back and faltered on her high heels. She collided with me and Garrett dropped the bag, moving forward to steady her. Sandwiches and soup spilled onto the floor. A pumpkin pie did a wobbly flip and landed with a deafening splat.

"Ouch!" Whitney yelped as a splash of hot liquid marred her suede boots. She stifled a cry and scrambled away from Garrett. "You! What are you doing here?" Her voice was brittle and shrill and threatened to smash into a thousand pieces. She blanched as if she'd seen a ghost and blinked at Garrett in disbelief.

My breath caught in my chest as I saw her initial look of fear turn to pure, white-hot contempt. All of her effervescent happiness was gone, replaced with a deep look of dismay.

Whitney murmured an apology and slipped out the door. Once she'd put some distance between her and Garrett, she seemed to recover enough to feign politeness and call over her shoulder, "Thanks again, Mallory! We'll talk soon." She nearly ran down the drive to her Jetta and didn't look back.

The unfinished B and B hadn't rattled her, but seeing my new beau nearly drove her apoplectic.

"I don't blame her." Garrett tried to salvage what was left of lunch. He crouched down in the hallway in his three-piece suit and mopped up steaming, fragrant puddles of potato and chive soup. He was one of the few people who could manage to look sexy cleaning up remnants of lunch, and I would've enjoyed the view if I hadn't been so rattled by Whitney's reaction. I wiped the wax-paper wrapped sandwiches and distributed them to the contractors. My stomach growled as I mourned the loss of half of lunch. Garrett and I settled on the top step of the front porch to dig in. It was a cool day, but the sun warmed our faces and the wind was still. I couldn't enjoy the weather, remembering Whitney's bizarre behavior.

"She nearly fainted when she saw you. I wasn't sure if she was going to deck you or run away."

Garrett put down his turkey on rye and turned to face me. "Ten years ago I defended the man convicted of murdering Whitney's mother." He winced at the word "convicted," no doubt wishing, even now, for a different outcome. Ever the defense attorney, he didn't say the man who *murdered* Whitney's mother.

"It was my very first homicide case. If I could go back in time, I would do it all differently. But I knew then, and I know now, that Eugene Newton is innocent. Someone else killed Vanessa Scanlon, and they're probably still at large." He shivered.

"If you believe your client is innocent, then he is." I gently laid my hand on his arm and winced at the toll my attempts at construction had taken. My left thumb was blackened by an ill-aimed hammer, and the skin was rough and raw. I was clumsy and many hours of working on the house hadn't made me more handy. Mine were hardly the hands of a professional wedding planner.

"But I understand Whit's reaction."

Garrett was still beating himself up about the trial from years ago. Not for the first time, I wished we could spend more time together. I had been busy with the renovation and Garrett had his own commitments to his cases and his young daughter, Summer. We had yet to go out on an official date, and I doubted we'd spend much time together now I'd promised to deliver a wedding to Whitney in mere weeks.

Garrett took my hand and shook his head. "That poor girl insisted on attending the whole trial. She was fifteen. The murder of her mother was particularly brutal, and she heard every detail. I couldn't imagine if Summer had to go through that. I'll never forget Whitney's face, and I bet she'll never forget mine."

My heart ached for Whitney. But I was still having trouble processing her reaction to Garrett. Did